DEATH GOES VIRAL

A genetically modified murder mystery

Stephen Clarke

ALSO BY STEPHEN CLARKE

Fiction
A Year in the Merde
Merde Actually (US edition: In the Merde for Love)
Merde Happens
Dial M for Merde
The Merde Factor
Merde in Europe

A Brief History of the Future
Death Goes Viral (previously published as Who Killed Beano)

Non-Fiction
1,000 Years of Annoying the French
Dirty Bertie, an English King Made in France
How the French Won Waterloo (or Think They Did)
The French Revolution & What Went Wrong

Talk to the Snail : the Ten Commandments for Understanding the French
Paris Revealed : the Secret Life of a City
Château d'Hardelot, a Souvenir Guide
The British Invasion
Elizabeth II, Queen of Laughs

ABOUT THE AUTHOR

Stephen Clarke is a British author living in Paris, where he divides his time between writing and not writing.

His best-known novels are the worldwide bestselling *Merde* series, including *A Year in the Merde* (which has sold more than one million copies worldwide) and *Merde Actually* (a number-one bestseller in the UK).

He has also written several non-fiction books, including *1,000 Years of Annoying the French* (also a number-one bestseller in the UK), a biography of King Edward VII's "éducation sentimentale" in France, called *Dirty Bertie, an English King Made in France,* as well as *Talk to the Snail: the Ten Commandments for Understanding the French,* and *How the French Won Waterloo (or Think They Did).*

Clarke's book *1,000 Years of Annoying the French* inspired the permanent collection at a French museum, which he curated. It is the Centre Culturel de l'Entente Cordiale at the Château d'Hardelot in northern France.

He has written two stage shows – an adaptation of his novel *The Merde Factor,* and a words-and-music show in French called *L'Entente Cordiale en Paroles et Musique.* Both have been performed in France.

He also writes jokes for stand-up comedians and song words for singers, and has co-written a French radio sitcom and a radio play. He occasionally performs in music and comedy clubs – but mainly for fun (his own rather than the audience's).

www.stephenclarkewriter.com @sclarkewriter

A PAF paperback

Originally published in 2004 as *Who Killed Beano*, and since comprehensively updated.

ISBN: 978-2-9521638-3-5

Cover design by Scott Clarke

To ALL the readers

"If you're going to lie, *lie* ..."

The mantra of the modern politician

1 Coma On

About thirty miles away, a government Junior Minister was sitting up in bed, using her phone to buy shares in a multinational company with which her Ministry was about to do a deal.

Much closer, a police inspector was emerging from a crime scene, having been evicted by the forensics team. She took out her irritation on her sergeant by asking him why he always dressed as if he thought he was going to be on TV.

Meanwhile, I was just thinking to myself that I really shouldn't have eaten breakfast.

And all this before seven in the morning.

I have Beano's keys, so I let myself into his building and tiptoed up the stairs to his front door. I was going to barge in, but somehow the idea of sneaking into his bedroom and waking him up seemed too intimate. How far can friends go when one of them's asleep? I don't know.

I rang his doorbell for about two minutes solid, then stopped to listen.

Beano's antennae were retracted deep this morning. There was no tumble from the bed, no slashing back of the curtains, no obscenities through the door.

I rang again – sixty seconds, timed by my new watch, accurate to within a millionth of a second per light year or whatever. It cost about the same as a small four-wheel-drive car, but you've got to treat yourself occasionally.

Nothing, except a few predictable complaints about noise pollution from the ground-floor neighbour. Well, it was very early on a Monday morning. And Beano's bell is very loud. More of a heavy-metal bell solo than a polite ding-dong.

I apologized down the stairs, and heard the neighbour go back indoors, still grumbling. Then I rang again, and bashed the door a couple of times. Nothing. Well, if Beano didn't react to that racket, there was nothing for it but to go in.

The intruder alarm was off, which was no surprise: carefree Beano often forgets to switch it on. Especially when he's unconscious.

The apartment smelled like an alligator's larder, but then Beano is something of an alligator, always dragging things down, leaving them to fester, then coming back for another chew. It means his fridge is always disgusting and his ideas beautifully twisted.

When I first met him, he'd just created an app called Horrorburgers. This was a compilation of true-but-gross info about what goes into fast food. You pointed your phone at a big-chain fast-food place where you were thinking of eating, and splat! You were told (and shown) everything you didn't want to know about their ingredients. Best slimming aid ever.

Beano made a fortune from the out-of-court agreement to shut him down. Well, it seemed like a fortune then. Nothing compared to what we're all going to make now. Or so we're told.

I trampled on a phone, I skittled a few quarter-full coffee cups, I toe-punted two empty booze bottles, but made it to the window without collapsing in the chaos on the bedroom floor. No Beano. I opened the window and took several bodyfuls of air before trying for the bathroom. After one of his weekend benders, Beano often spends a day or two on his bathroom floor. It's cool, white, and easy for someone else to mop.

At last, there he was. His blond head under the sink, a crust of gunk on his chin, there was Beano, in crumpled sweatshirt and off-white shorts. His face was surrounded by dried pools of unmarketable colours – dishwasher-outflow grey and run-over-squirrel's-innards purple. His usual hangover make-up.

"Beano, it's Bernie, come to scoop you up!"

Nothing.

"Come on, Beano, you rich bastard, on your feet!"

I nudged him. His lips dribbled. I just got the bathroom window open in time.

I once saw a French movie called *Madame Bovary*. She really was quite a Madame. A doctor's wife in the 1800s who drinks a corrosive poison that takes ages to burn her entrails out and kill her. There was more to the movie – a botched operation, sex in a horse-drawn carriage, lots of French arguing – but what stuck in my mind was the black vomit. Disgusting. But that, apparently, is what the French were into before they invented Chanel handbags.

Anyway, I used Madame B's death-bed scene in my first "See Models Die" short. The film is (honestly) not as disgusting as its name suggests. You're standing at the foot of a brass bed. You see a beautiful, naked-shouldered girl, asleep – dark swept-back hair, dark lips, long body under the white silken sheet. Then you swoop down and hover along the beautiful bumps of her, and just as you reach her face, she grunts awake and her lips start oozing black gunk. Caption: "Sulphuric acid – for Christ's sake don't drink it."

OK, it is a bit sick, but the film was aimed at medical students, who tend to have a pretty high morbidity threshold. After all, what other degree course involves chopping up dead human bodies? None. Except maybe contemporary art.

It was one of the first films I made, and it instantly went viral. I still get messages asking for details (name, phone number, availability for stalkers, etc) about the "dying" model. Her name is Claudine – she's French – perfect skin, perfect body, about ten feet tall, like a computer-generated goddess, but all real. Claudine's 100% organic.

Soon, I guess, no percentage of her will belong to me any more, because somebody wants to buy all our company shares, and all our company assets, including my old films. Don't ask me *why* they want to buy us out. Perhaps they're just too lazy to set up a business themselves.

And talking of laziness, what about Beano? He should be up by now, and yelling at me for kicking him when he's down. Beano, my inspiration. The Claudine scene was inspired by a movie, yes, but also by Beano's Monday-morning dribbles.

His bathroom was no worse than usual. Except that this time Beano turned out to be dead. As in not breathing. With two wicked blue bruises on his gullet. I touched his forehead – he was still warm, yet somehow cold. His eyeballs were puffed out like poisonous mushrooms. The strangler was probably in the kitchen, getting a cool drink after the exertion.

I parked my breakfast on the floor and ran. I got down the stairs as silently as an exploding bottle bank. Beano's ground-floor neighbour jumped out of her apartment wielding a fat-encrusted frying pan at me. I tried to explain, but it only convinced her to take a terrified swing at my head. I ducked, belly-flopped across the hall, and finally managed to crawl to my car while the deranged neighbour woke the whole street, shrieking for someone, anyone, to save her from this dawn intruder with a penchant for noise pollution.

In the old-fashioned world I might have been failing to get away unnoticed.

****

For sale: one KIDNEY, blood type O+, hardly used, one careful owner.
US$40,000 ono. Buyer collects.

Members! Exciting medical investment opportunities coma-ing soon!

Check out Doctor Stock's latest blog.

****

2 To Question Or Not To Question, That Is The ...

Pigeon instinct took me straight to Coma, the office. In normal times, a labyrinth of bright corridors, revealing at every corner its clusters of screens and its wide-angle views across the bay. I stumbled through the doors and collapsed on the first chair I saw.

If you didn't know us, you'd probably never guess what went on here. Headhunting? PR? International arms sales? No, we're tapping into the motherlode of modern life (I hope): health.

We're a double-edged sword of a company. First, there's the doctors' service provider. The medics get an appointments diary, unlimited data storage, free file transfers.

They can set up their own blogs and websites, give online advice about embarrassing diseases, receive truckloads of freebies from the drug companies, advertise their skills at tummy-tucking and liposucking, all sorts of stuff. And we guarantee they'll get zero spam or ads – except ours, of course.

That's been ticking over nicely for a while now. Our advertising blurb says we've also invented a new economic sector, because we are, amongst other things, agents for medical professionals. For example, an Argentinian midfielder arriving in England needs help negotiating his multi-million-pound transfer fee, right? So does a Bulgarian or Filipino doctor. If your local hospital has a ten-year waiting list for hip replacements, we'll find you a cheap specialist within 24 hours. He or she might not speak English, but the patients will all be unconscious, so a capacity for chit-chat is not a priority, right?

And it works both ways. There's a huge market for foreign hospitals selling their services to Brits who are browned off with being on waiting lists. You type in your illness on our search engine, we'll find you the cheapest, fastest treatment deal. So I guess we're a sort of EsickBay.

We're making a mint and doing the nation a service. We ought to get a knighthood. Arise, Sir Coma.

And we've come so far.

We started out as a place where medical students could network, find jobs and accommodation, and have a laugh. And what made them laugh, they told us (well, the male students, mainly, though not exclusively), was anything sick. Hence my "See Models Die" movies, which all featured fatal mishaps and flesh-eating diseases. They're still up there somewhere, in our big, complex sitemap. I can hardly *believe* the requests for new death scenes that still come in from the medics. You don't get sicker than someone who works on the front line in health.

When I first met my main model, Claudine, we at Coma were all students. We'd just created the company. We being me, Beano, Phil, Mona, Louie and Des.

Beano and I were setting up websites, blogs and social media accounts that would get us talked about. Phil was stomping around telling pharmaceutical companies to advertise with us. Mona was sending out waves of spam about our online services. Louie was money, Des was tech.

We'd gone on line a few months before, but it'd only been a hobby till Louie suddenly came up with the cash to turn it into a real business. It was start-up capital from a big drug company, Nostrum. We'd have to repay it eventually, Louie said, but for now we'd got enough dosh to drop out of college and create something very special if we worked at it. And so we did.

Back then, the six of us were like a band, crashing on each other's sofas, together in various combinations for 24 hours a day. That's why we all had each other's house keys. These days, though, we're less inseparable. The only key I use regularly is Beano's. He's the only one who uses mine. *Used*, that should be. Hell.

Sitting in the office, I rubbed my neck at the memory of him. My fingers rasped on 36 hours' worth of stubble. Last time I shaved, Beano was alive. Last time he shaved was the last time he shaved.

The lights seemed to be flickering like strobes. The clinical, almost metallic-white walls were setting my teeth on edge. There was a brain-quake happening in my head, but I couldn't get access to my drawer-full of life-saving pills. My cubicle is in the same office as Beano's, and a plain-clothes cop was giving his desk a frisk. I wasn't allowed in. I had to sweat it out in reception.

A policewoman, the head one, was talking to Louie, who's now officially our Financial Controller, with an office door of his own. Waste of time talking to him, I thought. I mean, who found the body?

We really shouldn't have let Louie put "control" in his job title. To a little Napoleon clone, it's just an invitation to start acting like an emperor. OK, Louie's the one organizing this business of making us all rich, but he spends most of his time marching over my ideas with his miniature feet.

Right now, he would no doubt be feeling obliged to tell the policewoman about all the times Beano and I punched it out over who'd thought of an idea first. As a large proportion of our ideas were (I admit it) stupid, our fights could probably be classified as mindless violence. The cop would be writing it down and thinking she'd have my confession in time for an early lunch.

People were starting to arrive at the office. We've got half a dozen in-house staff, plus a nomadic set of interns and sub-contractors for all the boring, fiddly stuff like technical support. Each new arrival in reception received the news about Beano with a gasp, and began flicking their eyes about at each other, and at me, as if they wanted to know which one of us had done it, and who'd be next. Then they all came and stood over me, gawping down at this being who had just left the presence of a corpse they used to know.

I wouldn't have minded too much, but two of the gawpers were our smelliest nerdlings, Mike and Joe. People sometimes accuse me of being a bit of a nerd, but these two are Nerdo Sapiens, Nerderthals, the type who don't wash because no one's figured out how to connect up a shower nozzle to a games console. Still, I guess at least that means they won't be able to mate and perpetuate their species. I don't know what their job title is exactly, but I hope it's nothing to do with public relations. Their collective body odours were making me want to recycle some more of my muesli.

Mona joined the crowd. She was crying. She's half-Egyptian, naturally tanned, but somehow she was pale. To break the spell of the others' gaze, I stood up and gave her a hug.

"Bernie, I'm so ..."

"Yeah, me too."

"He was ..."

"I know, Mona, I know."

She went to the loo to wash her face. Finally the others went away. Off for a gossip about whether I'd done it, no doubt.

I whipped out my phone. I'd only just got round to recharging it, so I hadn't looked at my messages since the previous night. Way too long to be out of touch.

Des, our in-house techie guru, who no longer works in-house, had sent me a message of condolence. God knows what he's been hacking into to get the news that quick. Perhaps he's permanently logged on to our DNA and knows automatically when one of us goes down.

There were other messages, but nothing from Beano, which is unusual. I hadn't heard from him since Friday. He must have been out of action for the whole weekend. Or otherwise engaged. Maybe he'd taken a stronger-than-usual woman back to the flat. Perhaps his death just proved what the doctors have been telling us for years now – you really have to be careful who you invite to your bed.

Rita walked by, crying inconsolably. Rita is our office manager. I hugged her, too. Her tears soaked through my shirt, and it might have felt inappropriately erotic if the wetness on my shoulder hadn't reminded me of Beano's clammy forehead. She also headed for the loo to dab her eyes. There was going to be a toilet-roll shortage before the end of the morning.

I couldn't believe it. How could Beano get killed? Today of all days? If one day can be worse than another to die, this one was pretty bad. Beano was due with me and Rita at a meeting at eleven, after which extra-strength credit cards were going to be ordered just to cope with our increased demand. This was nothing to do with the buyout. This was a job, a commission, courtesy of a certain Ms Greensands. My phone was blinking her name at that very minute, in big red capitals.

No one had ever merited such a flashy entry in my diary before, but then this was the first time I'd ever had a meeting with someone so close to the heart of the country's power. Ms Greensands is a Junior Minister. I usually associate the title "Junior" with inadequate American sons trying to live up to Dad's name. But Ms Greensands is nobody's son. And from what I've read about her, there's nothing inadequate about the woman, or the budgets at her disposal. As Juniors go, she's pure Senior.

"Anyone else got the shits this morning? Fuck Nell."

This was Phil, shouting the length of reception. Phil is exactly the guy in the old TV ads who used to drive into the Andes village to inspect the new coffee blend and sleep with Juanita the half-dressed waitress. Blond and hunky, in ever-fresh khaki Bermudas, Phil Harrap from the Cockney jungle.

"Oy, Bernie, got any ya gut drugs on ya?"

He obviously hadn't heard about Beano. I didn't have the energy to tell him.

"Not on me, sorry Phil. And my desk is –"

"Well any fin in a tube den – vitamins, aspirins, glucose ..."

"Nothing that'd cure the shits, no."

"I don't wanna take the stuff, I just wanna ram the fuckin tube up me arse to block it."

Typical Phil. He tramped off down the corridor in his rock-crusher boots. Strange that no one's told him about something as vital as Beano's murder. He knows *everyone*. His address book takes up a whole space station. When we all met at college, Phil was playing bass in what he called a thrash-metal electro-reggae band. He was claiming to be the only son of a bank robber. I think he just mispronounced it. If you're permanently stoned, you could say "robber" when you mean "owner". The offspring of minor criminals don't usually have access to the kind of money-people Phil deals with. I'm sure his parents paid for a six-month total immersion course in Estuary English for him. No, not Estuary English, sewer English. Everyone loves Phil for his foul manners, and says he's an unspoilt, gifted young man, the bastard.

"Mr Bridges?" At last. "Sorry to have kept you waiting," the plain-clothes policewoman said. She was wearing jeans, but I doubted whether her questioning would be as casual as her clothes.

"That's OK." I followed her into Louie's office. Louie had disappeared. On the sofa in one corner there was another cop, a young guy in a sharp grey suit and tie, who was introduced as Sergeant Milner. I nodded to him and settled into Louie's star-guest chair. Inspector Armlock, as the head cop called herself, sat in Louie's own swiveller at Louie's tidy desk.

Louie's office is bigger than mine, of course, and looks out towards the mercury sea. The window blind was down, and it rattled from time to time in the gust from the overhead colonial-style fan. I haven't got a ceiling fan – I'm afraid it'll fall on my head – but Louie (ironically for someone with the same name as a guillotined king) is oblivious to the blades hanging over him.

"OK, Mr Bridges. Thanks for taking the time to speak to us. Now, could you –"

"One thing before we start, Inspector? Will you be wanting me to, um, return to the scene of the crime?" (That didn't sound too well phrased, but never mind.) "Because if so, can it wait a bit? I've got a really important meeting at eleven."

The Inspector ran her hand through her short-cropped black hair.

"We can discuss that later, Mr Bridges. Now –"

"Have you been to Beano's place? Have you seen him?"

"My colleagues from Scene of Crime are –"

"But – sorry, last question – is Beano's murder the first of its kind hereabouts?" I crossed my fingers under the desk rim.

The Inspector exchanged a silent glance with her suited colleague. Well, she glanced at him while he just sat there staring.

"We suspect it isn't," she finally said, "but I'm afraid I can't tell you more."

"You can't tell me more? But that means you do know more, you do have suspects?"

The Inspector fussed about with her pen and pad, her hair and her thoughts, obviously trying to think of a way to say, "shut the fuck up and let me get on with my job." So I told her what happened, sparing none of the fear and the stink. She didn't squirm once, even during the bits of my account that made me stop and swallow to steady my voice. It must be tough on the street.

"That's all very graphic," she said. "Beano was Mr Wright's nickname, I take it?"

"Yes, because he was so blond."

"Sorry?"

"His name was Alan and he was very blond."

"No, sorry, still not with you."

"Al Beano."

"Right. Very clever. Go in for a lot of binges like that, did he?"

"We've both been known to over-indulge and suffer the consequences, if that's what you mean. We tend to have our best ideas drunk."

"Yes," she said, the voice of someone who has all her ideas sober. "We're having the substances on the bathroom floor analysed. But I don't think they can all be his, can they?"

"Yes, they are, except one bit. Mine was the thick brownish pool by his feet. Breakfast cereal. It should tally with the stuff outside his neighbour's door."

"And with the stain on your shirt?" She was sharp, this one.

"Oh no, that's Rita's make-up."

I explained about the tears and the hug. The Inspector looked at me coolly, soberly, as I spoke. I finished. She said nothing. The fan blades swished above our heads. Seemed like a good time to end the meeting.

"If I think of anything else, I'll call you," I suggested. "What's your number?"

I almost heard the click as her stare switched down a notch from Cool to Chilly.

"I do have a couple more questions, if you *don't mind*," the Inspector said, the sarcasm oozing across the desk at me. "Like motive. What about you? Why would *you* have wanted to kill him?" Instead of bending forward and turning an angle-poise lamp on me, she leant back and stared from under her symmetrically-plucked eyebrows, as if she was wearing bookish reading glasses.

"Bollocks!"

"What was that, Mr Bridges?"

"Sorry, that didn't come out right. But you know what I mean."

"No."

"Did you ask Louie the same question? Will you ask Phil, Des, Rita or Mona?"

"You just happened to arrive in the victim's flat around the time of death?"

"Yes."

"At the crack of dawn."

"Look, Beano was my best bloody friend! We worked brilliantly together. We're just about to – we *were* just about to" (I was glad I'd made the slip so naturally, most suspects must stumble over it) "cash in on all our hard work together."

"Hard work? Which is what in your case?"

I explained how I create online content, for us, or for outside clients. At her request, I described the original "Models" movie starring Claudine. It was the first one that came to mind, for obvious reasons.

"That's repulsive," she said.

"Yes it is, isn't it?" I said.

Then I saw that she hadn't meant it flatteringly. She probably had kids at home, and was scared they might go knocking back sulphuric acid like lemonade.

"Though it's a health advisory film," I added quickly. "We are a medical company. It says 'don't drink acid', you know."

The Inspector shook her head.

"What else have you two worked on together recently?"

"We did a website for a company called Woodlanders Rest? That was very tasteful, very respectful." This was for a chain of ecological crematoriums, where the clients' ashes are scattered over an area of picturesque woodland. A brilliant scheme – people paying money to have themselves used as compost. The site was all twittering sparrows, rustling leaves, not a vulture or maggot in sight. I described it to the Inspector.

She nodded. "Does everything you do have something to do with death?"

"Much less than everything you do, I expect. But I work in health. And health, good or bad, always leads to death, doesn't it?"

The Inspector stared at me while she considered this. Louie's desktop hologram sundial said ten o'clock already. My new watch said five to. Damn.

"In these, er, 'See Models Die' films. Does anyone get strangled?"

"No. Yes. In one of them ..." Dammit. I closed my eyes. "I was a student at the time."

It was my only defence.

****

Hello sick British!
You must to wait long time for operation?
Come with us! Here, no waiting list!
You want hip exchange, artery unplugging, fake teeth?
We do all operations, at cheapest price, with private bathroom.
Color catalogue here.
SPECIAL OFFER! Until 31th December, two new hips for price of one!

****

3 Go West

"In one of them ...?" The Inspector tightened her grip on her pen. She thought he was on to a lead.

"A crucifixion scene."

"Crucifixion scene? With strangling too?" This confirmed it – I was the perfect suspect, the serial killer with a sense of humour warped enough to power the Starship Enterprise.

"Yes," I confessed. "A girl gets tied to the cross – with ropes around her wrists and a big loop holding her feet together. But she's so thin that her wrists slip out of the ropes and she slides down and hangs herself on the loop that was round her feet. It was a student joke about anorexic models. Nothing more."

"A joke?" The Inspector had obviously never met a medical student.

"It was saying anorexia can kill. It's not me that's sick, it's the fashion industry. I was just saying so in joke form."

"Making a joke of anorexia."

There was an unpleasant silence in the room. I could feel the fan getting lower, coming down to decapitate me.

"Listen, Inspector. I know I'm making a cock-up of this. I should get a lawyer in here, shouldn't I?"

"For an informal chat like this?"

"Informal chat? When I have an informal chat it's usually: 'have a good weekend?'. Not 'murdered any friends lately?'."

The Inspector simply raised an eyebrow. I was like Tom Hanks in that classic movie, *Bonfire of the Vanities*. He's in the clear till he starts acting all guilty with the cops. Though, shit, he *was* guilty.

"I'm innocent!" I shouted.

"Pardon?"

Luckily my vocal cords had panicked and made me sound more like an infuriated parrot.

"Nothing."

"Hmm," said the Inspector. "Did you see any rope in the apartment?"

"Rope? No. Why?"

"Did you never consider the danger of inspiring a copycat crime?"

"Copycat? You think ...?"

"What if someone has decided to set up a – what do you call them? – 'See Webmasters Die' page?"

"God. Have they?"

"No. Not as far as I know. Not yet."

"Anyway, we're not webmasters, we're content providers, designers, filmmakers ..."

"Oh, well, you're in the clear then, aren't you?" She snorted scornfully. It was clearly the wrong time to be pedantic about my job description.

"But you just said this isn't the first case of its kind. So you do know something?"

"No. Just looking at theories."

This took a minute to sink in. Beano killed as a sort of homage to our work? *My* work? If it was the model movies they objected to, they got the wrong guy. I could be next. If I'd turned up at Beano's place ten minutes earlier, I *would* have been next. Or first. Holy shit.

"Perhaps we can return to the subject I wanted to discuss before you sidetracked us off on to crucifixion and strangling ..." She paused, but I resisted the temptation to react. "You have a motive for the crime. As do all the other founders of the company. Money."

"Oh. Yeah. Yes. Of course. Louie must have told you about the company being bought out? I mean, us six, the founders, we're going to make millions. I don't know how it'll work now, whether Beano's share gets divided out or what. But he had sixteen point six six per cent of the company."

"Sixteen point six six. That's an awkward figure – twenty per cent is much rounder."

"Now you're talking like Louie. You should ask him about the arithmetic."

"I did. He said that Mr Wright had slightly fewer shares than the rest of you. Any idea why that might be?"

"No." That was weird. I could only think he might have swapped some of them for booze. Or given them to a woman in exchange for her favours.

"And you don't think any of your colleagues would have killed for a larger share?"

"I bloody hope not. No, we're all old friends."

"Good, because if one of you did kill him for his shares, you were wasting your time. They're all in individual accounts. Mr Wright's shares will go to his next of kin."

"So it couldn't have been one of us, then."

"Unless one of you didn't understand how the system worked, and killed him because you thought you'd benefit ..."

She let the accusation hang in the air like a particularly noxious fart.

"No," I said. "It has to be an outsider." I thought this one over, and received a cruel flash of inspiration. It felt like a posthumous message from Beano zapping into my phone. Thanks, old friend. Now it was my turn to lean forward and turn my angle-poise eyes on my questioner. "Do you think that the bruising could have been caused by a frying pan? His neighbour is hysterical. She –"

But then I noticed that my suggestion had had a strange effect on the Inspector. A kind of nervous ripple ran up her forehead, and she took a long in-drawn breath. I thought she was about to hiccup, but no, it was much worse.

"You know, Mr Bridges, to my unsophisticated eyes, you seem to be treating all this as an enormous game."

"Game? No."

"This is a murder inquiry and you're not taking it at all seriously."

"Not taking it seriously? What do you –"

"You're flippant."

"No. No! It's not flippancy. I'm just making suggestions."

"Flippant suggestions."

"No. It's a – an occupational hazard. I'm an ideas man. All day, every day, I have to have ideas. Some are good, some are garbage. It's part of my job. You don't criticize a fishmonger because he smells of kippers, do you?"

"Kippers," she said, and nodded to herself. I thought maybe I should have chosen something more neutral, like "sole" or "salmon". The Inspector said the next words as if talking to a paedophile who's just invited her seven-year-old daughter for a walk in the woods. "I don't like your sort, Mr Beidges. You're the kind of rich-kid joker who'd run someone over and then say 'well he didn't have a job, so what's the loss?' No one matters a damn except you, do they?"

This woman didn't have a chip on her shoulder, she had a whole chain of fish shops.

"Look – I may have a new sports car and a new watch, both on credit I might add, but that doesn't make me a psychopathic snob," I told her. "For Christ's sake! I see my best friend lying dead, and instead of trying to catch the killer, you sit about telling me you don't *like* me. What else don't you like? Decaffeinated coffee? Green socks? Belgium?"

"See what I mean?" she sighed. "Flippant." She shook her head towards her buddy, who just stared through me, playing the stooge.

The Inspector turned back to me as if I was something she had to wipe off the bathroom floor.

It must be a trick they teach in police school, because every little crime and misdemeanour I've ever committed came flashing to the front of my memory in a burst of telepathic confession. Yes, I did break that school window. Yes, I stole Rebecca Johnson's yoyo, because she told everyone in class I wore girl's knickers. Yes, I set fire to granddad's newspaper, but only to see how long it would take him to wake up. And I threw a bowl of washing-up water over him to put him out, didn't I?

The Inspector interrupted me before I could get on to more recent mischief.

"Now then, you two were good friends, weren't you?"

"Yes, I told you that. "

"Very good friends. "

"Yes. "

"And you arrived in the apartment at seven AM. You didn't, ah, spend the night there?"

"What? Oh, right – you don't like me, therefore I must be a spurned lover. Logical. But two guys can be good friends without ... you know."

"No, what?"

"For God's sake. What the hell difference would it make if I *was* gay?"

"Was your friend gay?"

"Beano? No."

"Current girlfriend?"

I realized I didn't know. Weird. Why didn't I know?

"Sorry, Inspector. I don't know." Inspector Armlock just "hmm"ed again. She was obviously planning her speech for the midday news, when she'd reveal to an outraged nation the details of this gay SM-and-murder orgy ring. "But we weren't lovers and I didn't kill him," I added.

"Did I say you did?"

"You implied it."

"Did I?" She looked with fake astonishment across at her colleague, who, as usual, didn't move a muscle, facial or otherwise. I wondered if he wasn't inflatable. "Perhaps I do sound as if I'm accusing people all the time," the Inspector said. "I suppose it's an occupational hazard." She raised her eyebrows to bludgeon home her irony. "Now, you said you had an important meeting this morning?"

"Yes. It's –"

"Well, we've got to talk to your other colleagues, so we'll let you get on with your work."

"Uh?"

"Your desk should be free now."

"That's it?" I almost laughed with relief. She'd just been clicking my buttons. Goading me to see if I cracked. And I hadn't.

"Unless there's anything else you want to tell us?"

I shook my head. After all, granddad had only suffered singed trousers.

"Well if you think of anything else ... call me." She handed over a card with a mobile number. So we were friends after all. "Please don't leave town for the next forty-eight hours. We'll be in touch if we need you," she said.

Be in touch? Great. That's what people say when they have no intention of contacting someone ever again.

I was out of there before she changed her mind.

Louie was hovering in the corridor.

"Ah, Bernie, a word," he said, looking round to see if we could be heard. "No need to tell Ms G about, you know, is there?"

"You what?"

"Don't mention Beano to her. Having one of your partners die is not exactly good publicity for a health company, right?"

Beano hadn't even started to decompose, but he was already creating too much of a stink for Louie.

"Listen, Louie, I've just been accused of murder by Cruella there. It's not a subject I'm going to bring up over coffee, is it?"

"Good, yes, OK," he said, looking pleased. Too pleased.

"But," I added, "Ms Greensands is a government Minister. It's not going to take her long to find out about Beano, is it? What's she going to say then? 'Hmm, they never told me about their colleague's death. I wonder what other minor details they're keeping from me?' We'll have to tell her."

I was pleased to see Louie flinch.

"No," he said. "If it comes up, we'll say that the police asked us not to talk about Beano yet. Or that we naturally assumed she'd already know, or something. Believe me, Bernie, sudden violent death does not make for profitable meetings. We're not talking about one of your nerdy friends who wants you to spice up his Instagram profile. This is politics. Diplomacy. Decorum. Money. Great watch, by the way. Is it new?"

First I'm a psycho-killer then I'm a nerd. Good to know what people really think of you. I was surprised to find a tear escaping from my eye.

"Just fuck off, Louie." I ran to the miniature pharmacy in my cubicle. There was plenty in there to stop the flow of my rebellious bodily fluids. Much of it bought while travelling, and semi-legal in this country, but very effective. Luckily, most customs men can't read Hindi or Chinese.

As I fiddled with the key to unlock my magic drawer, I remembered an idea I had once: constantly flying west. Escaping from time.

It's the middle of the night here in England. But in, say, California, it's still yesterday. The world is turning eastwards, propelling me towards dawn and office opening hours, while my brain has run aground, totally overloaded, on the unfinished business of the day before. So someone should start an airline that simply flies people westwards around the world, staying ahead of time, grabbing some extra hours back from yesterday, never having to face up to the shit of tomorrow.

****

Asian nurses seeking jobs or husbands.
Photo gallery, all in uniform. Guaranteed healthy.
QualifiedAsianBabes

****

4 The Eyes Have It

As soon as the drugs had calmed me down, I called our company lawyer, who said there was nothing to worry about. All the same, she sent through an instant bill for the advice. Not reassuring.

A ding from my phone. I had incoming. It was Mona, back at her desk and communicating her sorrow, fear and incomprehension about Beano. Lots of "why would anyones" and "can't believes". Mona's great at communication. After all, she's our Communication person. She and I were a couple for a year or more, before I screwed up.

I sent her back some shock of my own.

That reminded me. There was someone I should have called. I hunched down in my cubicle and punched in the number. It was answered almost immediately.

"Hi ... What? ... How did you know? ... Louie *texted* you? A *text*? Heartless bast– uh? ... I found him when I went round there this morning ... I couldn't! ... I *had* to keep it switched off, I was being accused of murder for God's sake! You don't take calls while you're being interrogated! ... Granola? ... Sorry, I didn't mean to shou– ... Oh God."

She'd hung up. When I turned round, Rita was standing there.

"Huh," I said, "wives. Who'd marry 'em, eh?"

Apparently this was the wrong thing to say, because Rita's whole upper body heaved in a sudden sob. It crossed my mind that maybe she and Beano had been ... Lucky Beano. I mean, before he ...

When we'd both got back from our respective gender-neutral toilets, Rita and I started setting up a cosy corner in the main meeting room for our star guest, the ministerial Ms Greensands. We worked in silence except for our occasional snuffles and the disgruntled gurgling of my stomach as I pushed the chairs about. Since throwing up at Beano's, I'd had nothing to eat except half a goat's milk yogurt, and it hadn't done its usual calming trick.

Louie came and poked his little proboscis in.

"Crisis meeting tomorrow morning at eight, guys, OK? To talk about Beano and his legacy. Give everyone a chance to settle down first."

That's typical of Louie – his friend and colleague's dead and he wants to organize a fucking *meeting*.

"Fine," was all I could muster in reply.

"You're not looking too hot, Bernie. Sure you don't want to go home?" he asked.

You female private part, I thought. Male organ, too. Desperate to stop me spilling the beans about Beano to Greensands.

"No, Louie, I'm OK. I need to keep my mind occupied. Listen – when Lady Greensands starts telling us how many millions she's going to spend, do you want me to call you in?"

"I'll be sitting in," he huffed, and scuttled off back into his hole like some inedible species of shrimp.

Something else was bugging me. I nipped back to my office to fetch a small package, then went to see Phil.

His office is pure pop art. I envy him his office. He has this massive yellow fridge full of refreshments, an orange leather sofa, a blood-red bass guitar that he sometimes twangs in meetings. The walls are splattered with a mix of video-game imagery and framed graffiti art. He has an old-school reminder board with pithy notes on it. Today's selection was "eat with C!!", "fuck Friday" and "bank? wank".

Phil was on the phone. Pacing about the room yelling, "been shittin non-stop since last night!", "four pairs soiled so far this mornin!" I thought he was just gossiping with a friend until he finished the conversation with "OK, contracts wiv you later today, no worries. Ciao!" He hung up.

"Bernie. Come in an close the door for fuck's sake! You'll fuck up the thermostat." I should have guessed he was on the phone to a client – less than one "fuck" per second is meet-the-Pope politeness by Phil's standards.

"Right, yeah." I shut the door behind me. Phil was keying something into a tablet.

"Can't believe it about Beano. Fuck!" he said, finally looking up. "Poor fucker. Fuck!"

"Yeah. You should have seen his *eyes*, Phil. Staring out at nothing, like two huge, enormous ..."

"Eyes?"

"Yeah. Sorry, I must still be in shock."

"Don't do your fuckin ed in, Bernie. Wasn't your fault, was it? Was it? Anyway, if they catch the fucker who did it, he's fuckin dead, I promise you that. Fuckin promise, OK?" He prodded his finger at me. I don't think it was an accusation.

"You talked to Policewoman Plod yet?" I asked him.

"What? No. Seein er later on. Fuck lot of use the pigs'll be."

"You made an *appointment* with the police?"

"Yeah. Stuff to do." How does Phil make everything sound so easy?

"I brought you these for your guts." I lobbed over a little tube of pills that act like anal cement. I got them in India a couple of years ago. Even someone with dysentery, cholera and epilepsy of the sphincter would be constipated for life after one of these little babies.

"Cheers, saved my fuckin life." Tact isn't one of Phil's things. He guzzled half a dozen tablets.

"Er, Phil?"

"Correct."

"I wanted to ask you something. Were Beano and Rita, like ..."

"Fuckin?"

"Yeah."

Phil laughed, an explosion of mirth that ended as soon as it had begun.

"What fuckin planet you livin on, Bernie? Didn't you know?"

"No. Why didn't he tell me?"

"Probably fought you'd be jealous."

"Jealous? Me? Wedded bliss, mate. Me? Jealous?"

Another explosion of mirth from Phil, then one of his phones went and he linked up to his space station again and forgot mere Earthlings like me. As I left, I reminded myself that we're equals in the company. At least I *think* we are.

Rita had dotted a few vases of primary-coloured flowers about, and the meeting room was ready. A bit of sunlight would have been welcome but there was no chance of that. As it had been all summer, the sky was spread up there like reheated mashed potato, greying at the edges. Smelling like old mash too. Where are the sea breezes?

"You really up to this, Rita?"

"Yes. Thanks." She'd dabbed her eyes and was looking better, as if she'd only had a mild attack of conjunctivitis.

"Rita? You know, Beano never mentioned to me that you and he –"

"Why did Ms Greensands insist on an open window?" she interrupted. "What normal person would want to breathe that lot indoors as well as out?"

I took the hint and let it drop.

"Now now, Rita, no blasphemy, please. This is Ms Greensands we're talking about."

Our star guest was shown in five minutes later.

****

Dear Member,
Please support our petition in favour of a referendum to save the National Health Service. Let's put an end to waiting lists and management-heavy hospitals.
Yes, let's take back control and privatise the NHS now.
Vote "yes", and you could become a shareholder and end future waiting times.
TrulyYourNHS

****

5 GRINNING MAGGOTS

Ms Greensands' assistants, two guys with earpieces and suit-bulges, waited for her nod and then stood outside the closed door. Louie, Rita and I got up to greet her. Louie shot me a look to remind me of The Subject That Was Not To Be Mentioned. I avoided further eye contact with him.

We said our hellos and took our places, a jug of something fruity between us. I was sweating stickily. Ms Greensands emanated ease, as if she was fitted with personal air-conditioning.

She was so un-flash it was frightening.

She had on a bland white cotton blouse that hung around her reverently like a cloud of perfectly-schooled geishas. Body toned-looking without being showy, the sort of discreetly fine form maintained simply by expensive holidays and excelling at some martial art or dance genre. Black forest of hair tied up in a pony tail, royal-blue trousers, blindingly polished black high heels (no sign they'd ever stepped on a pavement – maybe they hadn't), and a good-shaped face with no flaws whatever as far as I could see. Just inscrutable brown eyes below lightly made-up lids, and regular features nicely covered in flesh. She was odourless. The sort of woman you instinctively want to impress.

Before any of us could commit the gaffe, she told us she'd heard about our "tragic bereavement". That was frighteningly quick. She must have been hooked up to the same psychic news app as Des. She thanked us for going ahead with the meeting under the circumstances, after "such a terrible, terrible loss." We all observed a respectful three or four seconds' silence, then she told me how much she enjoyed my "See Models Die" movies. I actually blushed. Louie was forced to utter more enthusiasm about me than he had in the whole of the previous year.

Again, after exactly the right amount of praise and polite questioning, Ms Greensands moved the talk on. She asked us to make sure we weren't recording anything that was said, and then began to explain her position.

Her first name is Angela, and I guess she is a sort of business angel. She's from the Ministry of Development, one of these new high-earning links between public and private. She and her kind have the power to decide which way the country's money will circulate. Cynics have said her ministry is just an agency for official bribery and mutual pocket-lining, but that's what cynics would say. Cynics are too damn cynical.

"But do you know what my real ambition was?" she laughed with genuine amusement. "To be an ambassador. Asia somewhere."

"Why didn't you?" Rita did the honours.

"My name," she explained. We didn't get it. "It's a crippling handicap to a diplomatic career. You see, Greensands is a lime-and-apple soda pop in Indonesia. We can't send them European diplomats called Mango Chutney and Curried Dog, can we?"

Bit racist coming from a government minister, I thought, but maybe it was a test. If so, I failed it.

"Not that Asia is a particularly attractive place to work at the moment," I said. "Isn't there some new flu bug out there?"

She didn't reply. On the other hand, she was totally upfront about her privileged position.

"I'm a Junior Minister," she told us, "but I'm also a businesswoman. I have a stake in everything I do. The government has decided that it is time to stop pussy-footing about and pretending that politicians are free of financial interests. We think that the most efficient way to get things done is to make it pay. Not in bribes, you understand."

We all chortled together at this ridiculous notion.

"No," she went on. "We get commission. Bonuses. All declared and taxed. The theory is that this is the only way to tempt the best movers and shakers away from the private sector. And it seems to be working." So she wasn't going to bother with any false modesty. "Now, we've been watching Coma for a while, and we're impressed." She embraced all of us in a congratulatory gaze. I for one felt childishly happy to have earned her admiration. "And, I might add, grateful. You've opened up the health market in a way we hardly believed possible. Huge numbers of patients are leaving our overworked NHS doctors in peace by knocking their names off the waiting lists. I think the Minister of Health will be writing to thank you personally. As soon as he gets back from having his face-lift in Bucharest."

She laughed, and we took this as permission to follow suit. Was she joking or not? Impossible to tell.

"As I understand it, you conceived the design for Coma's online presence, didn't you, er, Bernie?" She held out a hand towards me, palm up, as if she wanted to cup my testicles in some ritual gesture of bonding.

I shook the testicle-weighing image from my head. That, and her calling me by my first name, had sent a thrill through my body, and this wasn't the right time to react.

"Beano and I ..." The name hit me like a thumb in the throat. Angela (for some reason, it felt weird to think of her by her first name) waited politely until I went on. "Beano and I designed the logo and the basic look – what you see when you use any of our services. And we've also created a whole bunch of other stuff under the Coma tag. Fun, quirky things to get us noticed."

"Which they have," she flattered. "And you've designed quite a few things for outside clients?"

"Yes, we've started to put together content for online pharmacies, cosmetic-surgery clinics, health farms and the like."

"Which is why I'm here," she said. She got into the meat of the subject. Her eyes no longer took in all her audience. Now they were fixed on me. "Before we go on, I would like you to know that we're interested to hear absolutely any ideas you can come up with, however extreme you might think they are. Don't censor yourself at all."

So that explained the bad-taste jokes. She was showing us she's one of us. One of me, anyway.

"We are a remarkably free-thinking Ministry," the Junior Minister went on, "and all we care about is results. OK?"

"OK."

"And in view of the urgency of the matter, and the budget at stake, I'd like this project to be given first and complete priority, if that's possible."

"Of course," Louie answered, as if it was his decision.

"Good. Now." She kept her eyes on me. "I want you to go out to ..."

There was a scare story a few months back. A possible new strain of that flesh-eating disease. What's it called – Ricotta? Hezbollah? No, Ebola, that's it. In a matter of minutes, this mutant strain rotted your insides, filled your body with methane, and then you exploded in a ball of flame. You caught it off badgers or migrants or something. Every TV channel and newspaper had a different theory. It hit that village – what was it called? – everyone knew its name for a week or two. A class of schoolkids visiting the place on a field trip roasted a cow (so it was said) by simultaneously self-combusting. Some motorists who were parked outside the village church fireworked themselves through their sun-roofs.

Anyway, it took government medics a month and three splattered nurses to declare the disease a dud. Either it was collective hysteria, their report claimed, or a simple coincidence. One human body in a hundred million may bloat with methane and combust for perfectly natural molecular reasons related to the creation of the universe, the government health Twitter feed told us, just as one wave in a billion is a ferry-capsizing monster. It happened to Spinal Tap's drummer, a commentator said, why not a whole village? And of course, there were enough people out there hitting "like" to make the government report believable.

Angela Greensands made no comment on all this. She simply said the village's name and got the required nod of recognition.

"Perhaps it isn't surprising that the region's income from tourism has tailed off somewhat," she went on, deadpan. "You probably know that the village is just a few miles from one of the country's most popular spa resorts. Very big hydrotherapy business, a small water-bottling plant, the perfect place for stressed-out professionals to get a massage, lose a bit of weight, then put it all back on consuming the local gourmet cuisine. And stressed-out professionals do not like the idea of exploding in their jacuzzi. The spa's brand image has gone down the toilet," she went on. "That's why the regional tourist authority, via my Ministry, would like some ideas. We need to showcase all the beauty spots and hook people up to hotels, restaurants and the rest. And we want something that will appeal especially to foreign clients, who will have retained a more, er, *receptive* attitude towards the place, untainted by slurs about its safety. You know, we want picturesque, quaint. But lively. Healthy fun. Whatever you want – music, video, games, anything."

"Any video will have to be fairly long just to prove that nothing in the scene exploded," I said.

She laughed. "Right. That's the kind of attitude we're looking for. This region needs a few positive thoughts directed its way."

"No problem," Louie put in, "Bernie never has negative thoughts, do you, Bernie?"

"Never." Was that supposed to be a jibe?

"Perfect," Ms G said. "And I must also tell you that this is part of something much bigger that we have in mind."

She let the suggestion, and its budget, sink in.

"Can you give us any hints as to what that is?" Louie finally asked.

She pretended to give this some consideration.

"Let's just say health education for the masses," she said. "And pharmaceuticals. Exactly Coma's domain. If everything goes well, we'd be very interested in working with you further."

Louie looked across at me. He seemed to regret that everything depended on me and my ideas.

"So can I get this clear?" I asked. "You just want an outline on this village revamp? The basic idea?"

"There isn't time for more. You've got 48 hours, tops. Give me a brief outline, an *angle*. Keep in mind what you did for the Woodlanders crematoria. I thought that was very clever. Selling a place that's all about dying, but where you feel that death doesn't exist. Nothing but trees, birds, rebirth, hope. That's what I'm looking for here."

"OK. Great," I said. Nothing I like better than re-selling my old ideas.

"It took us a long time to find the jokes," she said.

"Jokes?" I asked innocently.

"Jokes?" Louie squawked.

"In your visuals, " she said. "By the oak tree? The grinning maggots?" She grinned like a maggot. "And in the grass, the worms holding knives and forks? Very funny. But I'm sure your clients, and their clients, will never notice."

No one was supposed to find that. I must have been doing a goldfish impression, because she added, "Don't worry, Bernie, I won't be telling them."

Them or the police, I hoped, because Armlock was still somewhere in the building, looking for more proof of my psychopathic tendencies.

But I was more awe-struck than terrified.

"The only way you could have found those," I said, "was by downloading the images in full high def, then blowing them up – ooh –"

"A thousand per cent," she said. "Yes, when we're interested in someone we get out the magnifying glass. That's why I say don't censor yourself. Tell us everything. We'd prefer all your clever ideas upfront in our material. We'll be the judges of how apt they are. OK?"

"Perfectly," I agreed again, more impressed with the woman than ever.

"Good. Read the report I'll send you. It tells you all you need to know about the neo-Ebola scare, including our basic brief and a summary of the medical investigations carried out. The PR agency handled it well, don't you think?" She asked this casually, but I felt that no question of hers could ever be casual.

"Yes," I said. "Genius. They were never going to convince everyone, so they went straight for the big lie that would get the believers on board. People believe only the best and worst about health these days. They love disasters and miracles, nothing in between. A clever social-media campaign can convince people that immigrants are stealing babies to sell their DNA. Or a good ad can shift megatons of useless pseudo-herbal anti-hair-loss vitamins. But nobody wants to hear the boring, reassuring stuff, or pleas for moderation. Drink only one glass of wine a day? 'Boring!' Drink red wine and you'll live for ever? 'Pass the corkscrew!' "

She nodded, still studying me carefully, before replying.

"Yes. It's a lesson that the pharmaceutical industry needs to bear in mind. When can you go out there?"

"To the village? This afternoon."

"Excellent. I'm glad I came. You're not the explosive type, are you?"

We all laughed. Louie and Ms G made a date to talk about money, then she got up to leave.

"Your 'See Models Die' page is sick, you know that, don't you?" she asked me.

"Yes, I suppose it is," I agreed, non-committally.

"But very promising." She laughed again.

Promises, promises. I know enough about money to realize that this share buyout is just that – a promise.

But a fee, a commission, that's different. My share of a big-budget project will be hard cash. Even Louie, whose role in our company finance is that of a condom in sex (you know you're getting money/sex, but it just doesn't feel like it), can't avoid paying me commission.

So I went to my cubicle and dialogued with Des. We shared our sorrow about Beano, and then I told him how well the Greensands meet had gone, and where I thought it could take us all. Des's technical magic is an integral part of my work, and my commission. He sounded enthusiastic. He sounded as if he was with me. I was deeply glad.

Because if Beano's killer strikes the company again, I have an order of priority for avoiding premature death. First is me, of course, second is Des. He mustn't get Des. That man is my kidney. He cleanses my ideas of their impurities and makes them fluid and useable, which is surprising in someone as impure as him. He works at home most of the time, nerding away in his nest by the sea, alone and vulnerable to attack.

"Watch out for yourself, Des," I told him. "Remember to put your alarm on."

"It's always on."

"Good, talk to you tomorrow."

"I'll be here."

"Yes, be there, Des, please."

As an afterthought I asked another question.

"By the way, did you know about Beano and Rita?"

"Yes. Didn't you?"

Of course. Des knows everything before it even happens.

As we said our goodbyes, I heard the patter of tiny footsteps approaching, and an indignant voice.

"Bernie!"

Louie alert. I didn't feel like talking about grinning maggots just now. I grabbed laptop and phone and prepared to make my second escape of the day. Time to head out to the exploding village. My guts were still grumbling, but at least there was elation in there now, as well as fear, shock and pills. Hell, I even felt like another yogurt. Beano loved goat's milk yogurt. He was the one who introduced me to it. Nothing gets rid of a hangover like it, he said. Except death, of course.

His joke, not mine.

****

Dear Member,
We are sorry to inform you that one of Coma's founders, Alan Wright, died recently.
This was a great shock to all of us, but we are determined to carry on with the work that Alan helped us begin.
Meanwhile, see our tribute to him here and send his family your thoughts and prayers with one of our downloadable condolence cards.

Civil servants? Boring? No way.
The Ministry of Development is recruiting for its dynamic marketing team.
Join us and do one of the most satisfying jobs in the world – hacking away, day to day, at the red tape that has held this country back for generations.
We offer very competitive salary packages and generous commission.
Ain't no stopping us now. We are on the move.
Movers and shakers look HERE. The rest of you go back to sucking your thumbs.

****

6 Berk Nerk

I opened up the soft top and dodge-drove through the lines of dawdlers. The motionless sea gave me some instant mood-massage. The boats out in the bay were bobbing prosperously.

I remembered that I hadn't listened to the voicemail on my old work phone. Back at the beginning of Coma, we were given phones for work-related stuff, the idea being to keep our private life private. Ever since my work-life balance evened out, so that work more or less became my life, I've centralized everything on my personal phone. But I still have the old work number, and it occasionally picks up calls. I hadn't listened in over the weekend, and did so now.

There was just one voicemail, and it had me almost veering into the sea wall.

"Bernie ... Berk ... Nerk."

OK, transcribed, it doesn't sound too throat-squeezingly nasty, but I'll explain. The first word, my name, was hoarse, but I recognized the voice. The next bits were just croaks. I looked up the call time. Six fifty-one this morning. And its origin. Beano's number.

Holy excrement. I mean, if you're getting murdered, the killer doesn't usually give you a break while you phone a friend and warn him you won't be in to work this morning. Keeping a careful eye on the whipping traffic, I played the call back again. There were clunks before the words, and a grunt of pain just before the message cut off. Maybe he'd had time to speed-dial my number before the killer closed right in. In his haste, he'd dialled the old work phone.

And his phone probably flashed up my name for the killer to read. Help.

I called the Inspector. She said she'd have a listen. She hung up before I could ask her how she expected to listen in to my PIN-number-protected voicemail. I stopped at a parking spot and shot undigested yogurt over the sea wall. It plopped in little atolls on the glistening water. A seagull swooped down to taste it.

I was leaning on the car, gulping bottled water, when the phone rang. My personal one.

"Bernie?" It was Rita, not the Inspector.

"Yeah."

"You OK?"

"Yeah, yeah."

"I've got some good news." She didn't sound happy about it, which was understandable in the circumstances.

"Yeah?"

"Our PR people just called. There's been another article about immorality on the internet in one of the national papers. Apparently they went into great detail about 'See Models Die'. There's been 1,000 hits a minute all morning."

"Wow. Did they give you any other details?"

"Other details?"

"About the alleged immorality."

"Oh. Yes, they didn't like the Turin shroud."

"The what?"

"Apparently, seen in negative, Claudine in bed under the sheet looks exactly like the Turin shroud."

"A spitting image."

"Very funny, Bernie."

"Oh, God. Sorry, Rita. Shit. Still, no one'll take that crap seriously."

"Well, the reporters have been calling."

"Hell."

"I thought you enjoyed getting people's backs up, Bernie. People talking about you."

"Yes, but that was before ..." Was that a sob I heard? "Look, Rita. I really didn't know about you and Beano. I'm so sorry."

"Yeah."

"Why didn't he tell me? We told each other everything."

"I don't know."

"Why didn't *you* tell me?"

"I don't know." This time it was definitely a sob. It nearly punctured my eardrum.

"Shit, I'm sorry, Rita. You, er, I'll ... See you later."

I can't handle direct emoting. It's OK when it's *my* emotions. But other people's I can't take. I never know what to say. I usually dive in for a hug. But you can't hug someone over the phone.

I risked my life pulling out into the traffic and drove on out of town. When the Inspector got back to me, I apologized and said I couldn't come into her office to discuss Beano's phone call. I tried Phil's trick and asked if we could make an appointment. The Inspector growled and threatened and tried out a few ultimatums on me, but I really didn't feel up to facing her again. I needed a change of scenery.

****

Dear Member,
Looking for cheap nursing staff?
Ever considered *nuns*?
Cheap and mobile and they won't go on maternity leave.
Discount for groups of ten or more.
Check out DevotedSisters

"We met on line and we clicked straight away!"
BedsideManner is the place where doctors and nurses get to play doctors and nurses.

Coma to sign major government contract? More details at InvestorNews

****

7 The Target

Mere minutes (and a few pills) later, I was zipping through primeval forest. Well, as primeval as a Christmas-tree plantation can get, anyway. The flat sky was giving the scene some soulful lighting. My slipstream was whipping up whirls of dust. I switched the radio on.

"According to a new government study, the most common cause of death amongst –"

I changed channel. I know it's good for the health business, but anyone would think we were all going to drop dead tomorrow. These so-called journalists must get paid per corpse. It's always bad news, scare stories.

You never hear, for example, that last night, for the 1500th consecutive Saturday, happy science teacher Jean Smith, 55, achieved simultaneous orgasm with her faithful husband John, 59, a well-paid factory worker with a healthy prostate. The couple plan to have a quiet Sunday lunch at home with their employed, home-owning kids and their asthma-free grandchildren, as usual. You never hear that, do you? And people accuse *me* of being sick.

I found some music, something cloudy, something really cirrus. I wished I had a helicopter's eye view of me in my car, my hair rustling like wheat, the forest forming a guard of honour either side of my shiny, eco-friendly car.

Then it occurred to me that I would look exactly like the target in some fighter-plane game. *Shootin' Up the Highway*, or something. I couldn't resist looking up into the sky to make sure there were no jets diving down for a strafe.

After that I just drove and tried to keep my mind empty of everything except the music. A couple of times a song reminded me of Beano. But then straight afterwards a record came on that reminded me of a holiday, school, or sex, and somehow my thoughts for Beano switched off again each time.

Sex, yes. Not much of that about at the moment. Things aren't too hot with Granola. Need to look elsewhere, perhaps? Yes ...

I squeezed the phone as if it was a snake that had swallowed my car keys.

"Allo?" At last. Superb, no hint of an anglicized accent, just straight oyster-slurping vowels.

"Claw Dean, hi. It's Bernie here. I'm ringing about how are you by the way? Sorry, what manners, I'm up to my ears, still, no excuse really ... er, OK I hope?"

"Bare knee." She said the name as if just remembering me. True, when I last saw Claudine we weren't alone. The whole team was there, all of us high on cash, having just learnt that the buyout was a possibility. Phil did a lot of talking, so did Mona and Beano. I did some too, all of it in Claudine's direction. Several times she turned her head partly towards me. Of *course* she remembers me.

"How are you, Claudine?" Got to get a grip on my voice.

"Fine, thank you, how are you?"

"I'm OK, thank you," but I didn't phone to give her a bloody English lesson. "There's something I want to discuss with you. Merchandising to sell on the 'See Models' page. It's still really popular, you know."

"I will get royalties, yes?"

"Of course."

"OK, yes."

"Yes what?"

"Yes, we can discuss."

"Great. So maybe we could I think we ought to it's better if we meet up what are you how about *lunch*?"

"Lernch? Today?"

"Well, if you're not I mean tomorrow in fact yes I can't today actually tomorrow would be if possible best."

"Lernch tomorrow?"

"Yes."

"OK. Where?"

"I'll pick you up."

"Uh?"

"I mean I'll come round."

"Uh?"

"I'll come shay twar."

"Ah, yes, come round. You'll come over me?"

"Right, I'll come over you." Like I said, I'm not her English teacher.

That is one of the many reasons I hate Louie. I don't understand how money works, and everyone thinks that ignorance about money equals total ignorance, whereas Louie knows loads of things about loads of money, so everyone thinks he's Einstein Junior. Which is pretty accurate, assuming Einstein Senior had an extra-marital affair with a Vietnamese pot-bellied pig. Even Claudine thinks Louie's fascinating – at the party, she talked to him for ages about the buyout, preferring his banal numbers to our red-hot wit.

Numbers are all that interest Louie. He'd rather sleep with a calculator than Claudine. A long time ago I suggested to him, why don't we produce action dolls of the model girl in my movies, real collectors' items? And he said, no, we don't need merchandising, or if we do, we only want low-cost, no-brainer stuff. Cheap, unbreakable crap like T-shirts and tote bags.

Look, Louie, I'm going to get these action dolls made whether you like it or not, I told him.

The company won't pay for them, he said. These movies of yours aren't expected to make money, he explained slowly, as if saying it for the hundredth time (when in fact it was the twentieth, max). But they're not expected to lose any, either. And anyway, he said, all that gimmicky stuff is not one of my priorities, Bernie. We're using your movies to attract members, small ads and sponsors – merchandising is way down our agenda.

You have to hate someone who says "way down our agenda." But I also hate him because he's always so bloody right. With him, two plus two always equals the same thing, and it's incredibly annoying.

Now, though, maybe two plus two will equal four plus a little extra for me.

I reached the turn-off towards the exploding village. I could see it, a mile away, crouching in its ancient rift in the landscape. I pulled over and looked at myself in the mirror. No chubby cheeks, no signs of puffiness around the eyes, surely the most explosive part of us. I reminded myself how much I needed a spectacular success here, and went in.

The village was unbelievably ... well ... village-like. It was an ad for organic biscuits. No outward sign of the recent "hysteria". Mainly because, from what Ms Greensands told us, the whole area had been hosed down with antibiotics.

From my open-top I clicked away at a farm worker, hair poking from his cap, his shirt-front and the arse of his trousers (they really ought to stop drinking the fertilizers, these boys). I got some snaps of old stone chimneys casually polluting the village air, the little church like a stack of soggy shoe-boxes, and of The Extra Arms, a newly converted ex-stable pub. It was run by a couple of former townies who came out and objected to the way I was pointing my zoom lens at their pubescent daughter in her butt-squeezing jodhpurs.

"Clear off!" Daddy told me.

"They'll arrest you as soon as you put the photos on Facebook," Mummy added.

"But I'm just ..."

"You're just a pervert, that's what you are!"

Another woman popped her head out of the pub door.

"Paedophile!" she yelled. "Wossie been doing?"

"Taking pictures of our Kate," Mummy told her.

"Wants castratin. Ear, George!" The woman called into the pub, presumably to the peasant who chops the balls off lambs and piglets. I'd have made a run for it if it hadn't been for Angela Greensands and her budget.

"Please let me explain," I smiled, regretting at once that I was trying to sound posh. I always imagine paedophiles as upper class, for some reason. "You've got it all wrong."

But they met all my protestations of innocence with insults and surgical threats. Until, that is, I managed to tell them exactly why I was in their village, at which point the landlord realized that "it must be thirsty work" and practically licked the road clean for me to walk upon as he begged me to accept a free drink.

I obliged by explaining how to make me a couple of Singapore Slings (no way was I going to sample their explosive local rot-in-the barrel brew) and by showing off my photo enhancement app to the customers as I zoomed in on the interesting bits. Apparently, none of the assorted neo-utang drinkers had ever enlarged any photos before, but that didn't surprise me. They clearly had several generations of technology to catch up on. Efficient razors, for example, soap. They and their village seemed deathly dull, but that was presumably what the region would have to sell: the lack of human methane bombs.

Back outside in the overcast heat, the world tinged pink by the afternoon sky and my cocktails, the pub looked snug and homely, a place where anyone would love to snooze a weekend away. Ideas were buzzing up like the first evening insects. I decided to accept the innkeeper's invitation to stay overnight, on the house. Armlock would be mad as hell, but who did I want to please more, a local cop or a Junior Minister?

I now understood why the tourists had come to the area before, and why they'd come again. After a mineral-water enema at the nearby spa, what better way to spend an evening than to come to this pub for a "Rusticke Fayre" blow-out. No, a *meal*, I mean. "Blow-out" definitely not.

I can't afford slips like that. No dodgy puns. And I'll have to warn the locals to cut out the wisecracks, too. The Extra Arms is the only pub I've ever been in where *everyone* pops their crisp bag.

As the sun belly-flopped on to the horizon, I went for a wander around the village. Curtains parted as I passed. A man stopped gardening to watch me. Whether the villagers had already heard about my mission or were just curious to see if this newcomer self-detonated, I don't know.

I walked and mused until the sunset set off my body-clock alarm. I tried to calculate how long it was since I'd last slept. It was six-oh-four, my watch informed me – three-oh-four in the morning in Tokyo. Tomorrow already for them, the poor lost souls. I hadn't slept the previous night, but the day before that I'd woken up late, about lunchtime, so that meant I'd only had ... Oh fuck it, I decided. It's rest my brain needs, not aerobic arithmetic.

I dragged my groaning limbs up the narrow wooden stairs to my room, turned off my phone, took off my shoes, crashed out on the bed and let myself drift down into merciful sleep. I then leapt up sweating, turned on the light, locked the door and lay down again. Then got up, double-checked the windows, balanced a brass flower jug against the curtains so that any intruder would kick it over and wake me up, and settled down for sleep. Rose again, wedged a chair against the door, put a shoe under my pillow to use as a weapon in case of attack, felt around the walls for a secret entrance in the panelling, bashed my head on the corner of the bedside table and passed out.

****

All your transplant problems solved.
Organs for sale. Live extraction on demand.
Guaranteed resistant to foot and mouth.
Check out HogHearts

Bernie
Where the hell are you?
Why is your phone switched off?
And why are Coma shares going into orbit? How come there are so many available to buy, anyway? Has one of you sold some? X

****

8 COCKTAIL SAUSAGE

I was woken by a male voice.

"He's asleep," it said.

I screamed, and ripped my eyelids apart. Two shadows were looming over me. One of them bent forward, holding out a hand towards my throat. I bit at flesh and suddenly I wasn't the only one yelling.

I jumped to my feet just as someone yanked open the curtains. Blinded, I lashed out at air with feet and fists, still bawling loud enough to wake the whole village. Where was the landlord? Surely even non-paying guests were entitled to be protected from killers?

"Mr Bridges?"

As my eyes focussed, I saw that the room was empty and the door shut.

"Have you finished?" The voice was outside the door.

Maybe it had all been a dream.

"Who is it?" I ventured, and picked up a brass jug from the floor, just in case someone answered, "we're the murderers".

"Police. Sergeant Milner." The name rang a bell.

"What do you want?"

"To keep all my fingers, basically." There was sniggering behind the door. "Can we come back in now?"

"OK."

I put down the jug as the adrenalin began seeping out of my veins. Unfortunately, as everyone knows, when adrenalin ebbs, pain flows. My head was throbbing. I looked toward the mirror on the back of the door to inspect the facial damage, but my reflection veered away as the door opened and a head popped round it. Milner. Of course. Armlock's dumb assistant.

"Sorry if we gave you a fright," he said. "But you were pretty scary yourself." He held up a hand with a love bite at the base of his little finger. "You could get life in some US states for trying to exchange bodily fluids with a policeman, you know."

He edged into the room, keeping a professional eye on me in case of any sudden movements. He was followed by a young blonde policewoman in a leather jacket. Milner himself had donned natty tweed for this trip to the country.

"Heavy night?" Milner asked.

"Uh?"

"You were on the floor. Drinking to forget?"

"Yeah. Didn't work, though."

"Oh, I don't know. You forgot that you weren't supposed to leave town," Milner said.

"Bloody hell. Is that why you're here? To arrest me?"

"No, we're just delivery boys." His female sidekick nudged him. "Sorry, delivery people. The Inspector would like an informal chat."

"Oh yeah. One of those."

"What was so urgent that you had to ignore the Inspector's request?"

"Work," I said. "For the government. Life doesn't stop just because ..." But I didn't feel like completing the sentence. Life does just stop. That's the problem.

"The landlord's making us all a cup of tea," Milner said. "We'll wait outside the door while you, hey, you OK?"

I'd just found a volcano on the side of my head and winced with the pain. "Yeah, fine. Be out in a minute."

"We'll take your phone and your computer for you, OK?" Milner picked them both up off the floor.

"And you'll be needing this." His partner handed me a shoe that had been poking out from under my pillow. I'm sure there was more sniggering as soon as they got outside again.

"OK, so what really happened was, I did in Beano, then I made hell of a row falling down the stairs, and threw up all over his neighbour just so I'd leave a good DNA sample lying around. That's what you want to hear, isn't it? Well, thanks for the solidarity. Of course I didn't kill him. Why should I? Look, we're talking about my best friend's death here, not who overcooked the fucking asparagus."

"Don't use language like that at me."

"Ugh."

I was sitting in the passenger seat of my car, watching Milner enjoy the drive and my pathetic phone call. His partner was already lagging way behind us in the medieval copmobile.

I'd had to watch the pair of them snuffling down a full cooked breakfast while I repeatedly listened to my lawyer's voicemail message. As a stalling tactic, I then refused to drive back to town in case I still had alcohol in my blood. As a stalling tactic, it was as efficient as offering a cocktail sausage to an attacking wolf pack, because five minutes later Milner was driving me towards Armlock in my own car at approximately double the speed limit.

My pathetic phone call wasn't to the Inspector. No, it was to Granola, who clearly thinks I'm enough of a bastard to kill my best friend. Or at least she doesn't think I'm sufficiently un-bastard-like for her to rule out totally that I'd kill my best friend.

"And another thing," she said. "While I've got your full attention. I looked at the credit-card statements yesterday. And unless you're planning to surprise me with a bucketful of diamonds to celebrate our decree nisi, you've got some explaining to do."

"Sorry, Granola, I don't do cryptic on an empty stomach."

"This bill from the jeweller's."

"Jeweller's? Oh fuck! Turn around!" I snatched at the steering wheel with my bare-wristed right hand.

"You fucking idiot!" Milner tried to prise my fingers off the wheel.

"We've got to go back! I left my watch at the pub!"

"Fucking hell. Is that all? Phone them up." We were back on the right side of the road again, but Milner was still shaken. Persuasion was out of the question.

"Sorry Granola." I rang her off, called the pub and hung on as the landlord went and searched my room. He felt obliged to keep up his patter as he fiddled for the key, moved chairs, opened cupboards and drawers.

"... and that's including wine. Ah, here we go. Down by the bed."

"Thank God for that. Can you keep it safe till I come and collect it?"

"Looks a little dented."

"Dented? It can't be. It's made of a metal specially developed by NASA for its meteorite shields. Just put it in a safe place and I'll pick it up as soon as I can, OK? Thanks."

Damn. I hope NASA kept the guarantee certificates.

I'm beginning to have my doubts about that watch. For a start, before buying it, I should have waited till Granola and I separated out our bank accounts. I'm sure a psychologist would have a field day with our bank accounts. How come, three months (I think it's three months) after we stopped sharing a bed, we still share salaries? Mind you, we still share an address, too. For all social purposes, we're still man and wife. I guess that just means sex isn't a social purpose.

After Milner, Granola, the landlord and fate, next up to take a slug at me on this fine morning was Louie. He'd left a terse message asking me why the (and I quote) "FUCK" I wasn't at the crisis meeting. I could imagine him sitting there in the meeting room, dictating his macho message for me as the others looked on. No way was I going to let him get away with that.

I hit call back, looking across to make sure Milner was picking up my aggression.

"Louie? Bernie. Listen, don't leave messages like that for me, OK? I'm a partner, right? I'm twenty per cent of the company now."

"Which is exactly why we needed you to be at the fucking crisis meeting, Bernie," he replied.

Like I said, how can you not hate someone who's so bloody right all the time?

To console myself, I started to chat to Milner. He turned out to be quite a nice guy. He'd looked up "See Models Die" since our interview yesterday, and thought it was "a killer". How come, I wondered, that everyone has their tact functions switched off these days? Or perhaps it was nothing new. Maybe I was just noticing it now that I had a chink in my usual armour.

Milner was keen to know more about Claudine. I bullshitted about how it had taken half an hour to get the bedsheet to cling exactly to her complex contours, and he groaned in all the right places.

But the male bonding stopped when they got me into Armlock's office.

****

"The NHS has announced that from now on, euthanasia will be available for patients in the terminal phase of certain diseases.
However, because of health cuts, there will be a two-year waiting list for treatment."

There are hundreds more where that came from. Sign up for Coma's daily dose of medical humour at KeepYourPatientsLaughing

****

9 Ten a Day

It was crude stuff. Inspector Armlock actually asked me at one point if I wanted to visit the cells "now or later". *Really*. My brain, although none too fresh, managed to work up some objections about warrants and innocence and citizens' rights. Just enough to make her laugh.

But her theory that Beano, shouting my name in incredulous horror as I loomed over him, unwittingly made his phone dial me and record his last croaks on my voicemail, doesn't stand up, does it?

Does it?

She let me go about two. I came away feeling almost grateful. Apart from the mind games, the police station's depressing colour scheme (mud-coloured paint and criminals' mugshots have never been my favourite decor) and its smell (cheap air freshener with a soupçon of jockstrap), my half-day with Armlock was an uplifting experience. I left with five important pieces of information.

One, no one stole anything from Beano's flat that morning. Two, there have been four other recent deaths in the area "in similar circumstances", including one the same day. Three, if the Inspector is so pissed off, it's because her Scene of Crime team didn't find enough evidence to arrest me, or anyone else. Four, our company lawyer clearly thinks I'm a waste of time, because it took her several hours to turn up at the police station. And five, I am a heartless, egotistical shit.

OK, so number five is not exactly surprising (Granola reminds me of the fact quite often), but I've only just seen it for myself.

It was when Armlock was talking about the inquest. No date has been set, she said. The post-mortem results were a long time coming. It occurred to me that if Beano's body didn't hurry up and tell everyone exactly how he died, he could be bumped out of line in the police's priorities. His case would take second place to a drive-by or overdose. My friend would lay in the fridge, his stomach stitched up, his organs bottled, until the cops just called off the investigation and signed the paper that would allow him to go away and rot in peace.

It wasn't that idea that made me see what a shit I am. It was the next stage in my thought process. I suddenly thought, à propos of nothing, hey, I was supposed to be having lunch with Claudine today. I'm going to miss it.

Yes, Beano had been bumped out of my line of priorities by a bloody *lunch* date.

Before leaving the cop shop, I asked Armlock to put a guard on my house. I wanted a marksman at every window and body searches on everyone entering my street. She finally agreed to listen in on my landlines in case of threats (my suggestion) and to provide me with an escort as far as the police-station door.

I got back into my car, scraped the skin off my knuckles trying to re-adjust the seat (Milner had basketball player's legs), and drove. I had a good idea who, apart from Rita, Beano might have seen last.

I couldn't tell the police about this. Partly because they'd have been too scared to follow it up, but mainly because of the possible tax implications. There was money at stake. Cash in hand.

I took the seafront road out of town.

The sea always does it for me, even the dull, grey English Channel on its dullest, greyest day. What is the point of living on an island if you don't live on the coast? Bournemouth's motto is "Pulchritudo in Salubritas". It means something along the lines of Health and Beauty, which sounds like the name of an old soft-porn mag.

Today, the sea looked healthy and beautiful in a kind of Terminator way. It looked so silver and metallic that it was impossible to believe anything was alive in there. Fish of all sizes – from hatchling to basking shark – were presumably going about their business, eating and being eaten, but on the surface everything was dead calm.

The Earth must look that way from orbit. Gazing down on the map-shaped continents, how can astronauts believe that people are shooting each other for believing different ideas about religion, politics, or drug-dealing territories? Or weeping uncontrollably because one person inserted a small piece of their flesh into a person other than the weeping one? Or finding it hard to breathe because one of the seven billion or so similar organisms down there has stopped breathing completely?

I stopped off at an ATM, then nipped into a service-station. Here I filled the tank, put up my car roof and bought a large brown envelope that would be essential for my errand.

I put in a call to Claudine. She hadn't sent me a pissed-off message about missing lunch. Didn't she care? I got through to voicemail, and left a message saying sorry, urgent business for the government, could we make it tonight instead? I'd call round at eight. If she couldn't make it, could she call me or send a message?

I'd like to see a breakdown of phone-company turnover: money spent on actually talking to a human being versus money spent talking into, listening to or writing to a machine. Bastards. They've turned me into a complete machine addict.

I drove on, and soon reached my turning. Mine was the only car to veer off here. Not surprising. I am where no one should be.

There are a hundred yards of demolition. Some hunks of rubble have lazing brown blobs on them, a few of which scuttle off at my approach. Rats, stray cats, four-legged viruses? I daren't look too close.

After that, there are rows of buildings. Well, "building" is a nostalgic name for them. None of these "buildings" show any signs of remembering when they were built. Crumblings, I should say, cavings-in. Roofs are balding, a window is no more than a scab of old cloth stuck to the inside of the empty frame.

The pavement is a sparse and saggy coat of tarmac stretched over (or sometimes under) exposed pipes, cables, sodden rubbish. The road surface itself is rutted, scorched, cracked, or debris-covered, depending on where I try to point my nose. Not my own nose, thank God, that is safe behind a screen of perfumed air-conditioning. The nose of my car, which twitches at a sudden movement in the gutter.

People. Alone or in groups they scratch, chew and smoke, all of them watching me. No one drives here, especially not in a brand-new car. Their faces, hair and hands are darker than mine, and only in very few of them is this because of muck. They lack new clothes, the occasional finger, but most of all they lack food, health and money. Any one of them would have every reason in the world to kill Beano: envy, poverty, spite, addiction, untreated schizophrenia, despair or just plain boredom.

Not everyone fits in very well with the town's motto, "Health and Beauty". These people are more Uglitudo et Insalubritas. Perhaps that's why they're on the urban fringes. These are the people who have drifted (or been drifted) beyond the town, beyond the welfare system, beyond any system. They're unemployable rather than unemployed.

This, surprisingly, is where Granola and I met. When I was at college, before all my time got eaten up by the business, I used to come out here with the university Community Group. A bunch of students in a minibus turning up every Wednesday morning to help the health visitors. I suppose we must have looked like Victorian ladies, arriving with our latex gloves and self-righteousness to do our bit for those less fortunate than ourselves, la-di-da. But the locals seemed to be grateful. I admit that I only joined at first as a chance to meet women. When I was a student, doing this kind of direct-action community work was a good way to show the ladies that I had a heart. But then I got hooked on the buzz of helping out.

I was helping people to write letters and make phone calls to the council, hassling them about unrepaired windows, leaky roofs, dry rot and bad plumbing. Some of the bathrooms these people had were too disgusting to use as frog ponds. The residents said that their complaints were always ignored, but when I phoned, my educated accent worked wonders. I got past obstructive switchboards, I made appointments for repairs to be made, I even got thanked for my calls.

Granola was doing drug counselling. I'd noticed her, but I didn't think I was in with a chance. Too prim, I thought. Too posh. Too serious. We talked, but I got the impression she thought I was a bit of a dickhead. Well, I was.

Anyway, nothing happened between us until one day when an immigrant woman was waiting for our minibus to turn up, and grabbed my arm as soon as I got off.

"Come look this," the lady said. She led me away, and I started deep breathing, in case I had to poke my nose somewhere that would require me to stop inhaling. I glanced around at my workmates for help, and a couple of them including Granola followed us, looking vaguely amused. Was there a prank about to hit me, I wondered.

"Here," the woman said, pushing me in front of her. We went into one of the houses, through a door that had been kicked in and hurriedly repaired a dozen times. There was dust everywhere. Shit, I thought, the ceiling's fallen in and squashed one of her kids. She pushed me along the hall and through another door. "We wait it for you," she said.

"You what?" In front of me was a gleaming bathtub with bright silvery taps, a new washbasin and mirror, and a perfect white toilet.

"They just finish," she said. "We want you first go toilet."

She went out and pulled the door shut.

I sat on the new loo and wept.

Next thing I knew, Granola was smiling down at me. She pulled me to my feet, hugged me, and then her mouth was on mine. I don't know what surprised me more: the new loo or the fact that a nice girl like Granola would burst in and stick her tongue down my throat.

For months after that, Granola and I were at it like newly released prisoners. She was as horny as I was. I still don't understand how you can go from that kind of sustained infatuation to our present state of mutual antagonism. Our ten fucks a day have turned into ten fuck-you's.

The immigrant lady has emigrated away from the area now. I don't blame her. All pretence at keeping the housing liveable seems to have stopped. Though there has been one change for the better. One of the industrial buildings has been renovated. It's this I've come to visit.

I am, as usual, feeling shit-scared about parking up. I've driven out here three times recently (you can't, unfortunately, do absolutely everything on line yet), and each time I've been convinced that I'd be leaving on foot, or at the very least with "cunt" scratched into my paintwork. So far, so good. Perhaps because the guy I've come to see is too scary even for the local car thieves.

Stanley, his name is, and he's the cheapest T-shirt printer in the region. In the world, possibly.

How about this for an idea? T-shirts as health aids. I've ordered two models so far. One of them gives simple instructions on what to do in case of a heart attack. A guy with a chronic cardiac disease keels over in the street, you open up his collar to give him air, and there you find the T-shirt that could save his life. I read that over 50% of heart-attack fatalities could be saved if victims got the right kind of help in the first ten minutes after the attack begins. The shirt tells you the symptoms to look for, and how to keep the patient alive until the ambulance arrives. All in four easy-to-read stages.

The other design I ordered is what to do in case of a diabetic coma – some sufferers get mistaken for drunks and left to die. This one says "Hi, I'm diabetic, if I'm acting strangely it may be because my body needs insulin", and then tells you how to get their blood-sugar levels stable again.

Louie can't say no to these, even if Beano won't be there to back me up. Beano was going halves with me on the initial outlay. This time Louie will have to admit I'm right. I'm going to present him with a thousand *fait accomplis* that he can stick way up his agenda.

"Stanley?" I call out as I lock the car doors. Best to let everyone know who I've come to see.

Stanley's printing works is in an old prefab warehouse that has had a new roof put on, bright red window frames and reinforced windows installed, and a large sign attached to the front wall: "Rottweilers like burglars. They're tastier than canned meat."

The dogs, though, are only loose at night. Stanley himself is the daytime deterrent. I hammer loudly on the open door and wait a few moments before going in. If he's printing counterfeit money, I don't want to be the one to see it.

But when I put my head round the door, there's no one there, and Stanley's four large printing machines are idle.

"Oy!"

I nearly have a heart attack myself as I swivel to see Stanley marching towards me. If I didn't know who he was, I think a heart attack would be preferable to facing up to him. There's something about the combination of unfeasibly large biceps, Maori-style neck tattoos and a carnivorous grin that makes me feel very vulnerable.

"Sorry about that, Bern. Just went round the back for a slash," Stanley says, and holds out his hand for me to shake. Even though there are probably no washing facilities behind his warehouse, it seems impolite to refuse.

"How are things?" I ask him as we go inside.

"All the better for seeing you," he replies, sounding unpleasantly like a certain fairy-tale character.

"T-shirts ready?"

"Course." He leads me over to a large table covered in a blue plastic sheet. "Here you go." He pulls the sheet aside, and there are my heart-attack shirts, looking as white and bright as a new toilet. Except for the black writing, of course.

"Great job," I say, picking one up. It is, too. The printing is crystal clear and the T-shirts feel good, they even smell good. I don't know how he sells them so cheaply – cheaper than Asia – and I don't care. If it turns out they're stolen, then I'm just a poor innocent victim.

I turn to another pile, the diabetic shirts. Again, the black characters are un-smudged and perfectly legible, with no ink spots anywhere. Even so, my smile fades.

"Fuck," I moan.

"What is it?" The muscles beneath Stanley's eyes flex at me.

"This." I point to the first line of text.

"Is it wrong?"

"Yes. How can it be wrong? I e-mailed you the text."

"Yeah, but I had a few problems with that one. You sent it as an attachment. I tried converting it various ways but I kept getting these gaps and weird characters. So I ran it through the spellchecker, and that's what it came up with."

"Hi, I'm diuretic?"

"Yeah, that's medical, innit?"

"Do you know what it means?"

"No."

"It means, roughly translated, 'I make you want to piss'."

"Shit."

"No, that'd be, 'hi, I'm laxative'."

Stanley laughs, then looks suddenly serious again.

"Not my fault if you sent me a duff text. That means you pay, right?"

Stanley is not a man you contradict without armed backup.

"Yeah, my fault. Mine and the fucking computers. I thought they were supposed to be able to talk to each other."

"No way, mate," Stanley said, all smiles now that he's sure of getting paid. "If everything was compatible with everything else, there'd be a lot less people making money out of computers, right? It's a tangled worldwide web we weave."

"Hey, that's good. Did you just make it up?"

"No, printed it on some shirts last week. Can have one if you want. Got the dosh?"

"Sure. I'll need a receipt."

I took the large brown envelope out of my pocket and handed it over. He counted the wad and nodded to himself.

"What about the rest?" he asked.

"We said nine hundred, right?" I began to sweat. Maybe this was the time I'd be leaving my car behind. With my balls still in it.

"A grand for your shirts, minus the ton deposit, and a grand for your mate's."

"My mate's? Beano had some others made?" Beano hadn't mentioned anything to me about doubling the order.

"Yeah." Stanley went around the table to another stack of shirts and threw one to me. This example of his impeccable printing read: "Protect your kids from obscenities. Download our parental control app, NoShitFuckOrBollocks".

"When did he order these?"

"Last time he came over. Friday I think it was."

"Friday?"

"Yeah. Said he'd be back Sunday with some dosh, but he never turned up. Far as I'm concerned, easiest thing to do is for you to pay me and get the money off him."

I tried to work out whether it was a good idea to tell Stanley why getting money off Beano wasn't as easy as it sounded.

"He didn't give you any money at all?" I asked.

"Yeah he did. On Friday he gave me the deposit for your shirts, and the order for his new ones. Without a deposit for them. And, generous dickhead that I am, I went ahead and printed the bloody things."

I wondered how many people knew that Beano was planning to carry large wads of cash about that weekend.

"When did Beano come out here on Friday? Morning or afternoon?"

"Afternoon. About four."

"He just turned up and drove away again?"

"Yeah."

"No one followed him? He didn't give anyone a lift back into town?"

"No." Stanley laughed. True, the idea of Beano letting anyone from around here within yards of his car was inconceivable. Almost as inconceivable as the idea of him getting killed.

"Anyone come out with him?" He might have brought Rita along to scare her a bit. It was one of his dubious sayings: scared girls are fun.

"No. Well, can't be sure. I wouldn't have seen if someone had stayed in the car. Those windows of his are just like mirrors. Why?" He's getting suspicious now.

"Was anyone else here in the warehouse with you?"

"No. What are you? Fucking part-time cop or something?" He looks dangerous. I wouldn't like to be a cop, routinely asking questions that get people as annoyed as this. Before Stanley can lose patience with me and engage in physical debt-collection tactics, I explain.

"He was murdered yesterday morning."

"Murdered? Shit. How?"

"Choked. Massive bruises on his neck. Couple of other people have been murdered in town recently, too. You haven't heard anyone round here bragging about coming in and killing off wage slaves, have you?"

"No."

"Be worth some money to find out."

"I'll ask around."

"And you haven't seen anyone out here flashing lots of readies about?"

"No. I'm the only one round here earning," he laughs bitterly. "And even I'm still waiting for one of my payments."

"Right, yeah. Can I pay his share by credit card?"

Stanley considers a moment, and then seems to decide that it'd be proper to make a gesture of condolence.

"Sure, I need to put some stuff through the books. Five hundred on plastic and you give me five hundred in cash. Say, before Wednesday midnight, OK?"

"And I can take the T-shirts now?"

"Yeah, I trust you." Meaning he trusted me not to want limbs snapped unnecessarily. "So, shit, cops got any leads on who killed Beano?"

"Yeah, they reckon it was me."

I told him all about Armlock as I did the business with my credit card and we packed up the shirts. We bagged the heart-attack ones first, and when he'd run out of bin liners, we stacked the remaining shirts straight into the car, filling every available space except the driving seat.

"Sure you don't want to swap this buggie for my van, Bernie?" he laughed. The laugh turned into a sneeze. "Must be the dust," he said. He wiped his nose, then held out his hand for me to shake. If it was a test of my courage, I failed, and felt something squelch against my palm. "Wednesday," he said.

"Before midnight," I promised, and he slithered his hand free of my fingers. As soon as he was out of sight, I emptied a bottle of hand gel into my palm, and sacrificed one of the diuretic T-shirts as a towel.

On the way back in, I called Rita.

"Where *are* you?" she asked.

"I'm cruising about two feet above Earth, where are you?"

"Louie's been going mental because you've had your phone switched off."

"Well it's switched on now. What was so important?"

"Ms Greensands called to ask where you were on the village project."

"Already? What did you say?"

"I said you'd got all your photos ready."

"Brilliant."

"She wanted to confirm your meeting this afternoon."

"Confirm it."

"I did."

"Brilliant."

"Will you be wanting to put together some kind of formal presentation?"

"No, that's not what she wants. Do you know where Des is? He hasn't been answering."

"He went out somewhere with Phil. Shall I check?"

"Out? Des? No, it's OK. See you."

"Wait – Louie's been trying to warn you that the press have been sniffing about. What with that newspaper article about immorality, and ... you know ..."

"Yeah, I know." Yes, Rita, your boyfriend is dead. But don't forget he was my best mate long before he mated with you.

"They think you might ..."

"Might what? Be some kind of sicko murderer, is that it?"

"No, I don't *think* so." Her italics were damning.

"Shit! Have the police been talking to them or what?"

"I don't know. Louie's mad. He's been going on about you sinking the boat for everybody. He says he's going to delete the Models films. Them and anything else that might make Coma look bad."

"What?" Driving while talking on the phone is dangerous at the best of times, but waving my steering-wheel hand about in exasperation nearly killed me and the occupants of an oncoming family saloon. "He can't do that!"

"He says we don't need them any more."

"Don't? Need? What!" In the past, I may have dismissed my model movies as student doodlings, but now that they were under threat, it came home to me that they are my babies. No one can kill my babies. Not that Louie would stop short of infanticide in his quest for world domination. "They're my shop window," I objected. "They're what brought the Ministry in."

"He wants you to talk to some journalists and do a, what did he call it? Mea culpa."

"He wants me to sing them a hymn?"

"No, it's a sort of, you know, grovelling apology."

"Has he gone fucking loony? They'll just think I'm guilty. I'm coming in now, OK? See you in half an hour."

I sped up and started overtaking. Once I'd cut up a few slackers I felt better, more in control. Simply coasting forward is bad for the mind, you've got to dash and dart. Predators are everywhere.

****

Dear Member,
Feeling fluey?
Prepare yourself against next season's flu strain now. It might be more urgent than you think.
Don't vacillate, vaccinate!
For conditions, see Nostrum.

****

10 Free Insurance

I stuffed a couple of T-shirts into my bag, and barged into reception, getting up momentum for my attack on Louie.

And stopped just inside the door. Phil and Des were there, sitting together over espressos. As I walked towards them, smile outstretched, they stopped talking. Up to something? Maybe.

I sat down with them.

"How you feelin, Bernie?" Phil looked concerned, or curious at least.

"OK."

"OK?" Phil repeated, as if he didn't believe me.

"Yeah, OK," if a little bored by this conversation. "Pissed off that someone's been dirtying my name with the press, obviously."

"That's not necessarily true," Des informed us. "Journalists regularly hack into police systems when there's a murder investigation going on." We nodded silent acknowledgement and he looked embarrassed. Poor lad, he knows it all, but he also knows we don't really want to know it all. He made a nervous hunching movement, lifting his right shoulder and tilting his head sideways for a momentary scratch behind his ear. The pale yellow shirt re-emerged speckled with white. Phil and I pretended not to notice. It was cruel Beano who first pointed out that Des is not only short for Desmond, but also for Desperate Dan, as in Mr Dan Druff himself.

Poor Des, it's wrecking his life. He's not a bad-looking lad, his hair looks clean, it lies brown and thick on top of his head, but if you look closely you can see the white dust wiggling its way to freedom. He never wears any shirt or jacket darker than beige. And he scratches his scalp compulsively when he's nervous, which is pretty well always, seeing that it's his crumbling scalp that makes him nervous.

"Yeah, and Mona won't even let me meet the fuckin paparazzi and tell em where they can stick their immorality bollocks," Phil spat.

"That's because the press would accuse you of murdering the English language and sodomizing its corpse, Phil," I bantered. The mood seemed to become less conspiratorial.

"Ready for the onslaught, Bernie?" Des asked with gratifying solidarity.

"Right on the fuckin nail, Des," Phil barged in. "Look at Bernie, fuckin luvvinit. He's gonna be in all the papers, a real *meeja star*. Reckon he'll still talk to us after, Des? What jah reckon it'll feel like, workin with a *meeja star*?"

"Well, as long as his fans don't take up all the parking spaces ..." Des quipped mildly, but Phil seemed to think it was the best joke since the exploding cigar. He was on his suntanned knees in an instant, praying for my autograph and the chance to give me a blowjob.

I was paralysed. I sat there simply taking punishment. I mean, I've tongue-wrestled with the best of them, but you can't banter with a hyperactive chimp. You say something clever and he'll win the laugh by jamming a banana in your mouth.

Phil's act was way, way overdone as usual, but it works. His Mockney buffoonery puts Des at ease. He lets Des feel superior without ever patronizing him. It's a brilliant piece of image-projection. If necessary, I'm certain Phil could clean up his mouth and manners and assume total control of Coma at an hour's notice. He's got the contacts to make it work. With him and Louie on the prowl, I thought, maybe it's lucky we're being bought out. The new owners might put a cap on all this power posturing.

"Know what, Bernie?" Phil was now back in his seat.

"No, what?"

"That's what I just said." I hadn't heard that one since primary school, and chuckled nostalgically. "No, seriously, guess who I phoned." Phil challenged.

"I give up."

Phil winked at Des and told me, "Clodeen."

"Oh yeah?" Shame Phil's attack of the shits hadn't turned out to be amoebic dysentery, I thought.

"Know what she said?"

"No, what? Sorry, you just said that."

"That's OK, it's not copyright. She said she couldn't meet me tonight cause she's seein *Bare Knee*." He mimicked the accent too well for a jellied-eel-eating slob.

"I'm seeing her to discuss some work," I said, stretching the frontiers of credibility.

Phil snorted. He turned to Des.

"See, Bernie don't let no one else get a look in. He's got to get a finger in every pie." Phil mimed squeezing a pair of buttocks but I knew he was talking about more than women. It's the Greensands business. She wasn't one of his contacts, and he doesn't like it. I felt Des's eyes on me. I held up my hands and studied the fingers fatalistically.

"For the moment there's not a pie between them, Phil."

He guffawed and marched off to his office. "Back in a sec."

Alone with me, Des looked even more uncomfortable than usual.

I immediately began trying to wipe the mockery and the rivalry from his mind by showing him my village photos and asking his thoughts. He made some solid suggestions on which ones to use.

"Perfect," I said. Des clearly liked hearing that word. "Now then, there's something really vital I have to discuss with you. My basic concept for the whole Greensands village gig. I'm not sure it's up to the mark. I need to try it out on you."

"Fire away, then."

"Right." I had to see Des's reaction. Fifteen seconds would be enough. But for some reason I couldn't go on. Phil was absent but somehow in control. My eyes were on his door, wondering when he'd reappear. My mind was warning me not to begin a sentence I didn't want overheard. "Let's go to my cubicle, shall we?"

"Well, I was, er ..." Des, too, looked over at Phil's door.

"It'll only take a sec." One sentence, and Des's face would tell me all I wanted to know.

"Less go." Phil was back again. Des gave me an apologetic smile and stood up. I didn't ask where they were going.

The impetus for my assault on Louie had gone. I went to see Rita. I thought she might be up to discussing last Friday's visit to Stanley – whether she'd been there or not. I now suspected that she was the last one to see Beano alive. After all, when you're screwing someone from work, you'll usually do it evenings and weekends, won't you? Not much opportunity at the workplace. Well, not my workplace, anyway. I've tried.

"Rita. How you feeling?"

"Bernie, at last. You'd better go and see Louie."

"Louie can wait. I wanted to ask you –"

"It's not just *your* stuff he wants to take down. It's half of Beano's, too."

"All right, I'll see Louie now." Emotional blackmail, but what can you do?

There was no way I was going to knock on Louie's door and wait around outside, so I phoned him from the corridor.

"Louie? I'm in the building. Can we meet now?"

"Sure. Your place or mine?"

"I'll come over you."

"Uh?"

I was in his office five seconds later, my rage refuelled.

"You can't just zap all our stuff like that, Louie. Who are you to decide whether content that I created – that Beano or I created – should be deleted just because a bunch of fucking bigots says it's too sexy?"

"I didn't."

"You didn't delete it?"

"No, I didn't decide."

"Meaning?"

"We voted."

"Who voted? No one fucking asked me to vo –" I saw the trap too late. Louie didn't even bother to push home the point. "You mean Phil, Des and Mona voted to delete us?" I asked. Why hadn't Phil and Des told me?

"Well, Phil voted against, but I'm sure he was just being his usual provocative self. That made three for and a maximum of two against, so I'm afraid we shut down 'See Models Die', 'Medical Accidents', 'Put the Lepers Back Together' ..."

"Put the Lepers ...?"

"One of Beano's games."

"I never saw ..."

"You don't want to. I've got a list somewhere. There are about five of your films and ..."

"Five? Come on. You know what this means, don't you?"

"It means that we can get the media off our backs and get on with the serious business of selling Coma for serious money."

"No, it fucking doesn't. Well, yes it does, but it *also* means that you have used Beano's death for the sake of your fucking office politics. If he'd been here, the vote would have been fifty-fifty. Beano's been dead for what – a day – and you're already ... Beano and me fucking gave this company its identity. We fucking –"

"Look Bernie, why don't you sit down? Here, want a Kleenex?" I shook my head and sat as assertively as I could. "I'm as sad as anyone about Beano," he went on. "Well, maybe I wasn't as close to him as you and Rita were, but we've all been together for over three years now. We've all worked fucking hard, and it's, well, I can't say how, how, *tragic* it is that Beano won't be here to cash in on it. But when I say we've all worked hard, I do mean *all* of us. Sometimes I think you and Beano don't – didn't – really appreciate what the rest of us are doing, just because we're on the less sexy side of things. But this is a business like any other. Your content was all part of our business strategy."

"A masterplan, right?"

"In a way, yeah." He looked pleased with the word. "It was a simple marketing strategy. You two created content that would get us talked about, even if it was a bit leftfield from our core market. Everyone knew we had to get people visiting us if we wanted to survive. Your stuff was just a new take on those old Benetton ads with sexy nuns. Have you ever seen them?" He pulled out a phone, as if he wanted to show me.

"No." He was trying to distract me, so I ploughed on. "You're saying Beano and me were just a line in the business plan?"

"We're all lines in the business plan, Bernie. That's why *we're* getting bought out, unlike all the over-valued, under-managed start-ups who've tried to fob the public off with their shitty services enabling people to do something online that they never really wanted to do anyway. We're a well-run firm, with major backers, a sharply defined target market and a business plan that's as tight as a duck's arse. And you know how tight a duck's arse is, don't you?"

"Should I?"

"Watertight, Bernie. And that duck's arse is why you're going to be rich. Don't knock it."

"I wouldn't dream of even touching the duck's arse, Louie. I'm not a duck's arse man."

"Just don't forget that word, Bernie. Watertight. We've all got to be watertight till the buyout goes through."

"Otherwise the water will get in our backsides and we'll sink, right?"

"Exactly," he said, not in the mood for levity about his *mot du jour*. "Your risqué movies served their purpose, and I know they're still popular, but we can't afford to let them put a spanner in the works now. We've found our niche and we've got to make sure we hang in there. Our business is about a hell of a lot more than jokey films, Bernie. Honestly, I hate to be saying this, especially now, but you're a decade out of date. The internet hasn't been the new rock'n'roll for years – you're just playing air guitar."

"You've been rehearsing that line in front of a mirror."

Louie shook his head. "I'm the first to acknowledge it: you and Beano gave us our original image, you created a buzz about us, but you know where most of our income comes from? It's the boring workaday stuff like ads, corporate sponsorship and the agency work. If this was a life raft, you and Beano would've spent most of your time lying drunk in the bottom of the boat, giggling about how funny you are. If we were a human body, you'd be –"

"The creative bit of the brain."

"No, you'd be ... you'd be the breasts. You attract the suckers, but mainly you just bounce around trying to look sexy."

"Well, the body won't look so good after its recent mastectomy, will it?"

"No, you're right, there's only one tit left now. Sorry, cheap shot."

"Yeah, well there's always been just one asshole, Louie, right?"

Louie laughed. It sounded forced. I should have put my guard up.

"I admit," he said, "if the Greensands business works out, you might bring in some serious profit. But it'd be the first time."

"And while we're on the subject of profit, look at these," I said, delving into my bag. I handed him a heart-attack T-shirt. He unfolded it and held it up. "What about this as a service?" I asked. "Doctors are always moaning about the lack of care in the community. This will take medicine into the streets, all thanks to Coma."

Louie laughed again.

"You sound like Mona. She's been hassling me about becoming more *caring*." He sang the word as if it was part of a hippie anthem. I could just imagine him battering poor Mona with his financier's irony.

"It's good though, isn't it?" I said. I could see that he approved. Well, didn't disapprove violently like he usually did. "I thought we could do others. You know, for diabetics, haemophiliacs, asthma sufferers."

"Right. Epileptics ..."

"Yeah, or with simple anti-malaria or anti-Aids precautions."

"Not bad," Louie conceded. "They're light, indestructible and – how much did you pay for these?" I doubled the cost and told him. "– cheap," he concluded. "How many you got?"

"Five hundred of the heart attack ones, and a thousand of these others. They weren't my idea." I showed him Beano's comedy shirt.

Louie laughed.

"Incorrigible to the end." He put Beano aside like a worn-out battery. "Let's stick to these health ones. We get sponsorship from the drug companies, the various charities and patients' support groups, the WHO even. Get a few more logos stamped alongside ours on the shirts. Some celebs wearing them. Bottom line, little or no financial outlay and some healthy PR. What was it you said? 'Taking medicine to the streets'? Neat. T-shirts are a mere gimmick compared to the other PR stuff we're doing, but they might be effective. And it was a good move to put Nostrum's logo on there. Your idea?"

"Of course, Louie." I could have added, "you patronizing shit." Instead, only my eyes said it. He didn't hear.

"You see the difference between these and those fucking dolls you wanted to do, don't you, Bernie?"

"Yeah, yeah. So you'll refund my outlay, then, will you?"

"Sure. Got a receipt?"

"Er, yeah." Shit, I thought, I only got the card chit for part of it. I gestured over my shoulder towards some theoretical computer, drawer or pocket where receipts might be stored. I was going to have to forge a receipt for the cash. Still, no one would dare go out to Stanley's place to check up.

"Great. We'll do a thousand each of all those diseases you mentioned, shall we? Once we've got the go-ahead for a few more logos. We'll run competitions to win them. And get them into hospital wards, direct to the sufferers."

"Right." Things were looking good. At these prices I'd be making 100% on every T-shirt. I'd even be able to slip Stanley a sweetener.

"Now ..." Louie pushed my T-shirts away to the far edge of his desk. "About these journalists. Mona seemed to think it'd be good for you to meet them."

"Mona did? Well, she might have told me herself."

"She's out doing some damage limitation with our sponsors. And with the Ministry, of course."

"So what I am supposed to do? Tell everyone I'm sorry I killed Beano and used naughty words on the internet, and swear I won't do it again?"

"Be serious, Bernie. Mona thought it would be good if you said, no problem, they were just some old films from our student days. We've never had any complaints before, but we're deleting them while we get on with much more exciting things. Then you hint that we're working on something that will contribute to the health of the nation, tell them health after all is our raison d'être, bla bla bla. Not mentioning the Greensands project explicitly, of course, but dangling a fish in front of them."

"Don't you mean a carrot?"

"Do I?"

"Unless you mean a red herring?"

"Bernie. For Christ's sake. We haven't got time for that."

"OK, OK. You want me to turn bad PR into good, right?"

"Right. Protest your innocence. Cry a bit if you can."

"Cry?"

"Yeah, like you did just now. It'd look good."

"I wasn't cr –"

"Just try to kill the story before it's even born. Abort it."

"God, Louie, you certainly have a way with words."

All in all, though, it didn't seem too bad. So what if our old movies get pulled down? Someone might start up a spontaneous grass-roots campaign to get them put back on line. If I asked them nicely.

"So what happened at the crisis meeting?" I asked him.

"Meetings plural. One at eight this morning, and another that ended just before you came in. Where have you been, anyway?" Louie was surprisingly laid-back about my absence now.

"I was at the police station, being accused of murder. Again."

"Bastards." He looked genuinely sympathetic. "On what evidence?"

"None. They were pissed off because I wasn't supposed to leave town, and I went out to the country to start work on Greensands' material. You know, making some more serious money?"

"But the cops aren't charging you?"

"No, it was all scare tactics. By the way, when did *you* last see Beano?"

"That's nothing to joke about, Bernie."

"Who's joking? Did you see him during the weekend?"

"No. Friday night. Went for a drink with him and Rita." God, even Louie knew more than I did. Thank you for your confidence, Beano.

Louie explained what went on during the crisis meetings. It was heavy financial stuff, and I found it hard to follow. My head was aching again from where I'd bashed it, and my attention wandered out the window, towards the sky, which was turning silver as the sun dipped lower over the bay. The horizon had almost disappeared.

Then I heard the word "danger", and I was back in the room. The big danger, apparently, was that the buyout might be delayed by an inquest, or the threat of one.

"Let's hope the coroner says he died of natural causes," Louie said.

"Natural causes? Yeah, a tapeworm crawled out of his arse and throttled him. Come on, I saw him, remember?"

"Exactly my point. The coroner's going to say misadventure at the very least. So you see the danger."

"Bad PR?"

"Right. Just think what that could do to the share price." Louie leaned back, giving me time to think. He stretched, putting his hands on his head and showing off an oval sweat patch under each arm. "Any hint that things are amiss at Coma, the market could get jittery and the price could go down the toilet."

I felt as if someone was pulling banknotes out of my pockets.

"How far down the toilet exactly?" I asked. "Are we talking, like, floating in the bowl or right down in the sewers?"

"Well, we might not be millionaires on day one, put it that way."

"Fuck."

"That was another thing we discussed at the meeting. I, ah –" Louie picked up a red file. It was the only file on his desk, which is one of those anally tidy work surfaces that I envy and despise in equal measure. "I suggested to the others that we cover ourselves." He opened the file and pushed it across the desk at me. In it, there was a form of some kind.

"What do you mean?" I glanced down at the form and my eyes seemed to blur. I don't mind filling in forms but I can't *read* them. My mind goes blank whenever there's a question longer than "name" or "age".

Louie leaned forward, frowning with concentration.

"Now then, you understand the terms of Nostrum's offer, don't you?" He stared hard just above my eyes, as if trying to look inside my brain and check whether it was stocked up with all his fascinating finance.

"Yeah," I lied.

"You'll be selling them all your shares, right?"

"Right."

He looked very pleased with my answer. "And you know how that'll work?"

"I ..."

"Because not everyone does. I'll take you through it again if you want."

I shrugged my assent. It wasn't 100% necessary, I implied, but if that was what he wanted, why not.

"OK," he explained, "now, as you know we haven't yet voted on whether to accept the offer."

"We haven't? I thought it was in the bag."

"Oh, it is. We're going to accept, obviously. But we won't say so formally for another week. Because we founders own all the available stock, we can hang in there for a while and let the price rise on the back of the offer. It's all been agreed."

"Clever."

"Aren't we just? And this underlines the importance of good PR during the course of the whole deal. What if the price plummets for whatever reason before we vote?"

"Shit."

"Exactly." Louie pushed his fingertips together, making a pyramid with his hands. "Now," he said. "What I suggested to the others is that we cover ourselves by each of us forward-selling a tranche of our shares in advance of the buyout. At today's price, which is very respectable, as you know."

"Yes. Right. And the others all agreed?"

"Why shouldn't they? I'm doing it." He fished a form out of his desk. It was signed at the bottom with his huge Arabic-looking scrawl. I looked from his form to mine. No differences I could see.

"So we're selling half now, half later?"

"Yup. An insurance policy."

"Right."

I signed. Why not? Usually when you take out insurance you have to pay. This policy was free. More than that, I was the one getting paid for being insured.

"How many journalists has Mona invited, by the way?" I asked, shoving the form back across the desk.

"Four," Louie replied. He filed my form away in his drawer. "It's not a press conference as such, just an informal chat."

I almost snapped Louie's pen. That phrase again.

I went and fetched Mike and Joe, the niffy nerdlings, to help me unload the car. I didn't want anyone making off with my valuable cotton booty.

They weren't exactly happy to be snatched away from their screens.

"The fuck's this?" Mike asked when he saw the car's neatly piled white passengers.

"Merchandising," I told him. "Er, you have washed your hands, haven't you?" I could have added "since your eleventh birthday", but it would have been counter-productive.

They both stooped their lank heads to look at their palms. I guessed they rarely saw that part of their hand, what with having their fingers permanently on a joystick or screen.

"Never mind," I said. I gave them the bin bags to start with. For the second trip I'd get them to carry the piles of "diuretic" t-shirts. It wouldn't really matter if those got smudged.

"What are we, fucking clothes shop now?" Joe grumbled.

If I hadn't been on the promise of a fat profit, I'd have reminded him who was boss around here. Instead, I came over all worldly-wise.

"You know who made the most money out of the California gold rush?" I asked them. "The man who sold jeans to the miners."

"Yeah, but they *needed* jeans. Who the fuck needs another T-shirt?" Mike retorted. This from one of the two youths outside the Third World who were most in need of a new T-shirt, preferably with odour-eater armpits.

It took us three trips to get all the shirts into the office and stacked away. Going up with the pair of them in the lift took a lot of willpower and breath control.

They mumbled and moaned throughout like a pair of hungry puppies. At the end of it all, I gave them each a T-shirt as a thank-you present. I didn't think they'd know what "diuretic" means. I wondered what the equivalent word for "so smelly it makes you want to heave" is. Retchoretic? Pukative? Gagogenic?

****

Coma price dips as director dumps.
The price of shares in the medical company Coma fell sharply today with the news that one of the company's founders was selling 50% of his shares, despite the prospect of a major dividend from a buyout by pharms giant Nostrum.
The director's actions are all the more baffling because of persistent rumours of a major joint venture with the Ministry of Development.
However, prices rallied again almost immediately when another of the founders made it known that he had bought a sizeable tranche of the available Coma stock.
The dip was a blip. Buy now.

Health managers:
Isn't it heartbreaking when you have to postpone or cancel a heart transplant operation for lack of intensive-care facilities?
That's why we've set up our chain of one-stop chest-care centres. You provide the patient, the organ and the surgeon, we do the rest.
For info and addresses check out ThorassicPark

****

11 First Catch Your Porcupine

When I went into the meeting room, all four journalists were there. Rita had been keeping them, a cameraman and a photographer amused with clinking glasses of non-alcohol and a coffee-table prospectus about our many inoffensive activities. The guests' low-slung armchairs were set out in a rough semi-circle. The hacks were all flipped back in snooze-posture. Mine and Rita's were upright chairs, with Rita's just off camera, outside the pool of light from the cameraman's spot.

"Good afternoon, ladies and gentlemen," I announced.

I'd never met any of them before, but I'd made enquiries about them.

One was a tabloid man. Jason Prince, a boy-faced and utterly perverse-looking guy, renowned for being first with the story when anyone big gets busted between a call-girl's or toy-boy's thighs.

Then there was Beatrice Crick, a 20-something with tightly-bunched blonde hair and classy clothes. She was from a news channel, but seemed to be wearing no make-up whatsoever on her tanned round face.

Paul Clifftop was a curly-mopped freelancer doing a story for a broadsheet paper that likes only fair-minded, articulate scandal.

And finally there was a religious reporter from GTV – you can guess what (or Who) the G stands for. I'd googled his group. They call themselves Christians but think Christ himself was much too soft on sinners. Turning the other cheek is for wimps, they say. Blow the goddam heathen away before he can get in a second punch. And send your credit-card details in now so you don't get left behind when Armageddon comes. All in all, it's not exactly what I remember from Sunday School.

GTV's representative on Earth had a beard and joined-up eyebrows, but he was disappointingly well-presented otherwise. Tasteful shirt, sober tie and socks, neatly-laced shoes. Not a sandal in sight. Still, inside, he would be a twisted knot of bigotry and spit. He'd make a foreskin of himself with his out-of-this-world arguments. As soon as I appeared, he started flailing like an overturned turtle.

"Please don't get up," I demeaned, and went over to shake hands all round. Then the four of them picked up their phones and set their recording volume on the sound of my bum hitting the seat. The TV camera began to roll.

I let them loose on me.

"Well, go ahead, I'm all yours."

At this point, Rita discreetly switched on her own phone recorder and pointed it at me. The journalists gave it a look and hesitated until she'd made sure it was working. A polite bunch.

All four mouths opened at once.

"Ladies first," Prince the tabloid man said, as unctuously gallant as only sexists can be.

"Thank you." Beatrice Crick gave him a withering look. "First of all, Mr Bridges, let me say that I'm very sorry to hear about your colleague's death. Can you tell us a little about him?"

"Sure." I nodded sadly. "He was my best friend. My *dearest* friend. We started out in this business together."

"Making sick films," the GTV man butted in. Philip Pigshit, misbehaving already. Or maybe I misheard. Maybe it was Prig-Shit. I'm not sure.

"Jokey films," I corrected him.

"You call scenes of ritual killing *jokey*?" he yelped.

Ritually killing you with a blunt machete would be a hilarious joke, I thought.

I took a deep, calming breath.

"Ritual killing? If you call that ritual killing, what do you call Macbeth? Or ninety per cent of computer games?" I shook my head sadly at the state of our decadent society. "And as you know, we have deleted all the material that was deemed offensive, though we have never, repeat ever, received a complaint about them."

"We're getting away from the point, though." This was Clifftop, the broadsheet guy. He had an actual notebook with questions. "You discovered the body, didn't you?"

"Yes."

"Can you tell us exactly what you saw?" he asked.

"No," I said, then, to counter the journos' barks of disapproval, "there's a police investigation under way. I'm not allowed to tell you *exactly*." I didn't feel like re-living it just for their pleasure, either.

A camera flashed at me. I was batting solidly, my face had not a crease on it, I'm sure. No guilt, no moral sickness.

"But he was lying there dead, right?" Prince asked.

"Just like the girls in your sicko films." Pigshit was heating up, giving off fumes. Prince and Crick grimaced at him, Clifftop glanced over neutrally.

"You're right," I told Prince, "my best friend was lying there dead, and I hope and pray –" I looked meaningfully towards Pigshit "– that the police will find his killer. Just as I hope that the press will not hinder the investigation by making an irrelevant fuss about some harmless films that we made years ago. You'd only be promoting censorship, and I'm sure you're in favour of allowing the public freedom of choice in our viewing, listening and reading. Yes, freedom of choice." I repeated my headline, bending forward towards their phones.

Journalists love defending freedom, especially freedom of speech. Standing up for someone's right to talk crap excites them as much as a really vicious OAP-bashing. On cue, three of the journalists turn accusingly to the bearded fourth. But Pigshit loves getting attacked, that's the trouble. All these hard-line born-agains are dying to be crucified. They thirst for those nails.

"Yes yes, that's all very neat and *open-minded*, but in a survey we did on GTV, ninety-five per cent of our viewers, who had all had a chance to see your films, were shocked by them."

"Just following your instructions, I'm sure," I quipped.

Pigshit either didn't hear or chose to ignore me. "Let's look at these films in detail." He lifted his right hand. Oh no, I thought, he's going to prove he can count his fingers. I hate people who count their fingers at me. "There's the one with not only a crucifixion scene –"

"Which has been deleted," I tried to interrupt, but as I spoke he simply raised his voice and repeated himself to drown my words. They baptise their friends and drown their enemies. Same water, just a few seconds difference under it.

"Not only a crucifixion scene, but nakedness, sick eroticism and, *and*," he holds up his uncounted thumb and finger like a pistol, "the taking in vain of the Turin shroud and the holy communion."

The other hacks look baffled but intrigued. I shake my head and raise my own counting hand.

"OK, I'll answer you point-by-point." Now my patience is the martyr. "First, the films have been deleted, as you know. The nakedness, well, the most you see in any of the films is underwear and a girl lying under a sheet, and anyway nakedness is nothing new on TV, the net or in newspapers for that matter." Moralizing look towards Jason Prince.

"That film about acid caused deep shock. Children saw it," Pigshit piped in.

"Not surprising if you showed it on your news programmes. If you deliberately shock children, that's your affair, I have no wish to do so. The film about sulphuric acid was aimed specifically at medical professionals who know the difference between a sick joke and real sickness. Children can see much worse things on the web, you know. Horrible things, *real* things." My eyes meet Clifftop's. He nods. The other two shake their heads gravely. They don't like hearing about kids being shocked. But Pigshit steams straight back in.

"What about the crucifixion, the shroud and the holy communion? You haven't answered those charges yet."

"Charges?" I raise a quizzical eyebrow. All of us, reasonably educated types, surely think of the Inquisition. Back to my fingers. "Secondly, what I'd like to know is where you get these ideas from. What on earth has a model acting out a scene from a French movie got to do with communion?"

"The slogan makes that very clear."

"Eh?"

"Sulphuric acid – for *Christ's* sake don't drink it."

"That's way too deep for me. It was just a joke for Chr –. Just a joke. And anyway, the film has been deleted."

"Don't we know it. That's the fifth time you've told us. Haven't you got anything else to say?"

"Dear Mr Pigshit, I would like to insert a porcupine into your colon and tickle it." That's what I'd like to say, but it wouldn't do my cause any good. I battle bravely on with more sober words.

"I mean, quite honestly, I don't know where you learned your vision of the world. If you think I've got time to mess about making films that secretly mock the holy communion, then you're wildly, insanely wrong. It's not in my interest to damage the company's reputation. My job is to entertain, to attract new clients, not find twisted ways of shocking people who like to watch films backwards, in negative, and upside-down." The three non-godsquaddies laugh. Pigshit remains expressionless.

"Will you apologize?" he asks.

"We've pulled the plug on the movies, and of course we hope that anyone who was offended can now use our online services without coming across anything offensive."

"Will you apologize?"

Like I said, "informal chat" is fast becoming a synonym for "bollock-kicking interrogation". But there are times, it seems, when grovelling is a good option.

"All I can say, at the risk of repeating myself, is that we never intended to cause offence, we apologize if we did so, and we have deleted any content that could have been deemed offensive. After all, this kind of humorous material is no longer at the top of our agenda." I hated myself for talking Louie-style garbage, but it was strangely satisfying. It made me sound authoritative. Yes, I *had an agenda*. "We at Coma want to get on with the serious business of helping doctors to improve the nation's health. Not such an offensive aim, is it?"

Looking around the journalists' faces, I reckoned it was three-one to me.

"Yes, and talking of health ..." Clifftop was pensive. "I was wondering whether you weren't in some way setting out your agenda metaphorically with your dying models' movies. Given what your company has done since."

I looked for help to the other journalists. Had they understood the question? Was it even a question? But their faces were as blank as mine must have been.

"I'm not quite sure I follow you," I understated.

Clifftop looked towards the ceiling and tried to work out a way of explaining himself to someone who hasn't got a PhD in philosophy.

"I mean," he began, "was the repeated killing – fictional, I know – of a beautiful woman a kind of warning metaphor? The idealized woman symbolizing a free, universal health-care system, who is destroyed by the company that intends to subvert, *poison* some might say, the system, as Coma has tried to do by publicizing all these private health-care schemes?"

He'd finished. Everyone seemed to hold their breath in awe. I put my finger up to my chin. Isn't that what brainy writers do on their book jackets? Never in my life had anybody accused me of being so incredibly subtle. What could I reply to do his question justice?

"Um," I said. Then, "No. See Models Die was just a bit of arty fun."

"Ah." Clifftop looked disappointed in me. I wouldn't be going into his Sunday supplement just yet.

"Great mis-interpretation, though," I added, to cheer him up.

"Pah!" Pigshit was on the boil. "We all know what that film was really about."

There was a collective groan at this. Beatrice told him he was hogging the press conference. The majority of the media was clearly on my side. Game over.

"And another thing." This was Pigshit yet again. "Whose idea was it to make the girl spit out black acid?"

"Mine," I admitted warily. "Just for visibility. And the rest of the team thought black was a good idea."

"And isn't it true that your late colleague, a member of this same team, was found with black liquid pouring from his mouth?"

He wasn't supposed to know about the black liquid. No one was. My shock must have shown.

"Black liquid?" Jason asked, and looked questioningly around at the others. They acknowledged ignorance.

"It wasn't pouring. And it was probably rum and blackcurrant, Beano's favourite tipple," I said.

"Hasn't been proved –"

I didn't know what more to say. Armlock had said there was a blackout, as it were, on the black gunk until the lab results came through. But now the visual link between my film and poor dead Beano's chin seemed to have set the journalists' minds a-slavering. I could just imagine the "BLACK DEATH!" headlines. I glanced across to Clifftop for support. He gave me an umpire's sorry-it-touched-the-glove look.

"Have the police told you anything off the record?" Beatrice asked Pigshit.

"Do you think he drank sulphuric acid?" Jason asked me. "Was he completely happy about the morality of your company's business practices?"

"Is the coroner's report already out?" Clifftop asked everyone.

"Isn't it true that the police suspect *you* of the killing, Mr Bridges?" Pigshit asked, smiling confidently now. I didn't believe that he was capable of tapping into a police computer system like Des said. So he must have been getting inside information via the hard-line evangelical wing of the local constabulary. The other journos gave him a look of professional respect. This was a real story coming out.

"No it is not true," I lied.

"That's not what I heard."

The others turned almost bodily towards Pigshit. He was the next interview they'd all be doing.

"Well it isn't true," I said, "and all I can say, Mr, er, Pigsh –"

"Pritchett."

"Pritchett, is that you've proved to us here this afternoon that you are saddled with a cruel and twisted mind. You distort a simple joke to your own ends, purely to mount a moralizing publicity campaign and get your TV channel into the news, a campaign to prevent all of us thinking or expressing ourselves as we wish. A campaign against free speech. The muzzling of the media."

Pisgshit wasn't budging a face muscle, he didn't give a damn. He'd won. The others were clearly hooked on the prospect of digging the dirt on me and Beano's gunk.

I kept talking anyway. Perhaps if I didn't pause for breath for a few hours, they'd all get bored with the story and leave me in peace.

"... And then you disrupt a perfectly serious press conference with your wild and groundless accusations. Let's get back to the real subject of our discussion – your completely unjustified attack on my company, your deliberately shocking children ..." I rambled vainly on.

Thank God Angela Greensands is going to make me untouchable as of tomorrow. At least I fucking hope she is.

In the end I had to storm out, leaving a smokescreen of "no comments" behind me, to get away from

Pisgshit's questions about why I'd murdered Beano and which satanic sect I belonged to.

****

hey j
u know those t-shirts bernie gave us?
i thought there was something funny about them.
look here MedicalDictionary/diuretic
m

m
bastard's taking the piss.
need 2 look 4 way 2 give him the shafting he deserves.
j

Dear Member,
We'll be hosting a webinar on sexual dysfunctions and their treatment.
Keynote speaker will be Dr Ross Douglas of St George's Hospital, Chicago, who published a groundbreaking paper on internet-related premature ejaculation earlier this year entitled "Online Porn, No More Horn".
To register your advance questions and obtain free samples of erectile medication, go to: ComaDebates

****

12 STEERING WHEEL COVER

Just when I needed it least, Granola called, demanding that I come home straight away. We hadn't actually seen each other awake since Sunday.

"I thought that's what you wanted, me not being there," I reminded her.

No immediate answer.

"There are some papers we need to look at," she finally said. That's the thing about divorce. There are always papers. It really brings a couple together.

"What kind of papers?"

"The bank, for starters. I've opened an account in my own name. And we need to look at the joint accounts."

Trouble was, I had planned an evening with Claudine.

"I can't. I've got loads of work to do for my presentation," I said.

"Come afterwards. I'm not going out."

"And when I've finished up my work, I've got to go and get my watch."

"So your watch is more important than discussing the lamentable state of our marriage?"

"You know how much it cost."

"So it *is* more important than our marriage?"

"Granola. It's only a *watch*."

"That's what I just said, you –" Granola controlled herself.

"Anyway, you're the one who said the marriage was over," I said. "There's stuff to sign, but is there really that much stuff to discuss?"

OK, that was a bit cruel, but it's true. She's the one who first mentioned the word divorce. We're both working too hard for us to stay married, she said. It's like owning a timeshare. We live at the same place, but not at the same time. Why not make it official?

Ever the softie, I cracked.

"Look, I'll finish up as quick as I can, then I'll come home. OK?"

"So you'll be claimin the condoms on ixpenses?"

This was Phil, gloating from the entrance to my cubicle. He'd been listening.

"Eh?"

"Shaggin Clodeen counts as work, does it?" Of course, he knew all about my real plans for the evening.

"Nice work if you can get it, Phil, and I'm not getting it."

"If I was you I'd give up on er. You don't stand a fuckin earthly."

"You think so?"

"No chance. Birds like that get bored fast as shit."

"The voice of experience, eh Phil?"

"Right. I mean, you've got to keeper amused *all* the fuckin time. And if you ain't got a six-foot dick," – he cast a critical glance at my trousers – "that means money, slick talk an generally a waste of fuckin time an energy. She's gonna jump the first billionaire she meets anyway."

"I'll watch out for passing billionaires tonight, Phil, don't worry." What was all this agony aunt stuff in aid of? I mean, as if I didn't know about Claudine already.

"You know you scare me, Bernie. You got the meeja bayin for your fuckin blood, but you're still totally fuckin sure of yourself."

"Sure of myself?" The opposite is true at the moment. Perhaps it doesn't show.

"Yeah, you reek of self-confidence. Mile off."

"Do I?" I made vague sniffing motions towards my armpits.

"Come off it, Bernie, you're the kind of bloke who always knows how his armpits smell. Roses all day long. But I'll bet any fin you want I get in there first with Claudine. We'll call it a sack race. You on?"

"Even though I'm seeing her tonight?"

"Yeah."

"Your guts completely cured then?" I asked with colleaguely concern.

"Oh yeah. Ace pills you gave me. Not even a fart since. Thanks to you, I'm fully active, my friend." He blew me a kiss and disappeared.

I don't understand, I really don't. How he manages to mash my ego at every turn. It must be something they teach you at public school. And why should he be looking so triumphant all of a sudden?

I called Claudine and told her I wanted to pick her up straight away. She'd become more vital than ever since the foul-up with the journalists. After all, if it comes to the moral election, which party will people vote for? The bearded nutjob, or the girl with the cute face and superhuman boobs?

"Sorry, no," she said. "I will meet whizz Phil in an arf hour. He said you are occupied." That swill-bucket Phil. He'd already called her. Hence the triumphant look.

"Yes, but Phil just asked me to call you," I said. I instinctively lowered my voice here. Phil was bound to have his satellite monitoring my every move. "He's just gone into a meeting. He has problems with the management. Money problems."

"Oh?"

"Yes. He might lose his position in the company."

"No! Why?"

"It's all very political. I'll explain when I see you. Are you ready? I'll, ah, come over you now."

She huffed. "You men sink you can pass me between you like a football."

"No, no. We just know how valuable your time is, and don't want to waste the chance of one of us seeing you." Entry-level bullshit, but she either didn't notice or didn't care.

"I must dress," she objected.

"Don't bother."

"Uh?"

"I'll be there in fifteen minutes."

"Fifteen? No. Twenty."

More like ten. And when I called from my car parked outside her apartment, she was ready, career-conscious animal that she is. As we drove out of her street, Phil's four-wheel-drive assault vehicle did not come charging round the corner at us. We rode smoothly away towards one of those male fantasy moments ...

I'm in a pub garden, sitting on a teak bench opposite the girl who's getting all the looks. She's posed like a living magazine cover – her long matt body, black and white, is set against the brilliant leaves of a glossy shrub. Her face is in profile to the floodlit garden entrance, and slightly tinted by the reflected green light. Everyone entering the garden gapes for a second before they remember how cool they are. They look at me, and the envy drips like tears from their eyes.

Claudine is dressed not so much down as off. Her endless legs disappear into a minute black mini. I swear she must have made a mistake when she bought it – the packet said steering-wheel cover, and she thought it meant skirt. I want to stare, but I daren't because I don't know where her eyes are. The sunglasses make her look so secret. Her hair needs no decoration – it is loose, bright and moving as if in water. Her mouth is big and red and closed. I can hardly bear to look at what she's wearing on top (on TOP). I keep my eyes welded to her sunglasses.

The fantasy came to life.

"What is ze problem with feel?" Claudine demanded. It took me a second to understand.

"Phil? Oh, something to do with drugs, bribery, fraud and false share certificates, I think. He'll be lucky if he manages to stay out of prison." My theory is, if you're going to lie, *lie*. "Terrible shock for us all. Such a promising career. Anyway, how about another drink? Excuse me!" The waitress responded with unbelievable speed: the Claudine effect. "One more Pernod for me, please. And ... Claudine?"

She waved no with one of her enormous hands. Not baseball-mitt enormous – they're long and slender, like two lithe animals dancing in the air. Call me a sexist bastard but I just couldn't help myself imagining what it'd be like to have them wrapped round my –

"Olives?" the waitress asked.

"Yes please. Now, this new ad I've got planned for you –" I turned back to Claudine.

"For farmer sir tickle industry, right?"

"Right, but I want to change its image – I want to make pharmaceuticals sexy."

"But you are in ze sheet for making sexy films. Why do it again?" She inclined her head. She honestly wanted to know.

"Well, I think maybe the way to resist is to show them that we're not going to let them prohibit our art. That we can rise above their petty moralizing and go on to greater things." I did my best to furrow my brow towards the distant better future, like some Communist statue celebrating innovations in tractor technology.

"I sink you are wrong. You cause more trouble, and your buyout will be ... Pfff!" Claudine swiped Coma out of existence with a scimitar-like hand.

"We'll see," I said, and veered the talk back to safer territory like my village visit, and Angela Greensands' promises (well, hints) of great things to come.

I explained to Claudine that the spa town and its region needed a face to symbolize its new-found health. Why not her?, I asked myself rhetorically. Claudine didn't look grateful or impressed. But she didn't look scornful, either. To be honest, I didn't know what the hell she was thinking.

The waitress returned. She put down the olives and the glass, and unsealed the mini-carafe of chilled water.

"Thanks." I mixed my drink, turning the golden liquid cloudy, watched in silence by my crusade-mate. I took a critical sip – a touch more water. Perfect.

"The death of Beano is a problem for the sailing of the company, no?" Claudine asked.

"The sale? No. It's sad to say but I don't think his death will make much difference to the business side of things. If anything, it might just give us survivors more power."

"His percentage will go to whom?"

She seemed very curious about our financial goings-on. But then I remembered the rapt attention she'd paid to Louie when he was talking money. So I explained, as best I could, the stuff about the share price and protecting myself by selling in advance. She nodded, apparently satisfied with my analysis of the situation. Perhaps I'd understood it better than I thought.

But it was time to move on if I wanted to win my bet with Phil tonight. I couldn't afford to give him time to contradict my slander about him.

"OK, let's go." To my surprise it worked. She followed me, and sat meekly (or maybe just indifferently) as I drove her she knew not where. The seat belt looked great on her, I envied its closeness. I took her for a speed-drive along the coast to a salsa club, a place so cool you could have committed hara-kiri with a pneumatic drill and no one would have deigned to notice. There, we drank some improbably expensive cocktails and jiggled around without the need to talk too intelligibly (or too much). She jiggled minimally but sublimely.

Between dances, she sat and listened attentively whenever I mentioned the Ministry and the people I'd be dealing with there.

"You'll have to come to the Ministry and meet everyone," I mentioned, off-hand. "You'd be so good for public relations." To show her approval, Claudine treated me to an enthralling towards-me leg-crossing show. The view caught a saxophonist full-face and he started to suck instead of blow. The reed lodged in his throat and the song petered out as one of his band mates grabbed hold of him and began to perform the Heimlich manoeuvre.

Driving back into town, with only me and the frame of my car to protect Claudine against the rushing darkness, I explained that I'd like something in return for letting her in on my world domination scheme. Something in advance, I should say. She seemed to understand, and didn't look at all offended. So when we arrived outside her building, I took a risk and clamped my hand below the rim of her skirt (which was all rim anyway). Her legs did not snap shut. Instead, she avoided my puckered mouth, and her long fingers all but burst my right eardrum with a whiplash karate slap. When I recovered consciousness, she was hissing at me.

"You don't know it is illegal to touch a woman without her consent?"

"Sorry, I thought I had it."

"No. It is also illegal to demand sex for professional advancement."

I was dazed from the nuclear left hook she'd just delivered, but awake enough to reply to that.

"I'm not demanding," I said, "I'm offering."

She tutted.

"I don't mind to fuck," she said. "Give me the choice between twenty years working in an office and one fuck, and I fuck. But I fuck when I say, how I say, and only if I get the contract. You understand?"

"Yes."

"One thing I will not tolerate is if you fuck, and then they don't give you the contract."

"Right. Absolutely. When?"

"Friday."

"OK, Friday."

"So you phone me to confirm about the Ministry."

"I phone," I agreed.

"OK. Goodnight." She reached for the door handle.

"Can I kiss you?" I asked.

"Why?" She looked genuinely baffled.

Before I'd worked out how to answer, she was standing on the pavement beside the car.

"One thing," she said, bending down to look in at me.

"Yes?"

"I will not blow your job."

"Uh? Oh, no problem. Just a fuck will be perfect. Thanks."

I tried to decide whether I was being a bastard. Or rather how much of a bastard I was being. OK, I was wrong to grab her thigh without permission, but I had an excuse, m'lud. I thought we had a tacit agreement. And I was suffering from acute frustration. Granola had kicked me out of her bed what felt like half a life ago. Besides, Claudine hadn't seemed at all surprised about getting propositioned. It sounded as if it was all in a day's work for her. And if I used her in this regional tourism campaign, and let her in on whatever else the Greensands team is planning, surely that was worth a fuck, wasn't it? Who else could offer a French model the chance to become the symbol of Britain's health, a sort of germ-free goddess?

But this was no time to sit and muse. A man alone in a parked car at night is never a welcome sight. I drove off before some nervous neighbour called in a rapid intervention squad.

****

Fed up with spam? Sign up to No Spam Please.
Do it within 24 hours and win a car!

Free food for humanitarian missions.
We will supply, free of charge, sacks of seed to charitable organizations. Rice, maize, peas, potatoes, tomatoes, and a range of cereals for every climate.
All seed guaranteed resistant to pests, disease and certain pesticides.
For details, see Nostrum Feeds The World

****

12A The Entrance

At nights, the city streets feel like a reef. I was hit by the same fear I've felt when diving in tropical waters – a nagging ache at the nape of the neck in expectation of carnivorous attack from any direction. One thing that used to reassure me in these streets was the late-night dog-walker, but we don't have so many of those any more, not since mugging became such a popular sport. And one thing that has never reassured me is the Neighbourhood Watch, even in my own neighbourhood where they're supposed to know me. Our residents' committee called in private security about a year ago, and they terrify me. If anyone in town has thumbs strong enough to crack a neighbour's throat, it's one of that lot.

I drove past two of them sitting on a garden wall, their truncheons on their camouflaged knees, their brilliant white "WATCH!" stab-proof vests bulging with pectorals and triceps and that sort of thing. They were leaning together over a screen, one of them punching at it with cudgel fingers. They looked up, stared blankly at my acknowledging wave, then resumed their game. I slid past them at a strict 29mph, and headed towards my building.

You brainless root-weevil. I pulled over and phoned the Inspector.

"Police, Dave speaking, how can I help you?" An anonymous night-voice, bored and obviously not dying to help anybody.

"Oh, isn't the Inspector there?"

"Which inspector?"

"Inspector Armlock. This is supposed to be her direct line."

"OK, just putting you through."

I heard the beep of a voicemail connection and a surprisingly pleasant-sounding Inspector asked me to leave a message. I did so.

"Good evening, Inspector, Bernie Bridges here. I've just had a thought. Have you asked Beano's, er, Mr Wright's, Neighbourhood Watch about his murder? If anyone was on the streets that early in the morning –"

"Good evening, Mr Bridges," she cut in. On duty, after all. "Of course I've asked them. But the trouble is two-fold, you see. Firstly, your friend was killed about the time when the night Watch would have been going off duty, and they were probably half-asleep at the very least."

"So they told you they didn't notice anything?"

"Which brings us to the second problem. You're well known in your friend's area?"

"Of course."

"And the Watch don't tend to record known vehicles or visitors. They're very enthusiastic doormen but not too good on the routine observation work." Like all cops, she's ruffled that the dear old Bobby has been found wanting and deposed from the beat in the better-off suburbs. "So they didn't pay any attention to your presence."

"Listen, who's talking about *my* presence in the area?"

"I am."

"Yes, well I was asking if any *strangers* were spotted in the area at around seven that morning."

"So I understood."

"I told you, I wasn't there when Beano died. You're supposed to be finding out who was."

"But you seem very well-informed about the time he died. Personally, I only found out this afternoon."

"You did? What time was it, then?"

"About seven, coincidentally, when you were in the neighbourhood, as you just said." Twisting words around her fingers, trying to knot me in them. She must be an insomniac, they're always the worst bastards, envious of everyone else in the world whom they suspect of sleeping.

"What else did you find out?"

"I'm afraid that unless you join the police force or become Home Secretary, I can't tell you that. But thanks for calling. I'm glad to see you're taking an interest in the case."

"But Inspector."

"Yes?"

"I thought you wanted me to visit Beano's place?"

"Why are you so desperate to return to the scene of the crime?"

"Because I want to help you to catch the murderer, Inspector, in case he, she, or ... er he or she tries to kill me."

"Well, the apartment has been sealed up."

"Sealed up? Why?"

She grunted, apparently not wanting to share her secrets.

"What about the inquest, Inspector? When's that going to be? Or the funeral?"

"The inquest isn't up to me. And as for the funeral, that depends when the body is released."

"Which is when?"

"After the inquest."

"God. One final thing though, Inspector?" She didn't tell me to get lost, so I asked it. "The reason why you refused to give me full protection, a constable on my door and all that – is it because you're afraid the Neighbourhood Watch might attack your people?"

"Sleep well, Mr Bridges."

"And fuck you, Arselock. You know you've got nothing on me." Sounded satisfying, even if the click of her hanging-up did separate the two voices.

I pulled up in the ex-garden of the ex-hotel building where I live and primed a couple of anti-mugger devices – one spray, one grenade. The call to the Inspector had successfully reminded me of psychos and corpses. My memory started to replay those "Berk-nerks" poor Beano had left to haunt me. I saw the black dribble and the blue scars again, and suddenly I couldn't swallow as easily as I used to.

Our only intruder alarm down in the entrance hall is old Grockel, the live-in caretaker. About as out-of-date as technology can get. If a prospective murderer did slip in the front door and start lurking about, Grockel would take three hours to get his brain and teeth out of the bedside tumbler and correctly slotted in his head, and another couple to remember the police's number. Nine er nine er ...? One tiny electronic box could replace him utterly, and the box wouldn't take afternoon naps or have days off to visit its sister in the old folks' home. But apparently we have to employ the aged until the population pyramid evens out.

It's disturbing to think that five minutes from now, or less, you could be lying as dead and grimacing as Beano.

Your watch (if you hadn't mislaid it in a village inn) would still be going, your hair and nails would still be growing, your digestion would still be digesting, but the rest of you would have stopped for ever. Sometimes I wish that I, and only I in the whole world, had a massive pump-action shotgun, unlimited ammunition and legal immunity. The world would be a safer place.

I turned my shirt collar high about my throat and dived out of the car. Head hunched and fists bunched around my glove-pocket self-defence kit, I sprinted for the front door, my spray and grenade primed, my trigger thumb ready to take out anything that stirred. I was only a couple of yards from the car when a shadow moved against the privet hedge dividing our forecourt from the next. Without interrupting my stride, I lobbed the grenade at it and clamped my hands hard over my ears. A couple of seconds later there was a monstrous bang, so loud my spine trembled right down into my rectum, and when I looked back, a large, obviously male, body was slumping head-first towards the tarmac. I hardly gave myself time to appreciate the heavy impact of flesh on tar. Luckily I'd been running away from the grenade.

I got inside and pressed my back to the hall wall, my shocked lungs slowly refilling themselves. What times we're living in, when a humble health-industry worker like myself has to become an urban guerrilla just to get home. An insect of some kind twitched on the wall and I neutralized it from three yards. It was paralysed before it hit the floor. I resumed my tensed search for human prowlers, pointing my spray wherever my eyes and ears led, listening hard for the nervous breathing of a would-be assassin under the stairs or round the corner behind

Grockel's door. Everything was brightly lit and as silent as my tingling ears would permit.

The floor creaked beside me.

Grockel nearly got the lot in his face. He poked his little head out of his door and eyed me like some somnolent grey turtle. He didn't seem to notice my paranoid crouch and home-made ninja get-up. Nor the dripping nozzle an inch from his nose.

"Evening, Mr Bridge, been for a check-up?"

He must be even deafer than I thought. Probably didn't even know what woke him up.

"No, Mr Grockel." What was the old nut blathering about? "Any visitors this evening?"

"I've heard nothing."

"That figures."

"Eh?"

I was tempted to spray him just to see if the gas would make his brain any more numb than it already was.

"Goodnight, Mr Grockel."

"Night, Mr Bridge," – he always gets my name wrong – "and don't forget the check-up. They keep talking about it on the telly."

"Yes, I'm sure they do." Anyone listening in would think I was about to climb my stairs in the certainty that the only threat to me was lying outside by the hedge. "Er, Mr Grockel?"

I leant close and made myself understood by mouthing, pointing and finger-counting. After some shameless haggling on my part, he agreed.

So I finally reached my front door behind the meagre protection of a stooping old man, half-asleep at the best of times, and now, in the middle of the night, as alert as a loaf of bread.

"I owe you," I promised him.

"You do," he promised me.

I went in, took my mask off, put down my remaining weapon and nearly screamed when a hot hand grabbed my shoulder.

14 NUMB

The hand pinches me, then punches me, and retreats into the darkness again.

I follow, and turn on the living room light. Granola's wearing her black kimono, sitting in a ball on the grey sofa with a phone in her palm, making a silent call, which means she's filled my work phone voicemail with nothing. She does this sometimes.

"Oh, you haven't." I try not to smile – it'll take me ages to zap all the mute messages. Half an hour of brailphone or invisible sign language. She waits five seconds then hangs up.

She refuses to answer when I ask if she's OK, frightened, angry, ill, Peruvian, human, etc, etc.

"Well give me your phone, I need to phone," I tell her. She doesn't move.

"Was that you, that noise outside?"

"Yes, and now I've got to call the police about it, please give me the phone." I don't know why I'm bothering. I could just as easily use my own phone, but something in our marriage makes me hang in there and argue about it. I move in closer for the grab.

"What happened, Bernie? Did you shoot someone?"

"Just give me the bloody phone, Granola, it's urgent."

"And don't talk to me like that." She doesn't swear much. Like I said, the first word you think of when you see her is prim. Prim and proper, well brought up, not stunningly beautiful but good-looking and sharp. Short thick reddish hair, which – how can I explain? – doesn't really need a style as such, no fancy cuts, just shaping around her slim face. Her eyes are dark blue, her eyebrows fairly heavy, her fair lips of average width, but much fuller when you kiss them. I admit it – she looks like Rita, but a posh, domestic version. Or maybe it's the other way round, maybe Rita's a racy version of her. I'd ask my analyst if I had one.

"Christ, Granola. You're exactly like the Inspector, more worried about good manners than killings."

"You mean you've killed someone?" She looks afraid of me suddenly.

"For God's sake." I leave her to it and make the call on my own phone, from my bedroom. I sleep in the "spare" bedroom now. I'm spare.

I undergo the same nonsense at the switchboard then tell the Inspector about the person lurking near my house.

"Can you give me a description?"

"A dark horizontal lump next to a hedge."

"Mr Bridges."

"Sorry, sorry, Inspector. No, I can't. He was in the shadows. You'd better do something before he comes round."

"What did you use?"

"A stun grenade. It says minimum twenty minutes' effectiveness on the label, but you never know."

"Twenty minutes? Are you sure it's legal? Where did you get it?"

"I don't know. On the web. Listen, there's a guy lying in my – "

"I'll get back to you." She rang off.

Again, something made me return to the living room, when I really ought to have thrown my body into a numbing bath and a numbing drink into my body.

I described the grenade incident to Granola.

"So you knew someone might try to attack one of us? I could have been murdered while you were having sex with your French tart."

"Listen, I have not been having sex with anybody. Not for a long time." Accusing stare.

"That would look great, wouldn't it – wife killed while husband boffs foreign model. And my dad thought that the next time I'd get my name in the papers would be in the birth announcements."

She rants, I feel like a dose of cystitis, the usual state of things.

"I've got to hang on to Claudine before some millionaire snaps her up and withdraws her from the public eye." Or Phil withdraws her from me.

"Oh, so it was purely business, then."

"For God's sake, Granola. Why do you *care*? We said we wouldn't ask each other where we spend our evenings. I didn't fuck – sorry – have sex with her, but that's beside the point. Here I am with a bunch of journalists clinging on to me by the lychees, the police sniffing round my arse, and then some stalker comes at me in the garden, and you do nothing but interrogate me about who I've been out drinking with. You're about three months late giving a damn."

I lift my arms and prance importantly back and forth, defending my case in front of our wide-screen TV, which has been silently flicking a black-and-white film at us. *Brief Encounter*, by the look of it. The opposite of our relationship. Granola pretends to be watching the movie through me.

"I have a right to know what you're up to if it could get me attacked in my own home," she says. "And don't give me that, that *rubbish*. Who do you think you are? Some great wheeler-dealer cornering the market in French commodities?" She works in a merchant bank, hence her vision of the world.

"You might not be far wrong." I sit beside her on the sofa. She pulls the kimono down to cover even her feet, and swings her legs out of my reach. I take the hint and stand up again.

"And what do mean by having the phone tapped?" She talks to my back.

"Shit sorry, I meant to tell you."

"They rang and asked me to say 'one two three four' into their damn machine!"

"Sorry, Granola."

"You gave the police permission to tap our landline? Are you crazy?"

"I didn't give them permission to tap the phone. I asked them to protect us against threatening phone calls."

"Protect us?" There is more than irony in her voice. "Is that what they're doing?" She doesn't take her eyes off the TV. "They asked me about you and Beano."

"My best bloody friend."

"And how you'd taken his death. And I had to say –" she shakes her head, she's close to tears, not for Beano, though, for herself, I'm sure. "It didn't seem to have affected you that much."

"You what? Fucking thank you very fucking much." I look for something unbreakable to thump. "What do you mean? I had to drink myself to sleep last night, I've been puking everything I eat, what more do you want? Christ!" I decide on the doorframe and give it a side-of-the-fist swipe. Ouch. “Come on, I said what more do you want?”

“I don’t know. I mean, OK, Beano was a drunk. Sexist. Foul-mouthed. Cruel. Irresponsible. But he was ... like family. And since he died, you’ve carried on normally with work. You haven’t even rung Beano’s mum.”

Shit, no that was true.

“I’ll do it first thing, Granola. But work, yes, I’ve worked. It’s the only thing to keep my mind off morbid thoughts.” I wave my arm at her as if to imply that she hasn’t been helping me very much, but she isn’t watching. “And I asked the police to send some men to protect you. They refused. Where’s fucking Armlock got to?”

“Oh, you’ve been very ... *efficient* about it all, but deep down you don’t really seem to care,” she says to the carpet.

“Care? That’s what the police were saying to me. Did they plant the idea in your head or was it some brilliant idea of your own?”

“If everyone’s telling you the same thing, perhaps it’s true.”

“Christ. I thought the cops were losing interest in me as a suspect and now you’ve been telling them I’m some kind of emotionless psycho. Is that it?”

Silence. I take it for a yes and shout “No!”

I slump into a chair and close my eyes to escape from everyone.

Beano and I used to be able to do that, to escape from everyone. We did together all the pleasant things in life that two grown men can decently do, plus several unpleasant things I think they ought to try. I could still picture him alive: happy, asleep, yelling, bouncing someone on his knee, puking merrily before going back for another bottle. Soon the memories would start to blur.

"Is that what you wanted, Granola? The kind of guy who tears his hair out over the coffin-lid just so everyone can say how caring he is?"

"No, maybe just the guy who comes home and commiserates with his wife over the loss of a friend rather than going out boozing with a French tart."

Put like that, I had to admit she had a point. But when you're in the divorce game, you can't concede even the fairest points.

"I've grieved, but maybe I'm just not Mediterranean enough about it," I tell her and the sofa. We talk to our furniture a lot. "Honestly, if James Bond had been invented today, he'd be weeping his way to the florist's every time a Smersh hitman got killed."

"So what were you doing on the toilet that time, out on the estates?" she asks, harking way back to my moment of tearfulness in the renovated bathroom. I laugh, even though it was unfair to bring up our First Kiss during a post-marital argument. "I mean," she adds, "anyone who can weep for joy over the fitting of a new loo must be fundamentally good. I think I married the real you, Bernie, but now someone else has moved in in his place."

She's wrong. She just doesn't know me. I spend so many night hours tiring my eyes in front of a screen, and Granola thinks I'm just thinking up sick jokes and checking out porn, but it's not true. Well, not entirely true. I'm also surfing around to check that everything is still intact out there – friends, family, coral reefs, species. I listen to the clunkings under the world's bonnet and I grieve that everything doesn't run perfectly.

But I have to get on. My languishing wouldn't do anyone any good. Just let me get where I want to get (and it's so close now), and then I'll have more time for the worthy stuff, I'll have time to help sort out other people's problems. Hell, if all the buyout money comes through, I'll go into semi-retirement in a year. If only she'd had the patience to wait for me, Granola and I would have been able to set up a charity trust fund and travel the planet, hand in hand, our consciences at peace. An eco-tourism cruise – on a solar-powered, zero-waste ship, of course. But that dream is dead, our marriage is dead, so why hassle me now?

"What about my medical T-shirts, then?" I said. Here was concrete (well, cotton, anyway) proof of my caring.

"What T-shirts?"

I explained about helping heart-attack patients and diabetics, about protecting people from Aids and malaria.

"Great, but what happens if someone has a heart attack when his T-shirt's in the wash?"

"God, Granola, you're so damn ... *practical.*"

"Come off it, Bernie, they're just gimmicks, admit it. I bet you're not going to be giving them away, are you?"

"Not all of them, true, but, I mean, even charities sell stuff, and with the right sponsors, the prices could be ..."

"God. When you started out, you used to talk about the internet being the new democracy, a way of sharing information and creating a sense of worldwide community. These days it's just another advertising billboard. A huge, shouting, shopping mall."

She huffed conclusively. She'd proved I'm a profiteering bastard and that was the end of it.

"Where's bloody Armlock got to? They ought to have a squad car round here by now."

I speed-dialled yet again.

"Police, Dave speaking, how – "

"Give me Inspector Armlock, please, I know she's there."

"You know more than I do then, Sir."

"I spoke to her a moment ago. Twice."

"If I remember correctly, I put you through to her voicemail, Sir."

"Yes, but I spoke to her."

"Strange. You sure it wasn't just the recorded message? You know, 'sorry, I'm unavailable at the moment, please leave your' –"

"Yes, I'm sure, now please put me through to the Inspector. This is very urgent." I was certain they were sitting side by side, keeping straight faces for their hilarious game. One playing the buffoon night sergeant, the other listening in until it got boring.

"Would you like me to put you through to her voicemail, then?"

"God. OK, yes please."

"OK, then. Have a nice night."

"For Christ's sake." I paced about as I waited for ten long seconds. "Hello, Inspector, this is Mr Brid–"

"Good evening again, Mr Bridges, I was just about to call you."

"Inspector? I wish you had. Have you picked up the unconscious intruder yet?"

"Yes."

"Well, who is he?"

"Intruders don't generally carry ID."

"OK, but you do accept that my wife and I are in danger and need protection."

"I don't know about that."

"What? But what about the guy in the garden? Was he just grazing on the shrubbery? I want round-the-clock protection, now, for my wife and myself." I turned to Granola as some sort of apology for getting her involved in all this, but she was still folded up, chin on knees, not participating.

Silence at the other end.

"My colleague's dead, Inspector, I'm being threatened, it's your duty to protect me."

"Mr Bridges, the man now suffering from perforated ear-drums is a policeman."

"A policeman?" My brain failed to fit this new information into the state of things.

"I sent him to keep a watch on your house. He got out of his car to have a pee."

"Against our hedge? Is that what you call community policing?"

"Personally I'm quite glad you bombed him – it'll teach him to take an empty bottle with him next time. I'm having him replaced with a less discreet team. They'll be driving by regularly in a big white car with blue lights on top. Try not to throw any grenades at them."

She hung up and I swung round on Granola, still in her foetus-that-refuses-to-come-out position.

"Don't you get it, Granola? She says she's protecting me, but really she's watching me. She thinks I killed Beano."

"You're the one who invited her to bug the phone, for God's sake."

"Oh, no. All this is your fault, you told her I didn't care about Beano, you dropped me right in it, you, you ... bitch."

"Don't you dare call me that."

"At least it proves I'm not totally emotionless."

"I didn't tell her you don't care." A muffled voice. She raised her eyes but not her face.

"What?"

She looked exhausted.

"Course I didn't, Bernie. Even if I thought it. I told her you were really shocked and frightened and hadn't slept or eaten since."

"Really?" Ah, my faithful soon-to-be ex-spouse. "I don't believe you."

"OK, don't believe me."

"Did you truly say that? Promise?"

"Of course. What kind of person do you think I am?"

"Really? Honest?"

"Of course. I just told you, didn't I?"

"OK. I'm sorry I called you a bitch. But in that case why the hell did you tell me all that crap before?"

And so on. Such is divorce.

****

Shares in British medical company Coma have fallen overnight as Asian markets reacted to the admission by Coma's financial director that the firm was expecting bad press tomorrow caused by "matters relating to the recent tragic death of a director in suspicious circumstances".
Full story here.

Being a GP is a moral minefield.
How do you explain to an 80-year-old that their heart op is not a good investment for the taxpayer?
Well, now you don't have to.
Just show your elderly patient one of our Moral Empowerment movies and the wrinkly will make the decision for him- or herself.
Made by qualified counsellors, our films (also available with large-print subtitles for the hard-of-hearing) will gently coax your patient out of that "save me at all costs" frame of mind.
Contact BudgetbustersVideo now for your sample copy of "You Probably Wouldn't Have Survived the Anaesthetic Anyway".

****

15 Nostrils at Twelve O'Clock

It's a cliché, I know, but it's after a row that I fancy Granola the most. When we're arguing, we're not being indifferent. And there she was last night, practically naked under her kimono. And there I was, still painfully horny thanks to Claudine and my long bout of abstinence.

I apologized for shouting at her, and we agreed not to separate all our bank accounts just yet, and we seemed to be getting back on the right track. I thought we could mark our new *détente* with a little physical *rapprochement.*

She didn't agree, so I went to my spare room to do terrible things to Claudine in my troubled half-sleep.

Half-sleep is an exaggeration. I didn't sleep at all. I spent the whole night in victim mode. Granola and I were boxed in better than Tutankhamun. The vibration-sensitive alarm was set on maximum, but I spent the night staring at the door and window, listening to distant engines, the Watch bawling out some of my neighbours, an early-riser's pre-ignition car alarm. I couldn't even listen to the radio for fear of missing the murderer's entry. It's scary sleeping alone.

In the street next morning I found a white police car with fluorescent stripes, crowd-control loudspeakers, and two uniformed officers pointing their nostrils straight at the roof. Trust the insomniac to send two somniacs.

I drove down to the seafront for an eye-toner. The water was its flat calm self but the weather was grumpy. Husband and wife, you might say. There was a blotch of something bright over the sea, but it was more like a shrouded fog-lamp than a sun. I sat in the car on the prom overlooking the waves, and got my phone out.

First I opened up Jason's tabloid news feed. True to form, here was a primary-colour headline with full-column exclamation marks. The other tabloids had picked up the story and were almost identical.

Next I checked out Beatrice's TV news channel. Same there, via talking head and slightly smaller print. Millions of people would go out of the house with one or other of those messages burnt on to their retinas and eardrums.

All in all, there was a morning's worth of outrage and barely-contained disbelief. But not about me and GTV. No, the country was much more pre-occupied with a panic story about favouritism in a TV cooking show. A real threat to world democracy.

Louie was going to be ecstatic. In all the mainstream media I checked out, Beano and I were safely tucked away in the minor news, amongst some footballers who'd bought a diamond mine, a trophy hunter and his pile of dead pandas, and a newly-divorced LGBT lady bishop. Nowhere did Beano merit more than the bare news of his body being found, and there were no mentions at all of my name. An afterword about Coma winning a government contract, and that was it. Everything was treated neutrally and factually, almost as if we bored them.

Poor old Pigshit. He'd probably be spitting his marmalade into his beard at this very moment over the injustice of it all.

I looked into the rear view mirror and told myself loud and clear. "You're a fucking genius." Beano told me to do it every time I really think I've been brilliant. Never deprive yourself of deserved self-admiration or you might stop wanting to achieve, he said. My reflection looked as if it believed me.

Pigshit would be wondering why the media was empty of badly-reproduced screen-grabs of Claudine spitting, alongside point-by-point comparisons with the Turin shroud. And why there were no "we have a right to know" demands for the truth about Beano's black gunk. No doubt there were, in all the GTV news bulletins, watched by maybe a dozen zealots. Pigshit desperately needed the other media to talk about his unknown channel, and I'd personally deprived him of the publicity.

How?

At two in the morning, after my chat with the Inspector, I'd sought out Jason, Beatrice and Clifftop (in that order) and bought their silence. Not with money, I had better than that. I offered them hints of Big News from the Government. A great idea to help the region that had been hit by the exploding Ebola. Plus a massive new nationwide public-health campaign in the very near future. I promised each of them the full, and totally exclusive, leak of something exciting very soon. They were deeply interested in the chance of a real leak as opposed to the endless deliberate government leaks, which, their journalists' pride tells them, are cheapening their profession.

It was a bit of a gamble on my part. If Angela Greensands doesn't like my idea, or fails to come up with the promised public-health contract, I'll be in the shit. Same if she does deliver, and then learns that I leaked something to the press. But I've thought that out already. I'm not going to leak anything she doesn't approve first. It'll all be part of my idea for the health campaign: fake real leaks. Ms G will love it, I'm sure. "Perfect," she'll say.

So there it was. Coma's reputation saved by a bit of bargaining. OK, I have to admit that the government news wasn't what won the tabloid reporter over. I had to offer Jason something more.

I told him I was on a promise with Claudine. She's a bit of a tabloid star already. She makes the celeb pages when she goes to a London party, and she's flashed her boobs a few times in the lads' mags. I swore I'd give Jason a kiss-and-tell story about her as soon as the deed was done.

I'm not proud of myself. I might even renege on the deal.

But who's worse? Me for exploiting Claudine, or the tabloid press for being less interested in a murder story than a model's sex life?

When I got into the office there was a pleasant surprise at reception – a biker had delivered my watch from the village inn. I opened up the little brown box, fearing the worst. I removed the menu, brochure and hand-written note about weekend breaks that the pub landlord had enclosed, and there it was. It looked surprisingly intact. Dented? No, the dork had exaggerated the damage out of all proportion. The only mark seemed to be a scratch on the glass. I'd get that changed and it'd be as good as new.

Time to boast to Louie about my media manipulation. I'd even gone out and bought paper copies of Jason's and Clifftop's rags. I unfolded them, knocked on Louie's door and went in.

He was sitting back in his chair, staring into space. Or rather, space seemed to be staring into him. He looked as lifeless as the Moon.

I wondered if he'd been strangled. No, his face was relaxed.

A bullet? There was no blood.

Maybe he'd been paralysed with some nerve agent. I walked up to the lip of his desk and peered down at him. His remaining hair was combed back neatly over his scalp. His florid shirt was fresh on and smelt of some pungent eau de toilette. His hands were locked to the desktop. He didn't move or speak. I stood staring, uncertain whether I should run for a doctor or poke my tongue out at him.

"Let's wait till it's ten per cent then sell, OK? Have a nice day." He jerked forward. "Sorry about that, Bernie. How are things?"

Shit, yes, of course. His tiny earbud phone.

"Great," I underestimated, wondering briefly who he'd been talking to.

I laid out my newspapers on his desk and let their significance sink in.

He skimmed through one or two of the non-articles and then laughed manically as if it was some big joke.

"This is perfect," he said, almost dribbling with glee. "As Confucius no doubt said, no bad press, share price says yes." Like I said, dribbling. "How did Mona convince them to kill the story?"

"Mona? Mona did fuck – well, I don't know what she did, Louie, but what *I* did was call these guys and talk them out of splashing bad publicity all over the place."

"OK. Sorry. You're a genius, Bernie. How did *you* do it?"

I told him. Most of it, anyway. Not the Claudine stuff.

"Great, brilliant. Even if Angela doesn't agree, you've bought us time," Louie said. "What have you got for her? Rita told me you were being very secretive, and even Des doesn't know."

Shit, the one person I'd forgotten to call was Des.

"Have faith, Louie."

"Faith? Even if you were a certified, card-carrying Greek god, I wouldn't have faith. This is not the right time for blind faith. So what have you got?" Small oases of sweat were forming under his armpits.

"Louie, if you'd been listening to your mate Angela, you'd remember that she said she didn't *want* any big presentation. A rough outline, she said. So I've got some photos and a basic concept. That's all she asked for."

Louie nodded slowly. "Yeah, OK, you're right. She knows what he wants. I've been working to convince her to come to us for a long time now. Ever since she was appointed."

"Yeah?" Here was Louie trying to sniff up a few granules of the credit for my work. "I was under the impression that she came to us because of my movies. Mine and Beano's."

"Who do you think got her and her team to look at the films? Do you think she spends her spare time surfing weirdo websites?"

Why not? I do.

"I met her at an investors' dinner last year," Louie went on. "One of these things organized by the Ministry of Development to put companies like us in touch with people with money to spend. I gave her our spiel about opening up the health market. Seems it's bearing fruit."

I considered turning Louie's brain into fruit purée with his sundial, but decided that it would only mean going home again to change into a clean shirt.

"Well, thanks for giving me my chance, Louie."

"Yeah, well don't blow it," he replied, ignoring or not detecting the irony. "We're all depending on you."

"I'll quote you on that when the payment comes through."

Leaving his office, I checked that the corridor was empty, then turned and mimed a grimacing micro-dick wank at Louie through his door. Ten full seconds of satisfying scorn.

"You belittle yourself," Phil said. Where did he come from?

"Glad you've noticed." I swivelled with a chummy smile.

He was eyeing me like those knitting Parisian hags must have eyed Marie Antoinette, who also made a misplaced joke that time. I must be careful who I wank at in future.

"You're a real cunt, Bernie."

"Come on, Phil –"

"No, I love cunts. All's fair in business and fuckin I always say, and Claudine's both of them." He sounded suspiciously unconcerned about yesterday night.

"I'm glad you're such a good loser."

Phil laughed at this, I don't know why.

"I hear you put up wither for the whole fuckin evenin yesterdee. I admire you, Bernie, honest. These models are tough work."

"So you phoned Claudine?"

"Course I fuckin did, to ask why the fuck she wasn't there when I arrived to picker up. But you'd got er to switch off er fuckin phone, right?" Despite his extravagant use of his favourite word, his voice was more amused than angry. "Still, never mind, I know you didn't fucker." He laughed yet again.

"You asked her?"

"Course I did."

"You mean you asked her straight out if I'd fucked her?"

"Course."

"And she told you?"

"No, to be quite honest, the look on your face just did. Sorry Bernie, nasty trick."

"You enema."

He gurgled at me. "With any luck, I'll ave better luck."

"She still wants to see you, then?"

"Oh yeah. And thanks for all that bullshit about me bein some kind of money-launderin drug baron. She's fuckin fascinated now. Great boost you gave me. Cheers."

"So when you seeing her?"

"Well it's not Friday, cos she's seein *Bare Knee*. And it's not tonight, cos Des is comin over to Mona's for tea. Why don't you and Granola come?"

I wasn't sure whether Phil knew about my divorce. Probably. He was just stirring.

"I'll ask Gra – what do you mean, Des is coming over to Mona's for tea?"

He grinned even more triumphantly than usual.

"Like, Des is gnu eat his evenin meal at Mona's place instead of eatin at ome all alone."

I was feeling almost physically sick. This was too much.

"No, Phil. I mean the 'come over to Mona's' bit. Are you her social secretary or something?"

"Oh, Bernie, even *you're* not that out of it."

"Shit. What's been going on around here? Beano and Rita, now you and Mona? How come I wasn't invited to this love-in?"

"Yeah, well, take your pick – you fancy Des or Louie?"

"No, seriously, you're taking the piss, right? You're not sha–, er, going out with Mona?"

"Why the fuck not? She's a great girl. You should know."

"But when did it all start?"

"If you'd just get your nose off a fuckin screen for five fuckin minutes you'd find out there was other things going on the fuckin world, Bernie. Like your own fuckin wife's nervous breakdown."

"What's she been –?"

"Granola called me up yesterday lookin for you. Didn't know where the fuck you'd got to."

"She called you?"

"Well she couldn't fuckin call *you*. You keep turnin your fuckin phone off so we won't disturb you while you get up to all your mischief."

For a few moments Phil looked like my old friend from university instead of the rival he's turned into recently. He seemed to be pitying me.

"Well if you've got Mona, why the hell are you chasing after Claudine?"

"Bernie, please. Don't lecture me about fuckin infidelity. Specially not durin dinner with Mona and Granola, OK? See you later." He disappeared into his office, leaving me to work out why I always emerge from a tussle with Phil feeling as if I've just been stripped naked and dumped in full view of a football stadium crowd with a daffodil poked up my backside.

Then it hit me. Of course. Phil and Mona. Logical. That's why Mona had left me alone to deal with the journos. She's sleeping with the enemy. Phil is shafting her to shaft me. He's an even bigger bastard than I thought. Which makes Des all the more vital. Got to get him on my side when it comes to putting together some concrete results for Angela Greensands.

I looked down at my watch. Still plenty of time to have a chat with Des and get ready for her.

Or was there? The damn thing had stopped.

16 Do the Twist

"Look at this – I've only had it a few days and it's broken already. You've got to replace it."

The jeweller took the watch reverently and examined it.

"Bit of an accident, Sir?"

He grimaced sympathetically at the scratched glass.

"Yes, damn thing fell off my wrist."

He tested the stretch metal strap, politely proving to me that he knew I was bullshitting.

"OK," I said, "I dropped it, but at that price it should be able to fall out of an aeroplane under the hooves of a regiment of cavalry and not get broken."

"Hmm." He fingered the glass. He seemed to be running the watch's price through his head, assessing my worth as a customer. "Yes, we can change the glass for you. Free of charge, of course."

"Thanks very much, but that's not much use. It's stopped! Can't you replace the mechanism or at least fit a new battery?"

"Oh, no, Sir."

"But what am I supposed to do?"

He looked at me pityingly. Why did everyone seem to be doing that lately?

"Sir simply winds this little button here, and it will start again."

The fucking watch was *clockwork*. He gently wound it up for me, torturing my ego with every twist of his delicate fingers.

"What?" I finally blustered. "You're winding me up. I pay all that money and I'm supposed to do all the hard work myself?"

I made him promise to have it repaired and delivered to the office next morning, and got out of there.

I mean, is that what the idle rich do? Buy things that have to be wound and polished every day? Ride in cars that are too long and heavy to be driven by a normal driver? Eat stuff that has to be carved or opened for them on the plate? I've still got a lot to learn about being rich.

I bought a sandwich that someone else had made but that I could chew with my own teeth, and headed back into the office. I'd just grabbed a coffee when Rita's top half poked around the partition, announcing that a Ministry car had been sighted down at street level.

"She's early!" I moaned, but Rita had gone. Still in a mood with me, it seemed. No time to call Des. I sprinted into reception and smiled as the lift door opened for my visitor.

****

Dear Member,
An offer not to be sneezed at! Are your waiting rooms full of cold and flu sufferers?
Tell us about it and win a two-week holiday in the Antarctic, where no germs can survive!
Go to NostrumCureAll

****

17 SCRWGNYNMNSKLGYKN

When you're drunk, drugged or shagging, everything seems possible. You can actually *see* your absurdest plots come true. Yes, my darling, we'll spend the weekend in Antarctica, what's the problem? You, me, a bed and lots of bear grease. Let's go, *now*.

Then, later, things don't seem quite so obvious. In fact, the South Pole is actually quite a long way away. And bear grease is so environmentally unfriendly. Besides, are there bears in Antarctica?

That's the feeling of inadequacy that hit me as soon as the lift door opened. The best ideas are simple, yes, but they've got to look as if you've spent days, weeks, hacking the dross away from your inspiration. My idea for the village looked so simple, you'd think I'd spent half a minute with a tube of glue and two matchsticks.

"Right, but what about all those people in the Louvre saying 'wow gosh yes' in front of a balding, grinning dead lady whose only claim to fame is that she was painted by the inventor of the helicopter? If we hadn't told them it was vulgar, they'd do exactly the same – 'wow gosh yes' – in front of a heap of money."

"Oh, no. Now you're going too far."

For the last five minutes we'd been wading through "what is art?" I'd recalled the first time I went to Paris, saw the Mona Lisa, and was disappointed. Except I wasn't allowed to say so at the time, because it was generally acknowledged that Da Vinci was a genius.

We'd got on to this subject because my conversation partner had recognized the Damien Hirst dots on our wall – they're posters, though a signed original might be up there soon if all goes well with the buyout. A meeting room full of preserved animals by Damien Hirst would be perfect for our brand image – formaldehyde is so health-oriented.

My chat buddy wasn't Angela Greensands. This was Kieran Gimble, her budget controller. Fortyish, his pudgy face pummelled into a tight pink collar. He had a respectable tan and an expensive suit, but he looked uncomfortable outside the strict realm of his job. And especially uncomfortable inside the realm of his trousers. Angela G had arranged to meet him here, and Gimble had turned up early. I just prayed she would arrive soon. I couldn't take much more of this. Gimble was balanced on the edge of one of our tipped-back armchairs, one buttock on, one buttock off. Excruciating. I hate being with uncomfortable people. They make me so uncomfortable.

Maybe he was never totally at ease, I thought. That would explain the ten-kilowatt gold cufflinks bolstering his obvious lack of self-confidence. Angela had surprised me again – I'd expected her underling to be like her, slick and aerodynamic, but this man was more of a fleshy teddy bear. Recently given a large hike in salary by the looks of it, and not yet sure how to handle the prestige.

"I can see what you're thinking," I said. He was thinking, God my butt hurts, why didn't I take another turn round the block? "You think I'm just trying to shock you. But I honestly don't see any real difference between the Mona Lisa, a Damien Hirst cow, and a well-designed logo."

"I suppose you're right in a way," he said. "But which would you rather own? A Rembrandt portrait or half a pickled cow?"

"Ha ha ha ha ha," I said, hoping vaguely that I could make the laugh last till Angela Greensands arrived. "That's the financial expert talking, not the art-lover."

He chuckled, and at last he sank back into the chair, discovering to his visible ecstasy that the tipped-back pose took all of the strain off his waistband.

After a few more minutes of politely creaking conversation, Angela finally arrived and both of us could have thrown our arms around her knees in welcome. What a tactician.

She made her entrance in a dark-blue ultra-light trouser suit and crisp white shirt (dressed a bit like a vintage UK passport), closing in with proffered hand. We smiled hard, but my non-idea still lay inert in my head like an old dog on the sofa, waiting to see if it'll get kicked off or not.

Ms G was soon lounging in a low-slung armchair. A screen showing my hi-res glossies was lying in her lap like a TV dinner. She was waiting for me to whet her appetite.

The instant I opened my mouth I had a wishful vision of Angela Greensands going into fast video rewind out the door, giving me another day to think. Give me twenty-four hours and I'd come up with something really solid. I was about to tell her my supposedly brilliant idea and she was going to nod to herself and say she'd have to consult the rest of her department (a lie, everyone knows she's the decision maker), then she'd go away and get her assistant to delight Louie and Phil with the news that this Bridges guy wasn't up to the mark.

"Well," I began, "you can assure the tourist office that they won't be saddled with a campaign using some awful slogan like 'a new tourist *boom*' or 'it's everything it's *cracked* up to be'."

She laughed politely. "No, what we want is a campaign that will blow people away." Like me, she'd obviously been hard at work on the puns.

She was pleased with the photos. As she swiped through them all, I commented on the pub, the barns, the fields, the grinning village idiots, and she approved.

"It's a beautiful, restful place," I told her. "Everything the countryside should be. No reason why tourists shouldn't want to go there."

"Did you ask the locals how they felt about the, er, problem?"

"I tried. Some, the ones who'd lost relatives I guess, didn't want to talk about it. Others did some great sound effects. Weird sense of humour, these country folk."

She laughed. It was time to say it. My idea. Straight out.

"In a nutshell, the, er, main thrust of the, uh, core of my idea is" – I could feel her eyes on me – "simple. We can do away with all the bad memories, and bring people back for the right reasons. The quiet, the landscape, the smell of wood smoke and horse dung." A little smile. "I may be going beyond my jurisdiction here, but what I suggest is that you simply change the village's name and –"

It was out and I suddenly remembered that the government, Angela's own firm, had thought of it first.

I'd come up with a dodo. I mean, there's that nuclear power plant in Cumbria. It started off as Seascale, then there was a big radiation leak so they changed its name to Windscale, which it stayed till the antis got too efficient, and so they changed it to Sellafield. I *think* that's right. A dangerously brilliant campaign. Protesters have to spend so long reminding the public of the place's old names that people lose interest before they get to the nitty-gritty. Next time there's an accident, the government will probably give the place a name like Scrwgnymnsklgykn. Just let the protesters get that on a banner and into the public consciousness. Or easier still, give it no name at all.

But what of Angela Greensands? Was she heading, disappointed, disdainful, for the door? Not yet. She was still listening to me.

"... then you give the whole region a new tourist tag. You know, something like Spa Country or Springlands. With the right social media co-operation, it should be very efficient."

She was still watching me. I had all my head muscles under clamps. There was not a grain of doubt on my face, of that I'm sure. But inside, my head was doing a Scrwgnymsklgykn, ready to start pumping out radiation or melt down. She took her time mulling it over, she looked back at some of the photos, then said one word,

"Perfect."

I loved hearing that word.

"I like your sense of priorities," she said. "You're not worried that we might be seen as, let's say, covering something up?"

"Covering what up? I went out there, and I'm OK."

"True," she said. "Yes, perfect answer, really."

We discussed timetables, meetings, tourist officers, a re-visit to film some video footage, and finally, just for a few moments, the tightness of ladies' riding pants.

Then Angela asked, "Have you thought any more about the pharmaceuticals industry?"

As I said, women like her don't ask casual questions. The answer was, yes I fucking well had. I'd *thought* about this one.

"I've done a little research since we last spoke."

"Good. What did it tell you?"

"Big," I said. "Huge, and still growing. One of the *healthiest*-looking industries in the world. OK, the global economy may have its ups and downs, but one industry that always remains immune is pharmaceuticals. And the human genome, well, that could provide cures for any number of diseases, which means that the drug companies are on the verge of a whole new generation of profits. Just imagine if they could come up with a cure for Alzheimer's, or breast cancer, or this new Asian flu bug people are talking about. They could ..."

My mind boggled so much at the sums involved that I dried up. My brain was suddenly dazzled by the brilliance of it all.

"Go on," she urged me, softly.

"Yes. Well, whatever else we do, we humans are all getting older and iller by the day. We'd all rip up the entire Amazon rainforest if it would guarantee us a full head of hair and no cellulite. Health and Beauty is what everyone wants to spend their money on. Growth in global turnover of pharmaceutical companies last year was, I think, more than two hundred per cent. Thanks not only to medication, but to their activities in the agribusiness. I must admit I got the idea I just outlined to you from the sponsorship and re-naming of Freevax Eritrea. A disease-free, pest-free African state. Brilliant –

your company's name in every atlas. And I've heard that First World governments are also starting to work as partners with pharmaceutical companies, to fund national entire health programmes in exchange for sole rights on medication in a given country. They say that in Europe this will be tried out in Britain first."

That last suggestion was just a rumour, widely denied, but I thought it worth pulling out here.

Angela G gave nothing away. No sign of shock or disapproval, just receptiveness. I'd come to the end of my little set piece, very carefully set and pieced together, and I wasn't going to risk improvisation. Besides, I'd been quoting almost verbatim from the abstract of a thesis I'd found by an economics student called Caroleen in Boulder, Colorado, and I'd run out of material. Even the internet has its limits.

"Anything to add, Kieran?" Angela asked.

"Two hundred and seven point three per cent growth in the last five years to be exact. With an advertising and sponsorship budget growing almost at the same rate," was the reply. Old Gimble wasn't such a bad chap after all. I let an eyebrow hover in wonder.

"Aren't you bothered by the speed of growth of the industry, and particularly its entry into politics?" Ms G asked me. She wanted the full profession of faith. Her Ministry is called Development, a synonym for progress, complexity, new-ness. No place there for negativity.

"It would be hypocritical of me to do the job I'm doing if I had doubts about that," I said. "Pharmaceuticals are our bread and butter. If we at Coma are trying to hook up to the biggest growth sector in the economy, it's because we believe that the expansion of the health industry," (I should have held my left hand aloft, slotting my right inside my shirt above the heart) "is based on the importance of quality of life. Pharmaceuticals not only keep us all alive, but keep us in the best possible condition, too. Which, ideally, is the duty of a government, I suppose. So I see no problem in a government working with a pharmaceuticals company. Both have ultimately the same goal – a healthy, and therefore productive and contented, population. The pharmaceuticals company knows that market forces will remain in operation. If they don't perform, if they don't provide the population with good health, then they'll lose their contract. Just as a government will be voted out. I see no contradiction there."

Angela Greensands looked straight into my eyes, assessing me.

"Well," she said, "this government is as yet offering no sole-rights agreement to any pharmaceuticals company, but we have received a very important proposition for a sponsored health programme this winter which will involve, as a trial only, a single company, Nostrum." She shot a glance at us to underline the name of our very own partners. "If the trial works, we will consider making it permanent, and extending it to other areas. Now –"

This is where Long John Silver would have got out his treasure map. I tried not to lean forward in greedy anticipation. That's the good thing about our armchairs, you need to be a masochist to lean anywhere but back.

She began unrolling her parchment. It was big. Massive. A whole cowskin.

"First," she said, "you'll need to sign these. I think you know what they imply." She passed Rita and myself a form each. Official Secrets Act.

want to underestimate its potential effects if it gets this far west, and isn't controlled."

She allowed herself a pause to make eye contact and underline the seriousness of what she was saying. A consummate performer.

"Did you know," she continued, "that more people died in the 1918-19 epidemic of Spanish flu than were killed in battle in the entire First World War? Forty million worldwide. If you extrapolate the effect of such losses on today's population levels, you'd be looking at tens of millions of deaths in Western Europe alone. Not that there's anything to panic about just yet." She smiled. "That's just a worst-case scenario. You know that it's a politician's job to predict the worst, and then take all the credit when things turn out less badly than they might have done. Which is where I need your help."

She gestured to me for a reaction. But I was still trying to get my head round those forty million deaths.

"We were thinking of some kind of online doctor," she went on. "GPs aren't keen to have their waiting rooms invaded by hordes of coughing patients. Doing it all online will be much ... cleaner."

"Right – you'd programme the online doctor to list cold and flu symptoms, take names and addresses, then prescribe the seven-day cure and send out the treatment," I said.

"Yes. We thought we'd need probably several doctors – men and women of all the major ethnic origins, for maximum patient choice. Obviously, if someone with a cold or flu types in their symptoms, their 'doctor' should direct them to the seven-day cure. But that's not all. This has got to be set in the context of a general health environment. You know, you type in your weight, height, diet, etc, and the system tells you your life expectancy and what to do to prolong it. Including, of course, taking the seven-day cure. You ask for dietary advice, and it asks you whether you're getting enough vitamins to protect you against flu, then plugs the seven-day cure. That sort of thing. There will also be ads for the cure dotted here there and everywhere throughout the system. If you log on, for whatever reason, and the system suspects you're infected, it has to sell you – or rather convince you to take – the cure."

"All roads lead to *rhume*," Gimble said. Rita laughed, but I didn't get it. "French for cold," Gimble explained.

"One thing I don't understand," I said. "I mean, it may be none of my business. But this seems a lot more urgent than your tourist campaign. Why did you get me to look into that first?"

Ms G nodded acknowledgement.

"Well, we needed to make sure that you were the right kind of person for us."

"Right kind of person?"

"Yes, someone whose thinking is ... in *harmony* with our own. Not everyone is happy with public-private partnerships promoting tourism in destinations recently affected by disease, or immunization programmes. Make no mistake, the Spa Country campaign, if that's what we decide to call it, is important. Vital, even, for the region's economy. But now the seven-day cure should take priority." She looked almost sombre.

"No problem," I assured her. "You decide how and when your money is spent."

"Exactly," she said, lightening up. "And the good news is that this public-health campaign will not be restricted by public-spending constraints. We already have major backing from Nostrum. Kieran?" She gave the nod to Gimble, who'd been trying to remove some papers silently from his case. A sheet of figures was handed to me. The budget. If it had been written in words my eyes would have needed half an hour to take them all in. As it was, I got light-headed from all the zeros bubbling away at the end of the figures columns. What was that bullshit Louie had been talking about me not making a profit yet?

"For matters of budgeting you'll be working with Kieran. He will handle both ends of the finance."

"OK. Right. Yes," I said, pretending to read. In fact I needed a breath between each word I spoke. I was at altitude. Finally I got myself under control and turned to Gimble. "This is what I call art." He smiled back at our private joke.

My dad's an artist, sorry, Artist. He hates anything and anyone that makes more money than he does. Every time I go to see him, I get another earful about computer graphics being sub-art, and he wanders about his studio going "click wow!", "download that, motherfuckers!" and the like. He'd have preferred me to be a painter or something similarly penniless and self-righteous. Digital art is non-art, he says. Anything that doesn't involve getting pretentious stains on your trousers is non-art. A graphic designer isn't a real artist. Artist fartist my arse.

He used to hassle me about a career in business being the slippery slope to nerve cancer, but it was all right for him and his pig bristles, he had a dayjob at an art college, as painting teacher to the impressionable. Every September dished up a new piping-hot plateful of free-expressionists. The irony is that these days, post #MeToo, he's the one taking nerve pills in case any of his former students hits him with a historical abuse case. Stupid old dick. Much safer to work with digital women.

The Ministry of Development is based in a new marina, called simply "The Marina", just along the coast. Its more important members can fly up to London in half an hour whenever they need to, but they spend a lot of time sniffing around the seaside in search of money and amusement.

When the government wanted to set up its new Ministry, some very influential people started moaning about inner-city crime, protest marches, pollution and the London traffic, and how it would be much easier for them to travel in from their country houses or offshore abodes if the Ministry was based on the coast. They could also get into work way before eleven on a Monday morning after their yachting weekends. So the Marina it was.

I've seen TV reports, I've seen its discreet motorway exit, its powerboats, but I've never been close. You don't get within a mile without a pass. And anyway, the buildings wouldn't tell you much. It's what goes on inside them that counts. It's the smell of concentrated power in there, and the beauty of the people who breathe nothing but.

Coma and the Marina were founded almost side by side at almost exactly the same time. That's what they call serendipity.

"We have the bare bones of an online service ready for you," Angela Greensands went on. "But it needs to be brought to life. As we understand it, Coma has developed some software that would enable you to put together a final product very quickly."

"Er, yes," I confirmed, surprised that she knew about Des's latest invention. Though I don't know why I was surprised.

"Can you tell me about it, in easy-to-understand terms, of course," she said, though we both knew she could grasp the technical fine points as well as anyone in the building.

"Well, basically, what Des, our technical director, has done is create a sort of intelligent image library. You tell it what you want, and it instantly selects the appropriate images, and then brings them to life. It makes image search engines look like steam engines. Des can make any animal, plant, person or landscape do what you want it to do in 3D animation. You want a miniature Napoleon paddling a Native American canoe into Hitler's backside, you've got it, in seconds. Totally realistic. And any colour canoe you want."

"Sounds incredible. I hope he's patented it," Angela G said.

"No, he says he won't even share it until he's invented something better for himself."

She laughed. "Well, I don't know about you, Kieran, but I think we've come to the right place."

Gimble gave me a chummy nod.

"Yes, I'm getting a good feeling here," she added. "I feel as if we're really going to start taking health to the people." She was already working on her slogans and speeches.

"Which reminds me." I nearly forgot my merchandising. "Look at this." I handed Ms G a heart-attack T-shirt. "Imagine the same thing geared towards cold- and flu-prevention, handed out by pharmacies."

She nodded.

"Yes, yes," she said. "We could have a photo of one of our online doctors, with all the contact info. I like it. Health care as streetwear. What unit cost are we looking at?"

I took a chance and tripled Stanley's price.

"OK, knock off, say, fifty per cent for bulk and we're in business. What do you think, Kieran? Start with kids' sizes. At that price, we'd use a million to start with, wouldn't we?"

"Minimum," answered my good buddy Gimble.

"Get the wording from Nostrum and we'll go with it," she told me. She made to return the heart-attack shirt.

"Please keep it," I said, feeling generous. "Not that you look as if you need it." She probably gets a new set of vital organs fitted every year.

"Here," she laughed, and threw the shirt to Gimble. "Take it to heart."

Kieran's expression suggested that life with Ms Greensands wasn't always fun and games.

I looked up the Ministry, and found an impressive list of projects, partnership deals and heavyweight sponsors. Angela Greensands was in a prominent position, of course. She's a director of several companies, it seems, including Nostrum. Nothing out of order there. As she told me, it's a rule in her Ministry that all politicians are also company directors. This "promotes streamlined government-business co-operation," its portal boasted. There was only one weird thing: its website address is "ministryofdevelopment.*com*". As in, "dot com" not "dot gov". A government ministry can't be a private company, can it? Perhaps it's only the website that's private.

Anyway, I also learned that Angela Greensands is thirty-eight, married with two kids, and divides her time between London and the Marina. No shit about where she *lives*. Living's not enough, she's got to have that extra dimension. Divides Her Time. Total control.

****

Up Is the New Down
After their overnight blip, Coma shares are on the up again, bolstered by a press release formally announcing a contract to provide a "major online service" to a "large government agency".
More news here.

For sale: VACCINES. Flu, smallpox, anthrax, all varieties of plague. Others on request.
Fast delivery for batches from ten to ten million.
Vaccines guaranteed to be latest strains.
Catalogue here.

Prizes!
Dear Member,
For the latest in genetic engineering equipment, go to Nostrum and win a year's supply of frozen mouse embryos.

****

18 CROTCH

Suppressing a delicious desire to go and fart victoriously in Louie's face, I went to my cubicle to compose a message to Des. As I tried to think up an opening line, I swivelled in my chair. It stuck at 180° and left me staring at Beano's desk. The police had searched for clues, but Beano's pens were still littered where he'd dropped them. There was his plastic 70s desk-lamp, rounded and nuclear orange. Illegible jottings which would never be deciphered were pronged on an old 'IN' spike with "Rottingdean Hotel" embossed on its wooden base. Beano had altered the logo to read "Rutting Beano Hotel", of course. A pair of sunglasses, a tennis wristband. It looked as if he was going to come back and bring it to life again. Which he wasn't, of course. Why the fuck hadn't they found out who killed him yet?

I got up and left my empty chair facing his.

I called Des from the car and told him I was coming round straight away to start work on our new content – for the village, which we'd cobble together quickly, then delegate to some of our youngbloods, and for the doctors, which we would keep for ourselves.

Cruising along the coast, I put in a call to my new Nostrum contact, getting into his contacts list, plugging into his power. He didn't pick up, so I began to leave a message. Seconds later, he cut in.

"John Sway."

"Ah, hello Mr Sway. John. We'll be working together, I see."

"Yes, I'm glad to hear from you. What can I do for you?"

"I've run through the basic concepts with Ms G, and I'll be needing some more info about symptoms and the like from you as soon as I start work on the concrete design."

"Which is when?"

"In about ten minutes, if the traffic doesn't hold me up."

He laughed, and promised to send me the addresses and passwords of places where I could get what I needed.

"And you don't have to worry about this political business getting in the way of things," he said. "The votes are as good as counted. We've got Crotch on it."

"Crotch. Oh right. Yes." I laughed. We both did. "I see."

"You see?"

"Yes, I definitely see."

The crotch he was talking about is Crotch Holdings, the lobbying agency. If you can scrape together enough billions to pay their fees, they'll make you President of anywhere, they'll get you planning permission to build your drive-through porn cinema in the Vatican.

I pulled over into a service area for a little bout of ecstasy about the sheer size of the operation I'd got into. I stuffed some surgical masks in my mouth and had a silent scream. I was still coming to terms with the massiveness of everything – not only Nostrum and the Ministry, but lobbyists, the Official Secrets Act – and I was in the middle there, in the public front-line of it all.

Granola once tried to convince me that a penis isn't muscle (my theory), but spongy tissue which fills itself with blood. Spongy? Mine wasn't spongy. I understood why some women want to get fucked by chairmen and presidents. Power gives you one hell of a stiffie.

There are people who are envious of pharmaceuticals. They refuse to believe that here at last we are being offered an end to pain and ugliness. They're the ones who will refuse the seven-day treatment. They seem to think suffering is in some way healthy or natural. My online doctors will have to win them over. No one will be able to resist Dr Claudine. "Com een to my surgery. Tek off yer shirt." Now there's an idea for a new health service: Claudine's clap clinic. "Pule yur pants don, yew notty boy. Wave yur willay at Docteur Clodeen." A thousand hits a minute guaranteed.

I hoped that Des wasn't feeling the strain. On tense days it's almost as if someone has emptied a bucket of desiccated coconut on his head. Luckily we'd be working side-by-side most of the time, looking at a screen rather than each other.

I parked my car outside Des's house on the cliff. An anonymous-looking family house, except that the windows are all blacked out, the door is unpainted metal and half the roof is obscured by a massive satellite dish. OK, not so anonymous-looking. Threatening, even. As I approached the front door, a camera eyed me suspiciously. Des's camera is live, 24/7. I should get one. Shit, if only Beano had had one.

The door clicked open, I went in and it swung shut behind me. At the end of the entrance hall, another door opened to reveal the staircase. The place is like a submarine, with sealed bulkheads delimiting every room and stretch of corridor. Perhaps Des thinks he's going to get flooded. On a clifftop? Surely global warming won't raise the sea level a hundred feet in his lifetime?

I took off my shoes and climbed the dust-free stairs. The upper floor has all been knocked into one space, decorated, if that's the word, with four screens and all their various plug-ins and drives and whatnot. Des sat in the centre of the room, surrounded by gloom, the only light coming from the screen he was sitting at. Everything hummed gently. Nowhere was there a scrap of paper. I wondered how he wipes his arse. Laser, probably.

"Hi, Bernie. Great work."

"Hi. Thanks, Des. You're the one who's going to be doing some great work now, though."

I joined Des at his workstation. Here, snow-flakes or no snow-flakes, he is king. With his new software, he could stick your passport photo on a horse, and the video of you winning the Derby would look like proof that your mum was a mare.

I had Des sign an Official Secrets form that Angela Greensands had given me for him. He scrawled on the dotted line as if he'd done it a dozen times before. Maybe he had. I couldn't ask – it would have been a secret, wouldn't it?

First we bashed out a plan for the village campaign. We decided that the only way to market the countryside is with corn, if you'll pardon the pun. So we put together some classic footage that captured the essence of Olde Englande. When people see these images, the last thing they'll think of will be an exploding vicar. We'll flash them back to childhood holidays they never had, with bouncing lambs, mossy thatch, and old 50s films full of rosy-cheeked maidens pulling pints of frothing ale. In under an hour we'd compiled a full catalogue of rustic clichés for our internerds to work on. If need be, they could go and get real footage, but to the untrained eye, Des's creations looked totally life-based.

I warned Des that he'd be needing plenty of images of Claudine if my idea for the seven-day service was going to work.

"I've already got some loaded up," he said blandly, and did a weird twitch with his face muscles.

Apart from the druff stuff, this is the only problem about working with Des in person – when he discusses his brilliance, he has this tragic tic. A kind of sorry-I've-sat-on-your-phone grimace, due I'm sure to his fear that people see him as a boring freak incapable of producing anything except dandruff. Like, for instance, when I asked him, with sincere greed and curiosity, how many images he had at his disposal, he screwed up his face in abject apology, and said,

"Basically, infinity." Twitch.

Why not just grin proudly? As usual, it was Beano who put it best. Would you go to a concert, he asked, where the singer shuffled on and started mumbling that maybe this wasn't going to be quite as good as the studio version? No, you want someone who'll lope on and yell, "open up ears, I'm coming in", someone who'll throw your mind on its belly and shag the shit out of it.

Beano was right. No one gives prizes for timidity. Come on, Des, I thought. You're a genius. Live with it.

"Best if we film Claudine," Des said. "She's going to be in tight close-up. Get her to act out a basic script. Give me some real footage to work with."

"You're also going to need some special effects," I told him. "There'll be plenty of snot flying about."

"You sure? This is serious business, Bernie."

I cut him off before he could give me some Louie-like disapproval.

"In the best possible taste, Des. Let me explain. This is about colds."

As I described my mucus-filled visions, I lost all sense of time. Des's blackout was great. You could concentrate all your attention on the screen and your ideas. Freedom from distraction must account for at least part of Des's genius. That's why I often stay up nights. Only time I get some peace.

Des reminded me that we wouldn't be able to make this an all-nighter – we were supposed to be having dinner with Mona and Phil.

"Oh shit. Yeah."

It was still only 6.30. I called Granola. My life is such a sham. When will I get up the courage to tell the others about my non-marriage? Des must have thought the phone call was weird, even though he could only hear my end of it (at least I think he could).

"Granola? Remember I said Phil had invited us over to dinner tonight?"

"No, you didn't."

"Shall we meet for a drink first?"

"Apart from the fact that you *didn't* tell me, Bernie, I really don't want to go to dinner or drinks with your work crowd."

"Then, after that, we can go over together to Phil and Mona's place."

"Phil and Mona's place? They're –?" She was starting to squawk. I walked away from Des, towards where the windows used to be, so that she could interrogate me more discreetly. "Bernie? You still there? Are Phil and Mona going out together? He never told me."

"Should he have?"

"I guess not, but an evening with Mona slobbering all over Phil is not my idea of a night out."

"Mona does not slo –" I controlled myself for Des's sake. He was still focussed on his screen, but his antennae were probably picking up all of this. "Oh, no, that's tough, Granola," I said loudly. "OK, I'll tell Mona."

"Tell her what?"

"See you later, then."

"What are you talking about, Bernie?"

I rang off.

"Bummer. Meeting. She can't get away," I told Des. "Don't think I can really afford the time, either." He didn't look as if he cared one way or the other. I called Mona to apologize. She did care. She always does.

"Oh, that's a shame, Bernie. I haven't seen Granola for ages. *You're* coming over, though?"

"Can't. I've got a ton of work. For the Greensands job. I'll tell you about it next time we meet up."

"How about a quick drink now?" she offered. "I can be in town in twenty minutes."

"Uh. Hmm. Is Phil there?"

"No, he won't be back till about nine. He's –"

"OK, see you in twenty minutes." We arranged to meet in the pub garden where Claudine had caught so many eyes. Swift drink and then home to get some more work done. Surely tonight Granola would allow me some quality time without having to "discuss things".

"Fancy a quickie, Des?" I asked him.

"No, I'll finish up here first," he said, as I knew he would.

"Great stuff. Genius."

I held up my palm to do a high five, but he misinterpreted it as a wave, and waved back. He realized his mistake, but by then it was too late. I waved as if that was what I'd always intended to do, and got out of there. If I had been Phil, Des would have known it was a high-five.

****

Dear Member,
Remember the good old days when everyone joked about your illegible handwriting on prescriptions?
Remember how respectful your patients used to be when faced with someone who could write in hieroglyphics?
Well, we've created a set of almost-but-not-quite-totally-illegible typefaces for your typed prescriptions.
Put an end to patients' time-wasting questions about drug names.
Software includes a translator for your local pharmacist.
Go to: MemberOffersYouWhat?

****

19 Froth

The pub garden was packed with babbling after-work drinkers. I waded through the crowd looking for Mona, and didn't see her until she stood up and waved just two tables away from me. Not like Claudine. There was no missing *her*. Though Claudine is about four feet taller.

We kissed, on the cheek these days, of course.

"How are you?" she asked, apparently examining my face and body for holes.

"Fine, fine. Knackered, mind. Been working with Des on this public-health thing."

"Yes, I heard about that."

"Excuse me." My frantic gesticulations had finally attracted the attention of a waitress. Service had been distinctly more reverential when I was with Claudine. "Beer, please. Craft porter," I ordered. "Mona?"

She lifted her glass of wine and shook her head. The waitress went away.

"Shame about dinner," Mona said.

"Yeah. Granola's got a meeting. And I've got no time."

"Right." There was an awkward pause. Mona clearly didn't believe me. She sipped her wine. I admired the shrubbery.

I don't think Mona would be too sad if Granola and I split up. She knows Granola doesn't like her – Granola says she's vulgar. That's exactly why I do like Mona. She laughs loudly, she talks loudly, she dresses loudly. She does *everything* loudly: she is, aptly, a serious moaner. She enhances her Mediterranean colouring with heavy black eye-liner and very dark lip-stick. She's plumpish at the rear but makes up for it (as if that were a fault) with one of the most mischievous grins you've ever seen.

Maybe she knows about me and Granola divorcing. Even if she does, I'm not in the mood for marriage counselling right now.

"Took me by surprise, I must say, Mona."

"What?" she asked naively.

"You and Phil, of course. How long have you been …"

"Oh, Bernie. I honestly don't think you'd have noticed if it'd been *Granola* who was shagging Phil instead of me."

"What? Why?" I remembered what Phil had said about Granola calling him. And why was Granola so pissed off that he hadn't told her about him and Mona? Was he somehow involved in my marriage breakdown?

Mona laughed at my agitation.

"Bernie! You see, you're really not sure, are you?"

The waitress brought a small dish of olives and my bottle of beer. I took my time pouring it, watching the cool beige froth settle and turn black, making sure the organic granules of whatever they put in craft beer to make it crafty stayed in the bottle.

"Well? How long is it now?" I asked. Mona's lips curled lasciviously. "You know what I mean," I smiled.

"Only about three weeks in fact," she said. "It just kind of happened, while we were at that trade fair in Paris."

I could imagine Phil's chat-up line: "Ear, Mona. See that Eiffel Tar? It's nuffink compared to my dick." Page 3 of his *Mockney for Toffs* phrasebook.

"We're really *good*," Mona was saying. "You know, he's not at all –"

"A pain in the butt once you get to know him?" I interrupted. "We've both known him for years, and he's always been a pain in the butt."

"When you get really close to him, he's got this, he's so ..." – she smiled to herself – "vulnerable."

Organic froth shot out of my nostrils as my body registered its disbelief at the use of that particular word to describe Phil. It took me a few minutes and several paper napkins to clear my sinuses of beer.

"Vuh, nuh, bull?" was my first attempt at speech.

"Yes," she said forcefully. "His public persona is just that – a persona."

Well, I'd suspected that for ages, anyway.

"In the privacy of his home I suppose he stops saying fuck, sucks his thumb and wears gold embroidered nappies?"

"Bernie, please. Jealousy doesn't suit you."

"Jealousy?" Perhaps she was right. Phil getting it on with my old girlfriend was a bit of a shock. "Yeah, I won't deny there is a bit of jealousy in there. Only natural, really." I smiled nostalgically. Mona and I had been getting on well as a couple until my dick got drunk at a party. That was just before I met Granola. Mona smiled back, slightly less nostalgically. "But," I went on, "I think I know Phil pretty well. And I can't help being afraid that – how shall I put it? You know, with the company just about to be sold and all, and the uncertainty about who'll be in charge afterwards, well, going out with you might just be a, like, shit, this is going to sound awful, but I've got to say it, a ... you know ... business strategy."

"Like I said, Bernie, jealousy doesn't look good on you."

"No, no. This is not jealousy. Phil's a tactician, you know he is. He's started playing these mind games with me, trying to screw me up before big meetings."

"Crap!"

"No, I swear it's true. It's almost as if we were working for different companies, as if we didn't both have the same goal." I couldn't really mention that the only goal we definitely did have in common was Claudine. "He seems to be playing some sort of power game, jostling for position. Using you could be part of that."

"Well thanks very much." Mona's long, dark eyelashes hid her thoughts for a moment.

"Sorry to say it, Mona. But if you're sure it's not true, then I'm glad, and please forget I ever said it. Another drink?" I'd exhaled most of mine over the table.

She nodded, and I began waving both arms in the air again in the hope of getting served. Mona drained her glass and looked me in the eye.

"You know, Bernie, I was talking to Louie, and he told me what you were saying about me."

The shit.

"What was I saying?" I adopted the trusty old Alzheimer technique.

"I didn't *want* to leave you all on your own with those hacks, you know. The reason I haven't been around much is that I've been doing the rounds of our biggest corporate clients, promising them that we're still on course for a successful buyout, and reassuring them that Beano's death won't have any repercussions on our business. Some of them are taking a hell of a lot of convincing, too."

"Yeah?"

"One client that isn't worried at all, though, is Nostrum itself."

She let this sink in. I stopped waving for a waitress.

"Yeah?"

"They say the whole Beano stroke Models scandal is no worry at all for them. You sure *you're* not the one being used, Bernie?"

"What do you mean?"

"You completely happy about working with this Greensands lady?"

"Yes. Have you seen the size of the budget she's given me?" I spread my arms out wide, taekwondo'd a waitress in the midriff and took the opportunity to order two more drinks as I apologized and helped her to pick up her tray and the broken glasses.

"You know she's on the board of Nostrum?" Mona asked when I sat down again.

"Yeah. That's no secret."

"OK," Mona said.

"What do you mean 'OK'?"

"No, no. It's OK." She wouldn't elaborate. The mysterious Orient in her genes, I guessed. Or a bit of jealousy on her part, maybe.

Mona gave me a short rundown of the meetings she'd had, and how shitty she felt having to play down poor Beano's sudden departure from the board.

"Don't you ever miss the old days, Bernie?"

"What? You mean, like, you and me?"

Mona laughed as if it was a joke.

"No, Bernie. I mean the old days at Coma. When we all agreed about what the company was for. When we were just a straightforward service, helping medical students to get jobs, giving doctors and nurses easy access to relevant information. Basic things like that."

"That's what we still do, isn't it?"

"I'm not sure. Half our new recruits are in sales. Selling drugs, doctors and nurses. They could be working for a double-glazing firm. So could I, almost."

No wonder I was the one having to do all the company PR nowadays. Our head of public relations had gone native.

"Come on, Mona. If you're asking me whether I miss the old days when I drove a ten-year-old car and had as much chance of becoming a millionaire as turning into a butterfly, then no."

She smiled to herself, as if I was somehow missing her point.

"I can't imagine you as a butterfly, Bernie. You're more of a rutting moose type."

"Hey!" I couldn't let this slur upon my sexual refinement go unchallenged. "This is Mrs Hyena talking, right?"

We shared another nostalgic laugh and the subject seemed to be closed.

"Did Louie talk to you about selling some of your shares?" I asked.

"Some? *All*, you mean. What do you think the buyout is? Honestly, Bernie, you're such a dork. To have missed the crisis meeting like that."

"You didn't sign a form or anything?"

"Form? Not yet, no. The buyout won't –"

The waitress interrupted us with the drinks. This time she didn't bring a dish of olives. Fair punishment for my assault on her, I suppose. I gave her a hefty tip and another apology.

"Sorry, shouldn't have called you a dork," Mona said. "The police arrested you, right?"

"No, not arrested, oh SHIT!"

People at the surrounding tables stopped their cool chit-chat to glance across at me. Afraid, no doubt, that after flooring a waitress I might just start on the customers.

"Sorry about this." I took out my phone and chose a redial number. A gruff voice answered.

"Hi, it's Bernie. Where are you?" I asked.

"At work."

"Can I come over?"

"Sooner the better. I was getting worried about you," he answered. "Thought you'd forgot."

I hung up, and turned to Mona.

"Come with me, I have to go for a drive."

"Where?"

"I'll explain as we go." I stood up. Mona didn't budge. The dramatic-exit ploy wasn't working as well as it had done with Claudine.

"Where to?" Mona wanted to know. I sat down again and explained quietly what I was planning. She wasn't too keen.

"Don't worry, you don't have to get out of the car," I assured her.

"How long will it take? I've got to be home when the food's delivered. We're having Thai-Icelandic fusion."

"Half an hour. Hour tops."

She finally agreed, and we set off, leaving the well-lit streets behind us as we drove down the social scale. Soon we hit rock bottom, and my tyres were complaining loudly. I was glad that it was too gloomy to see in detail what I was driving over. I wasn't too sure of my way in the dark, and this place was way off GPS. I paused at a street corner where there had once been a factory. All that remained was a shadowy field of rubble and the bottom right-hand corner of a wooden sign – "works" it boasted inaccurately. I turned my headlights up full beam, and saw Stanley's warehouse a hundred yards ahead.

"You have arrived at your destination," I told Mona, and gave Stanley a phone call in case his dogs were on the loose.

"No, they're in the van asleep, soft cunts," he growled. "Come on over."

We pulled up outside his premises and I opened the window a notch to listen. When I was satisfied that there were no two-legged attack dogs around, I took a fat envelope from the place I'd hidden it and got out. Mona jumped out of her door, too, clutching her bag to her chest.

"I'm not staying out here alone," she said, and grabbed my arm.

Inside, Stanley was setting up one of his machines. There was a small pile of reject T-shirts lying at his feet. On one of them I could see the end of a slogan – "OUT!" – and something that looked suspiciously like a folded Swastika. I didn't go any nearer. Stanley's not the kind of guy you'd choose for a discussion about the finer points of immigration policy.

He finished up and wiped his hands and face on one of the reject T-shirts before coming to shake our hands.

"How you doing?" I asked him.

"All the better for seeing you," he said, turning his cannibal eyes on Mona. If he is a racist, he's the kind who has got nothing against shagging women of any origin. "Not been so good. Bit of a temperature."

Mona and I took a simultaneous step backwards.

"You brought the money," Stanley said. A statement rather than a question.

"Yes." I handed over the envelope.

Again, he unselfconsciously counted the notes, and nodded his satisfaction.

"I put an extra fifty in there as an apology from Beano for being late," I said. He must have noticed, but presumably thought it was a mistake.

"Apology accepted. Poor bastard."

"You heard anything?" I asked.

"Heard? Oh, yeah. No. Total blank. Sorry, mate."

So he'd forgotten to ask around.

"Oh well, if you hear anything."

"Sure, let you know."

I told him I'd have some very big orders for him soon, but didn't go into detail. I didn't want Mona (and, by inference, Phil) knowing all my business.

"Gimme a few days, though, Bernie, yeah? Soon as I've finished these anti-government shirts, I'm gonna take some time off."

"No hurry." Now that I knew I'd misjudged his political leanings, I felt I owed him a little patience.

"Good. Been overdoing it. Need a rest." It was true, the drops of blood dripping from the knife tattooed on his right temple were looking redder than usual.

Mona and I took this as our cue to leave, and even managed to avoid shaking hands again.

"Scary guy. You don't think he might have had a hand in Beano's ...?" Mona's question tailed off as I started up the engine.

"No way." I saved her from mentioning the d-word. "Talk about geese and golden eggs. Did you see how fat that envelope was?"

"Hey, shouldn't you have got a receipt?" she reminded me.

"He doesn't give them for cash. Anyway, that's all taken care of." My forged, and vastly inflated, invoice was already working its way through accounts. No one would bother to check, especially now the money was about to come pouring in.

Soon we were leaving the poverty zone, getting back on safe territory. We joined a reassuring stream of cars heading into town.

"Thanks for coming with me, Mona. I really appreciate it."

"Oh, that's OK. I'm just sorry it came to nothing." She shifted in her seat, and I could feel her Nefertiti eyes on me. "I'm glad to know you're out there looking for whoever, you know, did it. You're the only one apart from Rita who seems to care about Beano. It's a really warm gesture towards an old friend." She touched my leg, briefly.

"Well, I went out there partly out of self-interest. If I hadn't repaid Beano's debt, Stanley would have broken *my* legs. And don't forget that if I can help find the killer, I'll be able to clear my name once and for all with the cops." I stared modestly ahead.

"You never could accept praise, could you, Bernie? You always have to say something. Usually a bloody awful joke. Don't do yourself down. Going out there –" she grimaced back at the place we'd just left "– to clear Beano's debt was a Good Thing." I smiled, not allowed to speak, and kept my conscientious eyes on the road ahead. "We haven't had a real talk like this for ages," she said, touching my leg again. "We used to talk so much."

"That's not all we used to do."

"Bernie!" She laughed her old dirty laugh.

"I suppose –?"

"Bernie!" This time she wasn't laughing.

****

m
think b is up 2 some fiddle with t-shirts.
will look 4 more when get chance
j

Dear Member,
Coughs? Sneezes? Tickly throat?
Not your own coughs and sneezes, of course. Your patients'.
Do you really want to inhale everything they exhale?
Spore-Tex© masks cut out germs and odours while allowing you to breathe coolly, comfortably and perspiration-free for up to four hours.
Get your free samples from Spore-Tex©

****

20 SITTING COMFORTABLY

"What were you rambling about? And why did you cut me off like that?" Granola was lying back on the sofa, flicking through the TV channels, a cup of tea in her free hand.

"Uh? Oh, I was at Des's place. Sorry, but I still haven't told anyone about the – you know. Divorce." I looked across to see how she'd take the other d-word. She was still staring at the TV.

"You told Beano," she said.

"Yeah, well he was my best friend. And he promised not to tell anyone else. Did you discuss it with Phil when you had your little chat with him?"

"No, why would I discuss it with him?"

"I don't know, especially seeing as we don't even discuss it ourselves."

"Exactly. Which is why I didn't fancy keeping up the pretence in front of your office lot."

She was right. Time to end the confrontation. In the olden days I would have kissed her. Now I was tempted, but she'd only have shrugged me off.

I sat down on the sofa next to her feet and looked at the TV, which was still lurching through the channels, playing disconnected snippets of sound and vision.

"Do anything exciting at the office today?" I asked conversationally.

"Well, yes I did, actually. I convinced my boss to offload a ton of stocks in a drug company."

"Which company?" I asked nervously. She told me. The name meant nothing to me. "Why did you get rid of them? They sell some duff pills or something? Going to get hit by damages claims?"

"Oh no. Quite the contrary." She switched off the TV and sat up. "Their price is soaring, but they're doing some very dubious stuff in the Third World. Patenting the DNA of Papuan tribesmen, and taking out copyrights on herbal remedies that they've stolen from healers in the Amazon. I told my boss I didn't think it was the kind of stock we ought to have in one of our big pension portfolios, and we sold the lot. That should make a little dent in their dividend, the bastards."

Granola is an eco-warrior. But unlike the people who bury themselves under motorways or nail themselves to trees, she has the power to really hurt the multinational eco-criminals. You concrete over the only remaining nesting site of some migratory bird, Mr CEO, and she'll make sure it costs you a lot of money. Your share price, and therefore your career, is going to get a kick in the balls.

She knows all about the stock market. I really ought to ask her about this business of selling some of my shares before the buyout, but I couldn't bring myself to do it. My ignorance would put me in a position of weakness.

"Good one," I told her. "You won't do anything like that to Coma, though, will you?"

"Why – you planning something unethical?"

"Ha. Course not. How can the internet be environmentally unfriendly? It's just a load of electronic signals."

"Hm. There's some weird stuff going on with your shares, though. Price is going up and down like a yoyo. And every time it goes down, the same two or three buyers come in for the grab. You're not doing any manipulating, are you Bernie? That'd be insider dealing."

"Me? I thought insider dealing was selling drugs indoors." She didn't laugh. "Look, Granola, I promise, OK?"

"Anyway," she said, "you don't need to do any insider dealing because this buyout is pushing the price up nicely. You just have to hang in there and you'll be quids in."

"Exactly." Though she had to be wrong. Louie said he was scared that the price would go permanently *down*.

"How was your meeting?" she asked.

Wow, I thought, such a long conversation. Two minutes and rising.

"Brilliant. Perfect." I got a flashback of Angela Greensands' satisfaction.

"Perfect? How come?"

"Uh. Can't say. Official Secrets Act."

She laughed. I didn't. She realized I was being serious.

"You're not serious," she said.

"Yeah, they made me sign the form. Can't breathe a word."

"So it was nothing to do with getting the contract to set up a public-funded online health service, then?"

"Who told you that?"

"Rumours are everywhere."

"Yes, well that was just guesswork. Now it's official and it's secret."

"You can't tell me anything?"

"Nope."

"Come on, it can't be *that* secret, can it?"

"It must be. Why else would they get me to sign a form?"

"It's not dangerous, though? They're not planning to put steroids in the water supply? There's not going to be some outbreak of untreatable measles that I ought to know about?"

"No."

"Because I wouldn't be too happy if I caught something because you had kept it secret from me."

"You won't catch anything because of what I'm doing. On the contrary." I regretted saying it immediately, but it was too late.

"Ah, so it's some sort of vaccination programme, is it, or contraception?"

"Stop it, please, Granola. I can't tell you."

"Forced sterilization of the poor? Euthanasia for the ugly?"

"Paralysis for wagging tongues."

"Or just for nagging wives?"

"Granola. For God's sake. It's an online doctor, that's all I'm telling you, and I've probably told you too much."

"An online doctor?" she said, as if she'd just opened a huge Christmas present to find a peanut inside. "They've been doing that for ages." She got up and went into the kitchen.

"Yes, I know. But now *I'm* doing it for the *whole* National Health Service. *Me*, OK? And if you saw the size of the budget, you wouldn't be so snotty about it."

But she was singing to herself in the kitchen. She couldn't hear me, or didn't want to. Fair enough. At least she'd stopped her interrogation. I followed her through and offered to make dinner.

"Great," she said. She took a glass of wine, handed me one, and we even clinked glasses. More intimate than we'd been since I could remember.

"To success," I said.

"To absent friends," she said, and left me feeling a total shit.

I put on some music and whipped up a typically English dinner. Snails in garlic butter, penne with langoustine sauce, and crême brulée with raspberry coulis. Thank God for freezers. We had a very civilized meal – no arguments – and talked fondly about Beano, without getting mawkish. Granola remembered our wedding, when Beano was best man, of course. For his speech, he'd cobbled together the filthiest collection of double-entendres I'd ever heard. Antique, all of them. He talked about taking me to the hairdresser's the day before the wedding to get a "shampoo and blow job". He informed us that "sometimes in a marriage, a man has to hold his own. If his wife won't hold it for him." He mused that "virginity is like a balloon. One prick and it's gone." A hundred of those, one after the other, groan upon groan upon groan.

Granola's mum almost died, and Granola glowered at me so furiously that I doubted the marriage would ever be consummated. Or re-consummated, anyway. Like I said, we'd been consummating like rabbits ever since our first date.

Now, though, it seemed that Granola had forgiven Beano for the speech, and for all the other times when his evil sense of humour disrupted her life.

"Death puts everything in perspective," she said, wisely.

I don't think she meant to bring me down after my victorious day. She just needed to talk. She was scared. She looked vulnerable. That word again. She caught me looking at her. Her eyes didn't flicker away as they had been doing for the past three months. Something in me stirred down at Calvin Klein level.

"The alarm's on," I told her. "We don't need to worry about intruders tonight."

A year ago, six months ago, less, she would have taken the hint. Now she just nodded.

"I'll go and wash up," she said.

Brilliant, so these days the prospect of sex with me is less exciting than doing the dishes.

I went and sat at my wide-screen computer. I saw that Des, using Mr Sway's list of symptoms, had already sent me a short diagnostic obstacle course that led the user, whatever path he or she took, to the seven-day cure. It needed Dr Claudine to liven it up, but it was already taking shape.

"Christ!"

I spun round, expecting to see Granola confronted by a masked assassin. But no, she was standing alone, staring down at me.

"Don't scare me like that, Granola. Please."

"Is that it?" she said, pointing to the screen.

"Shit." I quit. What a dork I'd been. "Granola, please. Forget you saw that, or I'm in deep shit."

"Nostrum and their so-called cold cure? Is that what you're plugging?"

"Granola, please." I stood and walked away from the computer, as if that would take us off the subject.

"Do you know what that is?" She was staring at the dark screen.

"It's a computer, Granola, and I think it needs to get some sleep. Let's leave it." I slumped on the sofa, furious with myself.

"You know what their so-called cure is, don't you?" She was standing over me, breathing hard.

"Yes. What I'd like to know is how *you* know. It's supposed to be a secret."

"There have been rumours about it for months. Word is, it includes a genetically-modified vaccine."

"What, so if I take it, I might become resistant to soya-bean rot?" I thought genetic modification was something they did to plants.

"Ho bloody ho."

"Sorry you don't appreciate my rapier wit, Granola, but what exactly is the problem here?" She was swearing. Something major had to be up.

"Rapier wit? More like drive-by wit. This is not a subject to be witty about."

"Please, Granola, I beg of you. Just tell me what you mean and then forget we ever had this conversation."

"A genetically-modified vaccine can cause the virus it is combating to mutate," she explained, bending down towards me as I lay on the sofa, as if I was some remedial science pupil laid low with lumbago, partial deafness and genetic stupidity. "That means it will render the virus harmless in its present form, but will also cause it to mutate to a new form that will make it immune to anything except the next generation of the vaccine. You see?"

"No, I'm afraid not."

She sighed impatiently.

"OK, a human disease is like a computer virus that makes your body crash, right?"

"Thank you, Granola, I do have some basic notion of human biology."

"OK, OK, but the analogy works quite well. Imagine a program that, instead of clearing out the virus, simply turns it into a different virus that will come back and attack your hard disk in twelve months time."

Fuck. What had I got into?

"You mean it cures you by changing the virus slightly, but if you catch the virus again, you'll have to take another dose? Doesn't sound too bad to me," I defended valiantly.

"And when it comes back, you have to take *their* vaccine, and no other."

"But I still get cured, right?"

"You do, but if meanwhile you pass the virus on to some poor soul who has no access to your treatment, or can't afford it, then no other treatment will work. That person will die."

"You sure of all this? It sounds illegal. What about all those laws obliging food manufacturers to label GM foods?"

"Who passed those laws? The government. Who's putting together a treatment programme using the Nostrum drug? The government. Who's got their pockets stuffed with Nostrum shares? The government." Granola is very practised in the martial art of political debate. "God, so they're really going to launch it now? I've got to let people know."

"No!" It was a cry from the heart. I leapt to my feet. "You leak anything like that and I'm finished. Unemployed. In prison. Fucked." This made her think for a moment. "I'm not joking, Granola. I signed a form headed 'Official Secrets Act'. I've already committed a crime by letting you see what I was doing on the computer. Now, what I can promise you is this –" I paused for effect, and to think what the hell I was going to promise her. "I promise you that I will look into what you've said. I'll ask Nostrum. Maybe you've got it wrong or they've changed their plans. Maybe it won't be genetically modified after all."

"I –" she was going to object.

"Look, it's no secret Nostrum and the government are working together. It says so on both their Facebook pages. Perhaps you're just being paranoid."

"I bet it doesn't mention GM vaccines on there, does it?"

"Let me ask them about it, OK? Let me find out if what you're saying is true. If it is, we'll think again. OK?" Fuck knows what I'd do if it was true, though.

Granola was still furious, but somehow, a little trust seemed to be seeping through. Her shoulders relaxed. Her fists un-balled.

"OK," she said. "You find out. But if Nostrum, the government and you lot aren't all in this together, why did they come to *you* to set up their online service?"

"Because we're the best, that's why. Believe it or not, they like my work."

Granola grunted sceptically.

"Now explain this genetic stuff again," I said. "Why would they do that?"

She sat me down and told me a story that I knew elements of, but had never realized they made a whole. About diseases that were becoming increasingly antibiotic-resistant. About these weird organisms called phages that could kill bacteria that were immune to antibiotics. Sort of Avenger bugs. Phages were hailed by some scientists as the answer to the antibiotics crisis. Only trouble was, phages were developed in the Soviet bloc, and the big drug companies of the west were pissed off because the patent was on the wrong side of the old Iron Curtain. So they decided that a western alternative had to be developed: genetically-modified vaccines. Damn good at killing phages, apparently.

****

Dear Member,
Have you treated a patient who recovered from an "antibiotic-resistant" infection?
Let us know, and you may be eligible to share in the profits from patenting their genes.
Go to NostrumGeneMarket and see just how simple it is.

****

21 Sooty Curls

I went into the office early next day.

The good news was that, like me, my watch also turned up early, with a bright new glass and a note from the jeweller: "Turn button to wind up." Couldn't resist it, could he? The watch made my wrist heavy, but pleasantly so. Hunky.

I didn't dare ask Des about the ingredients of the seven-day cure. No way could I afford to send out negative waves to him. So I had a nose around. I did a search on "GM" and "Nostrum", and found a few anti-Nostrum pages. I didn't open them up for fear of being traced. In the end I simply sent a message to my friend John Sway, asking if any part of our new service should be geared to lessening patients' fears about being knocked out for a week, or answering questions about the exact ingredients of the treatment, or anything else he could think of.

I also had another look at what Des was doing. As he'd said, we still needed some footage of Claudine in a white coat and glasses, doing a few stock expressions – concern, concentration, decisiveness, reassurance – and repeating some medical catch-phrases: "ow can I elp?", "do you ave a fever?", "click on ze link below". Stuff like that. Though maybe we'd overdub her. Would the Brits trust a foreign doctor? Even a sexy one?

Anyway, good excuse to call Claudine.

"Allo." She sounded half-asleep. Or half-indifferent. Only half, though.

"Claudine? Bernie here. How are you?"

"I sort it was tomorrow night?"

"What? Oh yes. Tomorrow. No, this is about work."

"So is tomorrow."

"Uh, yes, but I just wanted to make an appointment with you to shoot some film. You know that health programme I talked about?"

"Farmer sooty curls?"

"Yes. I want you to be the central character in the whole service. The nation's go-to sexy online doctor."

"Mm. OK. I get royalties or just modelling fee?"

"We can talk about money later. Why don't we –"

"I prefer to talk about money first. I get royalties? Or very large one-off fee?"

"I think a large one-off fee would be simpler." Her English was improving all of a sudden, but my budget was big enough to cope.

She named a price that was, objectively speaking, obscene, but again my budget was big enough to cope. I agreed.

"OK," she said, "you send me a contract today. We finalize details tomorrow night, before sex."

"I'll send you a draft contract today," I promised, "and we can sign it tomorrow. *After* sex."

"Before sex."

"After sex."

It was going to be a long argument. I turned and looked over my shoulder. This was usually where Phil popped up. Surprise, surprise – he wasn't there. Neither was Claudine. She'd hung up.

****

Give a lifetime of experience to your new baby.
IVF for the over-60s is now legal in several countries.
You have the womb, we can fill it. We have the eggs and the expertise.
For further information and confidential counselling go to: MatureMums

Struck-off doctors. You can work again. There are places in the world where they don't X-ray the past.
Visit us at Paradocs

****

22 Dancing Lobster

If Vietnam proved anything at all apart from the fact that a good exotic war sells more films than a commonplace European one, it was that leisure time is dangerous. If we're to believe the movies, so many of the American kids who died out there weren't killed while on patrol, protected by the world's most expensive weapons. They died while relaxing, in a bar-bombing or a night raid on their living quarters. The Viet-Cong even used to booby-trap the latrines. Ouch. And the Viet-Cong killers were rarely in uniform. I watched *Good Morning Vietnam*, and in that the kids planting the bombs wore shorts and T-shirts. Lethal leisurewear.

It was about one o'clock, mealtime. I'd walked out to eat, trying to get Louie off my mind. I had just left an empty plate behind me in one of the town's better luncheries. I was just getting used to playing host to the pleasant new weight I'd taken on, when I suddenly found I could neither breathe nor stand up straight any more. Someone helped me, or rather forced me, to unfold myself almost upright against a wall. I assumed it was the person who'd just pushed his fist half way through my abdomen. Between quivering eyelids I could see a clean-cut, handsome kid with hair almost as blond as Beano's. He was wearing a long gold chain round his neck. He and his two mates, all of them in sports tops, jeans and trainers, were looking down at me patiently, waiting for my wits to return. They were in leisurewear on leisure time.

I managed to wonder what they wanted. I hoped it was my pride and my money, and not my death.

We were near a street corner, a few yards from the café entrance, but I couldn't make a noise to call for help. They didn't need to bruise my throat like Beano's. Anyone wanting to suffocate me would only have had to pinch my nose between finger and thumb and lay a gentle palm across my mouth. I couldn't have resisted.

"Hold your hand out," the curly one said. He had a pleasant, business-like voice. What was this, I wondered, the new way of doing a high-five? That's why Des didn't recognize my attempt.

I held out my hand.

"Other one, shithead."

I obeyed. He slipped my watch off my wrist.

"Have a nice day," said the kid.

They had gone before I was in any state to shuffle away from my wall. I gestured up at a closed-circuit TV camera, pointing to where they were running. It didn't swivel to follow them. So much for city-centre security. No one walking along the street had noticed, or wanted to notice, anything.

I drove, one hand holding my throbbing entrails in place, to the hospital – not the private clinic, where I was sure to be met in the plush lobby by some nurse-cum-masseuse who would kiss my hand and groan, "oh, Mr Bridges, in bed, *now*." They're very hot on customer relations over there, but I wanted my bruising to be incognito. Getting mugged, I reckoned, would count in the stock market's book as a PR screw-up. One Coma director dead, one attacked. Not good. So I put on a couple of surgical masks and went to the A&E unit at the public hospital on the edge of town, St Plebs or something like that, one of those bright but depressing shopping malls of sickness that the government keeps public just to show what a good idea it is to take out private insurance.

A&E was right – Alcoholics and Extraterrestrials. The duty nurses were dashing about so fast, they didn't seem to realize I might have come for something more than a quiet chat to the guy with the pulped nose sitting next to me on the plastic bench where six of us had set up camp.

I don't know why they call us "patients". "Impatients" would be more accurate. Especially if you're an out-patient. We were all going crazy with pain and frustration.

Almost everyone in the room was groaning, picking at bandages, comparing wounds or hawking and snorting their globules of disease straight out into the air I was forced to share with them. I realized I ought to start spouting blood very messily indeed, otherwise I'd die unnoticed in the waiting room, and my body wouldn't be discovered until it started to smell even more than the homeless people's trousers.

I waited until a nurse was walking past my bench and then flung myself, yelling my agony, under her feet. She must have been used to this trick, because she stopped short and asked,

"In any pain at all, Sir?"

In fact my stomach was actually hurting quite a bit, so I clutched at the offending part and groaned up at her through my masks. This seemed to earn me some favouritism, because only an hour later the nurse finally shoved me into a windowless cell in the company of a bony little male doctor who looked about twelve. Working here was part of his GCSE Biology course, no doubt. He asked me a few questions, then put on a pair of those condom gloves and said he was going to stick his fingers up my bottom.

"You are not," I told him.

"It's the standard test for internal injuries," he said, flexing his fingers in the air.

"Haven't you ever heard of X-rays? Have you actually got a machine here?" I mean, this bum-probing sounded like something a private hospital would invent as an extra consumer service. Smoothly done, I'd be all for it, but in this place you couldn't even be sure that the gloves were new.

"Look, Sir, it's the quickest standard test, please take your trousers down and lie across the bed."

"Ooh, I haven't had an offer like that for ages." OK, so it was a dumb joke, but I felt genuinely uncomfortable about the appropriateness of it. He was just so *young*. What age do doctors qualify these days?

"Right, wait there."

You know the noises the schoolboys make in those old story books? Yaroo! and Yikes! Stuff like that. Well, that's what I heard myself saying next. The young intern had gone to fetch some yeti of a male nurse who had climbed on my back and whose finger was now rummaging around my anal passage like an epileptic lobster.

"Hey – yaroo! You didn't put any (yikes!) lubrication on, you're doing this *dry*!"

He pulled out the lobster with unnecessary (yowee!) violence, and examined it for blood. It was clean. Feeling marginally safe, I stood up and made a grab for my underwear.

"Christ. Was that your finger or your head? Shouldn't you have worn some kind of rubber balaclava?"

He kept looking at his finger, then smiled.

"Hmm, iss dat blood-spot, doctor? Mebbe I try again."

My trousers have never been belted quicker.

"Don't worry, there's nothing wrong with you," the doctor told me. "If there'd been any internal damage, Pavel would have made you scream much louder than that."

"Well sorry to disappoint you," I told the still-amused Pavel. Pavel? It had to be a pseudonym for Vlad the impaler.

The baby doctor clearly thought I'd atoned for my sins, because he agreed to prescribe me a carrier-bag full of cortisones, bruise suppressers and painkillers. I felt suddenly grateful, in love with the NHS.

"Thanks, doctor, and sorry if I made a fuss."

"You call that a fuss? You should come here on a Friday night."

Which made me feel a bit less shitty.

I drove back into town, almost pleased with myself. Sorted. I didn't need to tell anybody about my visit to the hospital. The external bruising was negligible, and pain in itself's not so bad really. There are drugs to cure it.

I'd just stopped off at the office to try and piss some blood when it came.

A flashback, I mean.

The kid with the chain. The one who hit me. He was wearing a crucifix.

He and his mates had all looked so neat. Surely muggers aren't usually so clean-cut? And you know what they say cleanliness is next to.

I sat down on the loo and called Armlock.

"It was the godsquad who killed Beano, Inspector, you've got to arrest that Pritchett."

"The who?"

"That GTV reporter at my press conference. He knew about the black stuff coming out of Beano's mouth. Only the killer could have known that."

"You knew," the pig-headed pig said.

"For Christ's sake, Inspector." My indignation echoed around the cubicle. "Don't you get it? It was the god-botherers, they were punishing Beano for his immorality."

"Why didn't they punish you, then?"

"Hah. They just di –" I stopped myself spilling the beans about my recent brush with the moral muggers. "Are you going to interrogate Pritchett or what?"

"Interrogate?"

"Have an informal chat. Whatever. Nail him."

Armlock grunted. It sounded almost like a laugh. Now who was being flippant?

"Actually we're working on a different theory," she said. "It's those bruises."

"The bruises?"

"On your friend's neck. They're the wrong way round. Left thumb pressed to left side of throat, right to right. That's not how you strangle someone."

"Maybe the killer hadn't read the rulebook." Nowadays, it seems that even murders have to be done according to health and safety guidelines.

"You try it," she said.

I gripped my phone between my teeth and mimed it, strangling the air in front of me, two-handed. It was true. If you're trying to choke someone, you press the left thumb on the *right* side of their windpipe, and vice versa. I wiped the spit off my phone and asked her what that meant.

"Self-inflicted," she said.

"What? So Beano strangled himself? Get real."

"We think it might be –"

"A sex ritual of some kind? No way, Inspector. I mean I can imagine him going in for a bit self-strangulation with a belt round his neck. But how's he going to bash the bishop if he's got both hands round his throat? He was a brilliant guy, but he only had two arms."

"You're suggesting someone was with him, doing the ... bashing?"

"You think it was me!"

"I didn't say that."

"What do I have to do to convince you that Beano and me weren't shagging each other?"

"I've never said –"

"Unless, wait, wait ..." Desperation had given my imagination wings. Huge flapping pterodactyl wings, too, not some pathetic row of sparrow feathers. "What if someone with very long thumbs crossed them over in front of his throat? The cross. A symbolic strangling."

"Mr Bridges."

"Try it. Put your phone in your mouth and try it."

Armlock did one of her sullen silences. Unless she actually did have her phone in her mouth.

"If you'd just stop talking for a minute, Mr Bridges, I'd explain that we're working more on the theory that he was first poisoned in some way, and gripped his own throat while choking. That might account for the black liquid. But thanks for calling. As ever, talking to you was ... illuminating."

She rang off.

But without the mugging and Armlock's ravings, it would have been a good day. In the afternoon, Des and I whipped up some beautiful, multi-coloured animated celebrity sneezes for the Marina presentation. I drove home humming to myself, listening to the painkillers splashing about in my veins, changing acute discomfort into little more than a tightness behind my navel. I made a recording on my phone of my humming to see if any pain was audible. Tremolo-free. We'd got it under control, pharmaceuticals and me.

"No, Mr Grockel, not this evening."

Trouble was, the old prostate seemed to have taken to our get-togethers between the hall and my front door. He enjoyed the captive audience. And the danger money. But this evening, having been attacked already, and with cops (awake!) cruising near the house, I thought I'd do without him.

No chance. He was out of his cubbyhole as soon as my engine had stopped.

"I miss that old winter nip," he wheezed, leading me up the stairs, a broom held rifle-like in his hand. At least he didn't have a saucepan on his head. "Either it killed the germs or it killed you. These days you never know what you're in for." He'd clearly been reading about global warming and thought a melting iceberg was going to come skating down the street any minute. "This unseasonal warmth – it's a breeding ground for sickness. Thank God it's changing."

"Look, Mr Grockel," I winced (getting up the stairs hurt a lot more than driving), "there's honestly no need for you, pardon? Changing?"

He stopped to explain. "The weathermen reckon there's a cold spell on the way at the weekend. North wind. It's going to freeze."

"Freeze?"

I grunted upstairs as fast as my ribs would let me, Grockel scuttling behind with his broom.

Des and I were in for some classic deadline work, a good old round-the-clock, ashtrays-overflowing-onto-the-carpet race against time. Des's dandruff was going to get dandruff.

I slammed indoors, dying to tell Granola the weather forecast. Then stopped myself. Best to keep quiet. It would only make her more anxious to know what went into the seven-day cure.

I found her under a book, draped sideways across an armchair.

"Hi," she said.

I sat on the sofa, glad to rest my ribs.

"How's it going, Granola?"

"Fine." She took a deep breath and announced that she'd been thinking. Thinking? I feared the worst. It's never good news when someone says that to you. Especially your wife. Or soon-to-be ex-wife.

She patted the arm of her chair.

"Come and sit here. We need to talk."

Oh, no, I thought, not a "Talk". I had no time or mental space for one of those. But I went and balanced one half of my butt by her side.

"We haven't really *talked* these past three months, have we Bernie?" Granola is a verbal chess master. Soft as a koala bear when it's called for, hard as a diamond when she wants. Now she was playing the koala. No one can be nasty to a koala.

"Well ..." I said, thinking of a few of our mighty rows which could be classified as talking. Very loud talking.

"We speak about things but we don't *talk*," she said.

"Right." I was waiting for the koala to rip its head off and reveal the mutant, diamond-toothed rattlesnake within.

"But now I realize that it's up to me to make the first move."

So that was it. The divorce. She'd got the papers and she wanted me to sign our vinyl collection over to her, something like that. No way. No one was getting my autographed Spice Girls album.

I could almost see the snake peering out of Granola's moody eyes.

"I've been worried about you, Bernie." She turned those eyes up towards me, and I was surprised to see that they weren't at all snakelike. "But the more this whole thing goes on, the more I think it's not your fault."

Hey, a no-fault divorce, so I was going to get custody of the vinyl after all.

"That's what I've been trying to tell you," I said. "I don't understand how we got into this state. I –"

She put a hand on my knee.

"Let me finish, Bernie." She smiled up at me. "What I've always liked about you is that you're a true ingenu." What's that, I wondered, some kind of naturally gifted type, isn't it? "I mean," she went on, "could you explain to me exactly how the Coma buyout is going to work?"

"Of course. Er ..."

"Sorry, unfair question. It's not your job at all." She saved me from proving my ignorance. This time she *squeezed* my knee. Getting really physical. "What I mean is, you're good at your own thing, and you're too wrapped up in that to be really blameworthy."

"Blameworthy? For neglecting you?"

She turned in her chair and the squeeze on my knee got tighter. It was now a borderline dead leg.

"Bernie. You're mixing with some people who are as far from being ingenus as you can get. Louie, for example ..."

I nodded. Except where numbers were concerned, he was as naturally gifted as a bowl of dogfood.

"This Greensands woman ...," she went on.

Angela? No, I thought, she's sharp as a razor.

"And the Nostrum people. Look, Bernie, I'm not being aggressive in any way when I say this, but they're dangerous people, and you've fallen into their trap."

I stood up, brushing her treacherous hand off my leg. There was a snake in there after all.

"Ah, so that's what this is *really* about? This isn't a talk, it's another bloody sermon. I told you I'd check all that out, and –"

She reached up as if to pull me back into her clutches.

"Bernie. Calm down, please. I'm not having a go at you. Not *you*. You don't know what you're getting yourself into. Beano's been killed. You've been forced by some religious fundamentalists to delete your films. And now you're involved in marketing a politically explosive vaccine. Don't forget that this windfall you're hoping to get is all virtual at the moment. What happens if the buyout goes badly? Your so-called money goes up in a puff of electronic smoke. It has happened before, you know."

"I've taken precautions against that."

"Are you sure? It's all too ... too ..."

She was lost for words and I suddenly found myself coming over all protective. I sat down beside her again.

"Don't worry, Granola. Angela Greensands is protecting me now. We're in safe hands."

"Are you sure? How come this new respect for politicians? You used to go on about what a bunch of power-mad shits they were."

"I told you, it's only because I'm working on a very important public-health campaign –"

"Are you sure that's what it is? Share-price health campaign might be more accurate."

This was going too far.

"Listen, Granola. I know what you're trying to do, and it won't work. I mailed Nostrum asking for guarantees that there are no GM ingredients in the vaccine."

"You did?"

"Yeah."

"What did they say?"

"Nothing yet, but I'll keep on at them till they give me an answer. What more do you want me to do?"

She laughed. "Honestly? To tell the whole lot of them to –"

I grabbed her shoulders and squashed her against my chest. It hurt but it worked. She stopped sermonizing. She almost relaxed in my arms, as if that was what she'd wanted all along.

"I feel threatened, Bernie," she finally said, her mouth against my ear. "They scare me."

"I know, and I'm sorry."

"He's dead. Beano's dead."

"Yeah. And I'm doing my best to find out who did it."

"When you can spare the time." She felt me tense up at this new accusation. "No, Bernie. Sorry. I didn't mean ... Oh God, how did we get into all this?"

She sobbed a little, we hugged some more, then suddenly we were in bed. I could hardly believe it. Nothing for three months and then this. Woman is a language that I definitely don't understand. She lay there, her arms above her head, her eyes closed, and I watched her as I shoved away her fears and doubts.

We both groaned a lot, but for different reasons. I for one was not faking.

She doesn't get it, though. I'm so close to the Final Solution (that sounds a bit ominous, but I know what I mean). The Greensands meeting at the Marina will be more than just a preliminary. We'll present the whole prototype. The timing will be perfect, just as the weather is breaking. The Marina people will love me. And I will emerge a happier, more pleasant person. Surely that's worth waiting for, Granola?

Later, only later, after the post-come calm had worn off, did I start to worry. Was this a good time to have a reconciliation? Reconciliations take time and effort. Flowers and phone calls and stuff. And being a prospective divorcee had freed me up to chase after Claudine.

"Bernie?" Granola wasn't asleep. Sex had lost its sedative powers. At first I didn't answer, but she knows when I'm awake. It's that female radar. She started going on yet again about viruses.

"Listen Granola, I'm not telling people to get the flu, I'm trying to help people get cured, there is a difference."

"Ah yes, but –" and she's off again, sounding more environmentally-aware and dolphin-friendly than I've heard since I first met her. Now she was giving me the full genetic Earth-dustbin horror story all over again. I had to interrupt her.

"Governments are really cleaning up their act. It's the smart thing to do these days. It's what consumers want. Organic kale milk and all that."

"No, Bernie, no." She turned beneath the sheet and her hot boobs were suddenly against me. "I'm afraid we in the West are all heading very smartly, very respectably, towards a catastrophe. All the multinationals, with their well-dressed marketing managers and their –"

"Money in your bank."

"Money in my bank, clean money, legal money, all of us buying things and throwing them away, filling the oceans with plastic, spilling oil and greenhouse gases and radioactivity, raising temperatures and sea levels, it's all going to fizzle out in filth and sickness. James Bond isn't going to jump out of a helicopter in time to save the world. It'll just be a nasty, an awful ..."

Fucking hell, I thought, do I need this? Do I really need all this?

"All right, Granola, yes. But it's not going to come to this sticky end next week, is it? I've got time to finish this job and get the payoff, OK?"

"Just one thing, Bernie. And I'm completely serious." She was almost whispering now, her voice somehow clearer despite the reduction in decibels. "If I find out that you're knowingly putting together a campaign to promote a genetically-modified vaccine, I'll shop your friends for insider dealing, and I'll make damn sure your campaign never even gets started."

It didn't sound as if she was faking it. If this was reconciliation, give me divorce any day.

****

For sale: SURGICAL MASKS, from only $1 per 100. Recyclable. Buy now while stocks last.

****

23 CH-CH-CHANGES?

The change finally came on the Friday night, a momentous start to the weekend. I'd been at home all day, dialoguing with Des, getting things done, and I emerged into the evening to find the sea and sky in almost forgotten activity.

The bay had its white frills on, the beginnings of surf were beating at the sea walls. The air was moving, and the cement cloud cover was being broken up by a steady, chilly northerly. Clouds were hanging in tatters from the first fragments of a clear sky that was dark as a pupil. I felt the ridiculous temptation to get out of the car and stand with my nose aloft like some Inuit trying to pinpoint the migrating walruses.

But this was it, this was what we'd been waiting for. The cold had got up enough energy to heave our weighty greenhouse roof away. I was looking forward to seeing some real clouds again. Not the solid-looking sheen of vapour that'd been suspended over us for the past few months, but storm clouds, real puffed-up ones, towering great clito-stimulus or whatever they're called.

"The cold snap is here," a radio DJ announced. "The season of sniffs and yellow boginess." This had me chortling all the way to Phil's place. I'd accepted an invite to go out for dinner – or tea, as Phil called it. Evening meal, anyway. I'd checked. I wasn't sure why Phil was suddenly brimming over with hospitality –

Mona's influence, perhaps – but this time I decided that a whole evening with Phil was bearable. Advisable, even. It would give me some idea if he was up to anything beyond his straightforward subversion vis-à-vis Claudine. I'd made a date to go and see her as soon as the dinner was over. And to make things easier for me, Granola repeated that there was nothing she'd like less than to spend the evening with other people who would be making money from the Nostrum campaign.

When I arrived at Phil's place, he was decorating a coffee table with thick stripes of white powder.

"Ah, Bernie," he shouted. "Get a noseful of this." He handed me a red-and-white length of kiddies' drinking straw. No rolled-up banknotes or silver spoons for Phil. That would be a dead giveaway.

"After you, mine host," I said. No way was I going to even smell anything that he hadn't snorted first. It'd be just like him to give me fart powder to liven up his evening. He took a deep snort and whistled his approval.

I followed suit gingerly, taking about a kilo less than him, but still getting an instant buzz.

"What is this, Phil? Only gangsters and diplomats get drugs this pure."

"Not bad, eh? Got it off this South American banker yesterday. Fresh out of the pampas, this stuff." He handed the straw to Mona, who bent over the table. Phil leered. "Takes it up the nasal passage, our Mona."

"God, Phil." This was Mona and I in harmony.

It's at home that he takes his citizen-of-the-gutter act to its most absurd extremes. We were surrounded by Phil's framed collection of airsick bags and his ghetto furniture (inherited, he claims, from "me gran" – what crap). We sat deep in Wimbledon-green leatherette, scratching our tender buttocks on fuzzy nylon cushions, made sixty years ago to keep the working class in their place. Even if the husband had got promoted to shit-shoveller-in-chief, he'd never have considered moving to a posher area – he'd have had to hire an aircraft carrier just to shift the three-piece suite. And his new middle-class neighbours would have bricked up the street rather than have the arrival of these globulous plastic monoliths bring down their house prices. Which is exactly why Phil bought them, for a fortune I'm sure.

There was an additional butt getting scratched this evening – Rita's. She wasn't in the merriest of moods, which was understandable, but at least she was making an effort to laugh at Phil's obscene banter. I refilled her glass to help her along the path to recovery. She didn't look at me as she said thanks.

Mona sniffed breathlessly. "Reminds me of the time I watched a gun battle in – damn. What's the capital of Colombia?"

None of us could think. Where was Des when you needed him?

"Wodger mean?" Phil demanded.

Mona wiped her nostrils with her fingertips.

"Well, people shoot each other for this stuff." Caring, sharing Mona as usual.

"Bollocks!" Phil snorted. "This is fuckin fair-trade import. Eco-coke. But if you're so fuckin worried about Colombian peasants, don't sniff the fuckin stuff. More for the rest of us."

Mona looked hurt. Phil leered and slapped her bum to show that he was joking. Mona still looked hurt all the same.

"It's going to pee down," Rita grumbled. "You sure you all want to go out?" She hadn't latched on to the importance of the weather change.

"Rain? Brilliant, yeah, less drive!" Phil leapt to his feet and yelled "shaddap!" The radio did so.

In two cars, me with Mona, Rita with Phil (he said I'd only depress Rita by talking about Beano), we raced into the wind and hit the rain just at the edge of town. Our lights were almost blacked out by torrents that stuck to the glass, half-frozen. This was one cold air belt. Then the game was to accelerate through the impenetrable spray of the deepest puddles, or to drive alongside your partner and force him or her towards the trees, swerving close, keeping them on the wrong side of the road in the hope of meeting someone else head-on.

The tyres gripped well, we never stopped laughing and yelling phoned threats. I'd have liked to take ten minutes in a lay-by with Mona. She'd been driving, making the maddest manoeuvres all the way, and yelping wildly around in her seat. Half-way to the restaurant, we swapped drivers, and Rita was even madder behind the wheel than Phil had been. She overtook me on bends that would have had a rally driver sweating. We all arrived breathless. The food tasted of adrenalin. We kept up the mood all through the meal and then zipped off into the darkness again.

Back at the house, we all started talking about danger, like landed plane passengers remembering the air pockets and flapping wings.

"Safternoon," Phil said, warming up his mouth for another bout of calculated glottal stops, "I was goin for a red light an I cut up this white van. I ad to stop, though, cause of the fuckin pedestrians, and next thing I know the fuckin van's alongside and two guys are gettin out with fuckin baseball bats. One of them comes towards me driver's door and the other one's comin round for a good swing at me fuckin win screen." We all cringed, me slightly more than the others. They were all with him in the car, but I was alone, bent double on my street corner.

"So I give em the finger, take off through the red light, an I didn't go near me fuckin brakes till I was parked up outside the fuckin cop shop."

"You should have run them over," Rita said, miming a change into reverse and a violent piece of pedalwork. Her armchair lurched back then forward, and she made flesh-squelching sounds with her lipsticked mouth. She was drunk.

"Yeah, yeah," Phil objected. "But you'd need to make sure you finish em off or they'll be after you, right?"

"You think they got your registration, they'll come after you?" Mona asked.

Phil inflated and deflated his cheeks. He'd thought of that.

"Nah," he said, though I could tell he'd feel more at ease knowing that those baseball batsmen were safely off the planet.

We all sat there, thinking how snug we were here together, and not outside at the mercy of whatever was there.

"Inspector fuckin Armlock arsed to bug my phones. I told er to fuck off," Phil said, slopping his drink over a leatherette armchair.

"So you had your interview, then?" I asked. He probably got tea and biscuits, too.

"Yeah. But where does she fuckin think she is, fuckin Kremlin?" Phil's entire existence depends on his communications. He farts on broadband. He can't do with anyone listening in on his dealings.

Mona started to have a bitch about these twisted times we were living in, with the moral majority trying to shut us down and politicians trying to take us over, but Phil told her to shut the fuck up with the fuckin politics.

He wasn't joking this time. He clearly wasn't feeling very "vulnerable" tonight. Mona looked hurt again.

I said he should cool it, but all Phil did was put on an overblown apology act that got us all laughing without knowing whether he was being sincere or not. The story of his life.

There were more drinks and more anecdotes. We started to spook each other over the likelihood of another strangling, and I decided enough was enough. I was due to go and perform with Claudine, and call me conventional, but I just didn't find Beano's death or the prospect of my own demise erotic.

"I'm tired. Can you run me home?" Rita asked Phil.

"Pissed more like," he answered.

"I'll take you," I offered.

"I don't want to take you out of your way."

"But I'd love you to lead me astray," I said. A joke, of course. Though from the look she gave me, jokes about this sort of thing still weren't allowed yet.

"Didn't you come in your car?" Mona asked her, looking a tiny bit peeved.

"Phil's right. I've had too much to drink." Rita stood up, and I watched her curves assume their upright proportions.

"Fingers, fingers," Phil mouthed, giving me a know-all stare which the girls didn't see. I shook my head, meaning Rita wasn't in my sights at all.

He already had his car-keys out.

"I'm not sure I trust Bernie," Rita half-whispered to Mona while I emptied my glass. Mona could hardly refuse such a woman-to-woman appeal, could she? And she couldn't say, "well Phil's no better."

"You stayin here, Mo, or goin back to your place?" Phil asked.

"What would you prefer?" Mona asked him, a mite huffily.

"I'm shagged out. Gonna come back and sleep. Let's call it a night, shall we?"

"OK." Mona stood up, a slightly larger mite huffily.

Did he mean call it a night or call it a day, I wondered.

Outdoors, there were only a few fat spits falling from the clouds, which were getting skimpier again, skidding away very fast. We were in for a clear night. The air was chill despite the drink. The road surface looked greasy, almost icy.

We all hugged and separated. I ambled to my car and heard Rita's heels clopping away behind me. I turned and saw Phil admiring her rear view. With Mona watching him watching her. Poor Mona, I thought. She never chooses the right bloke. Oh, well. It was a shame for her, I thought, but if Phil had decided to try and bed Rita, there was no way he could stop me winning the bet over Claudine. Within the next half-hour the contract would be sealed, and the sack race won.

****

Dear Member,
Strike while the iron's soft!
All the clever medical money is going into a great new alternative to Viagra.
For info on clinical trials, free samples, and merchandising including some fully leaded pencils, go to Nostrabonus

****

24 Perfect

The car heating was on full. My shirt was ruffling in a desert gale. Outside, in the inhospitable atmosphere of the new cold planet, the town's lighting system seemed to be on total overload. A halogen leak maybe? No, my folk memory reminded me, it was called the Moon.

After months of muggy cloud, it had been seasons since I saw the Moon so clearly, so big and round, fit to bring babies popping out at record rates, I'll bet. But as with people, a good clear view isn't always the best way to look at something. The old man in the Moon looked freezing out there in space. Spotty, scarred, pale and bald. Unhealthy.

Beneath its blank gaze, I drove on towards one of the healthiest zones in town: Claudine.

She had couriered her key over to me in case she fell asleep. I wasn't insulted by the idea that she wouldn't be waiting for me with baited breath. I just hoped she'd wake up for the actual sex.

Inside her apartment it was dark – I closed the front door behind me and remembered to put away my street protection. It wouldn't have been cool to let off a stun grenade in her face.

I could hear nothing except the tingling in my ears. I smelt the darkness for signs of life and picked up only the sweat of my own excitement. I wondered if this was how MeToo casting directors used to do it. A note to themselves in their diary: "10.30pm, sex with starlet number 325A". Even though I had Claudine's consent, it was about as erotic as an empty condom machine.

I pushed open a door. The Moon and the street lights shone through thin curtains. It was the lounge. Wrong door. I backed out again.

There were two other doors off the hall. One, I guessed, would be the kitchen, one the bedroom.

I got it right second time, after a brief and unhappy meeting between my left hand and a gooey dish of soft cheese. Don't the French ever put it in the fridge?

I opened the second door and smelt sleep, that thick, warm vapour that inspires tenderness in everyone but the most determined killer. I could just see the bed. It was big and white, almost filling the whole room. Her head was dark on the pillow, turned away, and my shadow fell weakly across her. I got undressed and sidled into bed. She was naked, lying in a foetal position. At last, the sheer warmth and smoothness of her, her soft womanly smell, added some sexiness to proceedings.

She stirred then gasped.

"Claudine ... it's Bernie," I whispered, not too proud to identify myself.

"Ah, yes." She rolled over on to her back. I took a chance and touched her belly. It was beating like a heart.

"Wait," she said, and got out of bed, throwing the quilt back over me.

Women often have little things to do beforehand, don't they. Gels, perfumes and who knows what. She disappeared into the bathroom and the light went on, revealing the primness of her bedroom. Not even a pair of tights dropped on the cream carpet. The walls were sparkling white, cupboards glossed and shut, the quilt smelt of nothing at all. The girl is hygiene personified. She probably pisses spring water, if she pisses at all. I lay back and waited. I could hear unusual tearings and scrapings coming from the bathroom, but for all I cared she could have been building a new shower cubicle as long as she came back to bed eventually. I make few demands. I don't ask for hypocrisy.

Mind you, she was taking her bloody time.

"Aren't you ready yet?"

"Wait!" I heard her puff disapprovingly to herself. The ripping noises were still going on.

Then in she came, framed against the bathroom light, and I nearly fainted. My butt twitched with panic, remembering Vlad at the hospital. Her outline was all female except ... The waistline, the hips were pure woman, but ... It had to be false – she's a real woman, I know. I've seen her picture in magazines, I've seen her (partially) naked during a film shoot, and she's definitely not a guy. But there it was. She had a dick, a dongler, a dangler of her own.

As she walked towards me, I noted that it was transparent, therefore probably not a real one, but even a falsie was scary enough. I'd heard about dick-toting ladies, beautiful women avengers who strap on a hunk of ebony and sodomize a poor lad just to show him what it's like to be lusted after. What's more, someone told me, apparently women's magazines are recommending it as the only politically-correct way for heterosexual couples to interact these days.

She came right up to the bed, her avenger swinging.

"What is that?" I asked.

"Condom," she said. "From Japan." But it was much more than that. Her boobs were squashed behind rubber like a pair of bank-robbers' noses. Her thighs squeaked. She was wearing a sort of neck-to-ankle diving suit, a second skin. And she had gloves on, too. She threw something on the bed and said, "Put it on." It was a mask, a surgeon's mask. "Japanese, also. Extra thick." She was putting hers on.

"How the hell does that thing work?" I asked, flicking gingerly at the swinging wang.

"You push that in like a female condom," she said.

"Great." I was still up for it, but suffering serious doubts.

"You want to fuck, right?"

"Yes."

"OK, we fuck. With maximum precaution." She lay on the bed beside me, creaking against the sheets.

"What happens if you fart?" I asked. "Will you start to lift off?" I mean, I was about to shag a hot-air balloon.

"Uh?" She didn't understand, but it didn't bother her. "You can begin. Please do not try to stimulate with your hand first. I have lubricated."

I put on my mask and gave it my best. Her rubber chafed my outer thighs, I lifted myself up on my arms to avoid scraping off my nipples. Down below me her clamped boobs weren't budging. Her eyes, as I'd feared, kept watch on me, so I closed mine. Now I understood her. This was how she stayed perfect. Surgical screwing, antiseptic sex. I couldn't even breathe at her.

It took me ages. Sex is not supposed to be surgical, is it? It's meant to be floundering, dirty, un-immaculate. Even grappling with a condom packet can add to the beautiful, frantic imperfection of it all.

I finally won over the doubts in my head and slumped down, making sure my torso didn't fall on to the latex hulk beneath me.

"Finish?" she asked. I mumbled something positive into the pillow. She squirmed around till I lifted my haunches and let her go. I lay there and listened to the new session of scrapings and crumplings in the bathroom. This time I could picture the scene. Bin bags, tweezers, the grimace as she tried to keep the squidge away from her skin. She came back into the bedroom in a dressing gown, still wearing her mask and gloves, with an empty bin bag, a huge pastel blue one, medical-looking. Probably for me, to send me off for incineration.

"I take the bed covers," she said. "You shower."

I obeyed. Alone under the blast of hot water, surrounded on all sides by gleaming chrome and enamel, I looked down and apologized. My dick was looking more shrivelled and drained than usual in this situation. Claudine came in and stared at me. There was no shower curtain – the whole bathroom floor was tiled to receive water. The drain was a brilliantly-polished grill in one corner. She smiled to herself, but it must have been in French, I didn't understand. I tried to look at my most nonchalant.

"How many people have worked on my 'See Models Die' films?" she asked.

"Why?" I took it as a snide way of asking how many other guys would be coming round to try and break into her diving suit.

"I am interested. Which others have contributed? Beano, who is dead, and who else?"

I let the spray spray on and gave a run-down of the roles of various people in making the films and posting them on line. It was one of our earliest ventures, so it was really hands-on. Beano, Phil, Des, Mona, myself, we all got our hands dirty, I told her. Claudine listened and watched me. I even felt that there might have been some closeness creeping into that sterile little room.

"So, all those people, they wanted just to see me die on the internet?"

"If that's how you like to interpret it."

"Let me take a shower now," she said.

"Come on under." I mean, a little skin-rub under filtered water can't give you any diseases can it?

"You finish first," she said.

I turned the water off, and went to stand under the drier. She had one of those public-toilet hand-driers fixed at shoulder height on the wall. Towels were clearly too unhygienic for her. She hung up her dressing gown and I almost gasped at the full, standing naked beauty of her. As she reached up to adjust the jet, as she twisted the tap on, as she squirted soap on to her belly, rising on tip-toe to bend her pelvis forward, it all moved and glistened, spanked by the gush of water. It was the biggest porn cliché since licking an ice-cream.

I realized, though, that this wasn't a show for me. She didn't care if I stared. She's a model. It's her job to be ogled at. The oglers don't mean a thing to her. She turned to look at me, emptily, as if I was just another lens.

"Do it if you want," she said. "But point over there." She motioned towards the corner drain.

I did it. She stayed under the shower, soaped herself, let the water stream between her buttocks, moulded a breast, ignoring me but giving me a peep show until I needed another shower. Before she got out, she directed the spray in my direction, sweeping the floor of my dying little tadpoles.

"Beano has come here," she said as she did this spot of nocturnal housework.

"What? Why? When?" Beano, you hot rabbit, you got in there first. I was astounded.

"He has promised me everything like you. He has promised shares in your company, even a real movie."

Beano was shameless. A "real movie," a great joke carrot, and she swallowed it. Or did she?

"When was this?" I asked. She was buggering up her grammar and making it sound so immediate. She was making it sound like Beano's promise still stood.

"I don't know, two weeks ago maybe, just as you, in the night," she said. "He has done what you have done, exactly. First the fucking and then the wanking. Exactly. Then he is dead," she added, "few days after." She shrugged, as if this was no more than a quirky coincidence, like going to a birthday party and finding that two of you have bought the same present.

She put on her bathrobe.

"We sign the contract now?"

I dressed and when I went into the lounge she was standing by a table, contract folded out, pen in hand. She watched me sign away a chunk of my fee.

"When we start work?" she asked.

"Tomorrow. I want you to do some filming in doctor's costume. You OK for that?"

"For this much money, why not?" she shrugged.

"I'll call you in the morning."

"OK." She turned away and disappeared into her bedroom. I followed her in there, but the light was already off and she was in bed, bathrobe still on. "Please leave my key on the table." She didn't even open her eyes to speak.

I slammed her apartment door, I slammed her street door, I slammed my car door and revved noisily away.

No way was I going to boast to the tabloids about this. Instead of a kiss-and-tell story, I'd got my fifteen minutes of shame.

She'd humiliated me like no one else has ever done. Pavel the nurse had been a model of kindness and consideration compared to her. Even lying back with her legs open, a woman can humiliate you. I didn't know that before. It was a tough discovery. I could picture her sneering into her pillow at the success of her rubber evening. Yes, that look on her face in the bathroom, it was scorn, pure scorn. No wonder I hadn't recognized it. It's not what you expect.

For the umpteenth time in a week, my wayward tear ducts sprang into action.

"No you don't, you bastards," I told the reddening eyes in the driving mirror. The tears looked big and clean. As each droplet emerged, I wiped it off my eyelid or cheek with a fingertip and licked it back inside again. This was no time to be losing valuable mineral salts.

25 The Call Comes

It's Saturday, early, and I'm back on an up. Mainly because of a mild overdose of painkillers, but then I've got a lot of pain to keep at bay.

And last night didn't end as badly as it could have done.

When I got home, I crashed out in front of the TV to take my mind off things.

What I saw did not look promising.

"Let me ask you again, Minister, do you or do you not agree that you have reacted far too late?"

Angela Greensands was being interrogated by the BBC's number-one politician-baiter. The type who can ruin Ministers' careers with one mercilessly repeated question.

She hesitated. You could see the glimmer of triumph in the interviewer's calm face. He was dying to wink at the camera and say, yes, we've nobbled another of the bastards.

"Minister, have you or have you not reacted far too late?"

She shook her head, apparently defeated.

"Yes or no, Ms Greensands?"

"Well ..."

"Yes or no, Ms Greensands?"

"Yes."

"No!" I shouted at the screen. I couldn't believe it. Surely my guardian Angela wasn't the type to let herself get humiliated on TV? Why weren't her armed guards wading in to slap the interviewer about a bit?

She looked straight into camera, waited for the director to zoom in, and said,

"Yes, I accept that wholeheartedly. We were late off the starting blocks. It was an error of judgement." Her handsome face was a picture of contrition.

I whooped. Now I understood. What a woman, what an invention – the honest politician. She was doing a whatsit. A mea culpa.

"Go for it Angie," I urged her. "I've been there, too, you know."

The interviewer was dumbstruck. His whole line of questioning had collapsed. Trooper Angela Greensands marched into the breach.

"To err, as they say, is human, and to forgive is usually beyond the means of journalists," she said, deadpan. "But this is no time for political point-scoring. We are talking about saving lives. There's no crisis yet, there's no epidemic, and there won't be one if we act now. So what I propose is to turn this interview into a public information session. Yours is one of the highest-rated current affairs shows on TV, and I think the viewers would probably prefer to learn something concrete rather than watch a professional interviewer and a professional politician play their verbal games. It may be good entertainment, but it's not really news, is it? What do you think?"

The interviewer interviewed. Gawping like a trout just out of the river, the host made a helpless gesture of agreement towards his ministerial guest.

"Thank you," she smiled, showing us the teeth of a movie star. "Now, I would like to share some vital information communicated to me by the Ministry of Health who are, of course, supervising this whole affair..."

I watched for a few minutes to see if she'd mention Coma, but she didn't. I wondered if this was because she didn't trust me to get the job finished in time. But no, I decided, she was playing her cards close to her chest. Shrewd move. Just because you do a mea culpa, it doesn't mean you have to confess everything.

I'd seen enough to help me forget Claudine's psychological castration tactics. I went to bed smiling.

"Where's your watch?" were Granola's first words to me next morning. "Haven't they sent it back yet?"

"Uh, no. I'll give them a call." I hadn't thought it necessary to mention the mugging to her.

I went and hid in the toilet. I seem to be making a lot of calls from the loo these days. I guess it's a throwback – we stopped using phone boxes, but subconsciously I still crave that snug, womb-like sensation of phoning without being overheard by the whole street, restaurant or train carriage. Or wife, for that matter.

In between making scary straining noises to keep Granola away, I had another chat with my friendly watch salesman.

I identified myself.

"Bridges," he repeated blankly.

I identified my watch, and he said "ah yes," as if smiling to himself about my last visit.

"I wanted to ask about the guarantee."

"Ye-es?" A long, suspicious vowel.

"I was just wondering – does it cover loss?"

"Losing time, you mean? Going slow?"

"No, loss, as in, I've lost the watch."

"Well, ha, that is not what we would define as a mechanical fault or manufacturing defect, I'm afraid. I don't think the makers would accept responsibility for that, Sir. Sadly."

"No, didn't think so. I paid extra for an insurance policy, though, I seem to remember. Have you got the emergency phone number?"

"Certainly, Sir. I'll send it to you. I'm sure they'll be able to help you. And if they do compensate you, Sir, let me know and I'll put a new watch aside for you."

Hence the politeness. Another sale in sight. That's why the customer is always right.

I phoned the insurance hotline, but they weren't interested unless I'd declared the theft to the police. Shit. I was trying to keep away from *them*.

There was a soft tap on the toilet door.

"Bernie, what are you doing in there?"

Why do people ask that question? What do they think we're doing? Watching porn? Re-enacting the Cup Final with our pants down? Making secret phone calls to cover up the loss of our atrociously expensive watch?

"Do you really want a description? What do I usually do while sitting on the toilet?"

Such low-level crudity was guaranteed to make Granola run for cover.

"Police. Mike speaking, how can I help you?"

"I want to report a theft."

"You are the victim, Sir?"

"No, I'm the fucking thief, turdbrain." Of course I didn't say it. I merely confirmed his shrewd hunch, and he put me through to the right department. I then told a female detective constable called Martin (so I presumed I was not on first-name terms with her, unlike their over-familiar switchboard) about being punched in the stomach and robbed by a crucifix-wearer right under a CCTV camera. She wrote it all down.

"Can you send me some sort of document that proves I've declared the theft?" I begged. "For the insurance."

"Yes, no problem, Sir. Do you know the serial number of your watch?"

"No."

"Well it'd help if you could find out. A watch that expensive might attract attention when those kids try to fence it."

"OK."

Shit. It meant yet another call to the bloody jeweller. This timepiece, I thought to myself, is getting to be a waste of time. Who needs a watch? I'm surrounded by clocks. My walls, computers, phones, car, TV, cooker and even my fridge are all fitted with clocks. They all tell a slightly different time, but who cares about being three minutes late for a date with a yogurt?

"Bernie! I need to go." Granola was pleading now.

"One minute. Literally. Just wiping."

Sixty seconds was all it took to call the jeweller and get him to send the serial number to the cops. But it was one painful minute. When will the humiliations end?

While Granola was occupied in the loo, I called and finalized the details of Claudine's film shoot. I'd decided to get Mike the nerdling to do it. I quite enjoyed the idea of one so beautiful being ordered about by one so gross. The unscrewable in charge of the inscrutable.

"I'm just going in to work for an hour," I told Granola. "I want to have a good search round to make sure about those Nostrum ingredients." It was the partial truth.

"OK. We'll have lunch together, though?"

"Great." First sex, now lunch. We really were going places as a couple again.

At weekends, the office is not generally empty. The internet never closes. So I was surprised to find that none of my fellow founders were there. Not even Louie, who doesn't have much of a life to go to.

"He's off," Joe told me. This was the other nerdling. He was sitting at Louie's desk, swiping away with a tablet on his knees. Didn't seem bothered that I'd found him there. Didn't even turn to face me as he replied to my questions.

"Off?" He made Louie sound like week-old milk.

"Like sick."

"Louie's sick?" The irony sunk in. The financial controller of the health company was not healthy. Who was committing the PR fuck-up now?

"Yeah."

"What's wrong with him? Hangover?" Louie drinks alone quite a lot.

"Don't know." Joe didn't care, either. But then, neither did I.

"Does Louie know you're working in his office?"

"Yeah."

"By the way, Joe, if you want another one of those T-shirts, help yourself."

"Uh? Oh, right. Too generous."

And they accuse *me* of having no social skills. Joe's of the generation that had Play Stations instead of teddy bears, text messages instead of parents. I mean, I only have followers instead of friends. There is a difference.

I went to one of the salespeople's cubicles and used a screen to do a search for Nostrum. Didn't want it tracing to me. There were dozens of hate pages accusing the company of doing everything from labelling GM quinoa as "organic" to plotting to kill the Hobbits. That's the trouble with the net. Democracy is all very well in theory, but the crazies have as loud a voice as serious folk like me. I gave up, too scared of getting caught at someone else's screen.

I'd just got back to my own cubicle when my mobile rang.

"Bridges?"

"Yes?" I didn't recognize the voice. It was very throaty, with a deliberate twisting of the vowels, an over-rolled 'r'. Brrr-idges.

"Exploiter of women, you will pay." A cheap melodrama voice.

"Very funny, Phil."

"Not funny. More dead."

"You're sick, Phil, you really are. And dumping Mona like that was just plain mean."

I called the Inspector.

"Hi, Police Station, Sara speaking. How can I help you?"

It took me half an infuriating minute to get through to the Inspector's voicemail.

"Are you there, Inspector? Were you listening in? I think it might have been a joke, but I'm not sure."

She cut in. "Morning, Mr Bridges. Glad to hear you're still with us." Her sarcasm sounded heavy and difficult this morning.

"Well, what do you think about the phone call?"

"So you only follow the news when you're in it, do you?"

"What do you mean?"

She sighed patiently.

"Three dead, choked, found yesterday evening between seven and twelve."

"Really? Shit. Last night? But this time you're out of luck, I've got a whole restaurant full of alibis, plus two carloads of friends and a French model."

"Mr Bridges. Will you please get off your paranoid hobbyhorse?" There was a heavy note in Armlock's voice. It was more sombre than usual, harsher. Something was definitely pissing her off.

"My what?"

"You're in the clear, as you well know."

"What do you mean, 'as I well know'?"

Another sigh, deeper this time, less patient.

"Look, Mr Bridges, I'm not a complete idiot, whatever you may think. That threatening phone call was such a bad fake. You disappoint me."

"I was the one who said it might be a joke, wasn't I? But who's to say it wasn't those religious nuts? Pritchett and his godsquad –"

"I wish you'd just forget the sodding godsquad. They've got their share of public attention, same as you. You've all had your limelight, and I've been helping you all get a little more famous. So now you can just go and stick your fake phone call where it hurts."

"What are you talking about? It's obvious, isn't it? The godsquad –"

"It won't work any more, Mr Bridges. Don't pretend you haven't been getting all the confidential information about the case."

"What? I don't –"

"And I'm removing your protection."

"You can't do that!"

"I'm only following orders, Mr Bridges. Complain to the Ministry. Get a drug company to send you some private security." In the past this would have been said with mockery, but now it was just plain bitterness.

"What confidential information? Someone's proved I had nothing to do with Beano's death, is that it?"

She laughed. "Don't bother with your naive act, Mr Bridges. Just tell me why you didn't report your mugging straight away."

"You know about that?"

"It's one of the few things I'm allowed to know, yes. Your name had a spectacular effect on our computer system when the theft of your watch was logged in. The duty sergeant actually walked upstairs to tell me about it."

"Ah."

"So why didn't you report it straight away?"

"Muggings must be two a penny. Didn't seem urgent. But like I told your colleague, one of them was a Christian."

"Slugged you with a bible, did he?"

"No, he was wearing a crucifix."

"Perhaps he stole it off a nun." She groaned, and not just at the lameness of her quip. "OK. Let's get this straight." She took a breath, as if she was just about to do something painful, like pull out one of her eyebrow hairs. "You really believe the godsquad are after you?"

"Yes."

"I'm almost a hundred per cent sure you're wrong, but let's forget that for the moment. And you honestly haven't been told the results of your friend Beano's inquest?"

"No."

"Hmm," she said. "I'll get back to you." And hung up.

I didn't understand. The strain is definitely showing. Armlock's going over the edge.

I headed for home straight away, my mind racing about Beano. I was driving through the town centre when my phone rang.

"Bernie, it's Louie." It didn't sound like him at all. He sounded small and weak. I looked into the phone with predatory delight.

"Joe tells me you're not feeling well, Louie?"

"Not too bad." He sounded on the verge of tears. So it probably was the booze. He's a mournful drinker. "Can you come over?"

"Now?"

"Yeah. Something I want to discuss. Something confidential."

"Can't it wait?"

"Confidential and urgent. Please, Bernie. I'll leave the door on the latch."

"OK." After all, he did say please.

****

m
got him. b's invoices 4 t-shirts = bollox.
have dropped him shitwards
j

****

26 Silent Rock 'n' Roll

Louie lives beyond one of the town's golf courses, Trump Park, which is abandoned at the moment. The official story is that diseased foxes were sighted in the woods. It's credible – no one fancies getting a rabid bum while rooting their ball out of the rough. Even if it was only the caddy that got fanged, there's the insurance.

But there are all sorts of rumours about who lives in those woods, and if they're true, the foxes have done bloody well to survive long enough to catch rabies. The latest story is that a bunch of illegal immigrants have built a bunker in there, and recently ate a couple of golfers. Who knows if it's true. I read it on Twitter.

Out here, on the leafy fringe of town, Louie has a house. It must have cost him a fortune. I turned off the main road into the deserted suburb, quiet with the self-assurance of wealth. The roads are wide and clear and pinkish-grey with new gravel. The pavement is never less than duo-jogging width. The houses are varied in size and style, though most of them are mock-something-or-other. Mature trees abound, the hedges are high, the lawns are vast, and now they were looking slightly healthier than of late thanks to the rain.

I parked in Louie's drive and ran for the door. It was raw out and I'd under-dressed. I still hadn't got used to all this weather we were suddenly having. His door was unlocked, as promised. The dork, leaving it open when there are killers on the loose.

It was unbearably hot in the house. Body-odour in the air.

"Louie!"

No answer. No sign of life in the hall. A few pairs of little shoes in a row by the door, incoming letters neatly stacked on a Chinese-looking teak hall table. So tidy it hurt. He'd be waiting in his study, I decided, relishing this chance to make me come running to him. I went in there and found Louie sitting on a sofa.

He looked dishevelled in a pale blue shirt and maroon-and-orange tie. Amazing. I'd never seen him so badly coordinated, so disorganized. He was unshaven, like some drunken bar-room pianist. I mean, who wears a tie at home? He probably hadn't gone to bed at all.

"There you are, Louie, you old soak. Now what did you want to tell me?" The sooner I was informed and out of there, the better.

He patted the space beside him on the sofa and I sat gingerly. He smiled and breathed hot self-pity in my face. There was stale alcohol on his breath.

"Louie? For Christ's sake, what have you been drinking?" I'd never seen him this bad, even when we were all students together.

"Claudine wasn't too impressed, I hear?" He laughed and winced. Aspirin not kicking in yet, no doubt.

"What?"

"Rubber man put you off your stride? The deep-sea diver's outfit."

"Fuck." I realized what he was talking about. "Is that what you wanted to tell me? That you know what happened with Claudine? Waste of my time and petrol if it was." He nodded and laughed again at my reaction.

"So was shagging her, if you must know," I said. "Cost me a fortune for nothing."

His shoulders shook as if he was tuning in to some inaudible rock 'n' roll radio station. I think it was meant to be laughter.

"I gave her some shares. Your shares," he said.

"My shares?"

"First she got some of Beano's. We sold them." He paused to let this sink in. "When you signed yours over, price went down, I bought a load. She bought more, too. Cheap. All planned."

"Bollocks. You're bullshitting me."

"You selling helped the rest of us. Make a killing."

"Killing, right. Good choice of word, Louie, as usual. What do you mean, 'the rest of us'?"

"Angela Greensands, too," Louie wheezed a chuckle.

"Bullshit."

"I told people. About your press conference. Price went down. We bought." He groaned, part pleasure, part pain. "You kept the story out of the media. Price went up. Cheers, Bernie."

I stood and watched him as he rock 'n' rolled mutely again. He was grinning like a cartoon cat.

"Who you think told Pritchett? About the black gunk?" he gurgled.

"What are you saying, Louie? What the hell have you been drinking? And popping? Did Phil sell you some of his duff drugs?"

Louie shook his head and flopped limply against the back of the sofa.

"No drugs," he said. "Coma ..." Then something like "god".

"What? God? The godsquad? Holy shit."

Keeping his reddened eyes on me, maintaining his moronic leer, he nodded, and carried on nodding.

Keeled forward, I mean, still grinning. He slumped to one side and gave one final gurgle. His last. His mouth was locked open but only dribble was coming out, and nothing was going in. He was showing as much eyeball as Beano had done.

Nothing short of a bullet could have stopped me getting out of that house. Time of death equals my time of arrival *again*. Inspector Armlock was going to love me for this one. I drove away too fast, and faces appeared at windows in two or three houses. I was back to square one, failing to get away unnoticed.

As soon as I was sure that no cop cars were going to block my way out of the neighbourhood, I called Armlock. I eventually got her voicemail, and for once she didn't cut in.

"This is Bridges. Louie's dead, same way as Beano, and it's your damn fault. I told you to keep a watch on everyone. Louie told me it was the godsquad just before he died, it's been them all along. I'm getting the hell out of here. I'll be in touch sometime soon, as soon as you've picked up Pritchett and his mob."

I had to get out to where I'd be protected. Correction, I had to get out to where and *when* I'd be protected.

****

Dear Member,
Road rage? Phone rage? Twitter rage?
Rage rage?
Keep your head while those around you are losing theirs.
Cannaboids are now legally available to medical practitioners, in gum, patch, inhaler, implant, suppository, cordial and condom formats.
Order yours now at trade prices from Nostrelax©

****

27 STOCKS AND CHAIRS

If there had been any eggs in mid-air they would have exploded. Any quiches hovering about would have got very hot. At least I think so. They use microwaves to send phone messages, don't they? Are they the same ones we cook with? Des would know.

In any case, as I drove, I sent those microwaves into aerobatics, warning people of the danger of attack, letting them in on the news about Louie. Neither Des, nor Phil, nor Rita answered, so I left messages.

I had to call Angela Greensands about the shares. Surely Louie was just bullshitting me. He'd been drugged or poisoned or something, and wanted one last joke at my expense before he shuffled off to wherever financial directors end up. A nouveau-riche corner of hell.

When I got through to Ms G, she didn't sound at all like someone who would help Louie to fiddle me out of a large dollop of my promised wealth. She sounded worried to hear that Louie had been topped like Beano. Worried for my safety, too. She agreed that it was a good idea to get out of town for a bit, and looked forward to seeing me on Monday. She also promised me that I'd have no police problems. Zero panic, zero stress. She is so fucking cool, that woman. When will I pick up the knack?

Her last words before ringing off were to assure me that our project was categorically, in no way, under any threat of cancellation or postponement whatever. From another politician I'd have taken that as meaning it was all off. But her word was good enough for me.

First stop, Claudine's shoot. I called to check that she was there.

"You come ear?" she asked, without real curiosity.

"Yes. Ms Greensands wants to meet you. I said I'd take you to see her today, if that's all right."

"Ah, OK."

"Er, Claudine?"

"Yes?"

"Did, Louie, er, give you any shares?" Angela Greensands I could trust, Claudine was much harder to read.

"Chairs?"

"No, *shares*. You know, stock."

"Stock? Like glue?"

"No, stocks and shares, the stock market, Wall Street, stock fucking options."

The phone went dead. I didn't blame her, really. I was starting to get hysterical.

The phone rang again, almost immediately. It was Armlock. Shit, should I answer it, I wondered. Yes, I replied to myself, I had to know what was going on.

"One thing I'd like to know, Mr Bridges, is why these victims call you just before they die. It's annoying, don't you think? Can you explain that?"

No I can't and I just wish people wouldn't phone me at such a delicate time.

"What happened to him?" Armlock asked me.

"Looked as though he'd been drugged, or force-fed booze or something. He was raving. Probably made to drink ten bottles of communion wine."

"You're being flippant again."

"For Christ's sake, Inspector. Arrest Pritchett. You heard one of his lot threaten me on the phone. Why don't you raid his offices? And please put a guard on my wife and all my remaining colleagues right away. My wife's at home alone and you've got to protect her."

"You know, you've actually convinced me, Mr Bridges," she said when I ran out of breath. "I really believe you're sincere about this whole business."

"Thanks a bunch, Inspector, but you're a bit late getting there."

"I think you're being messed about just as much as me. So why don't we help each other? Why don't you come and tell me everything you know, exactly what you saw this time." The last two words were spoken as if I'd been doing nothing except find corpses all my life.

"No chance. You think I'm stupid? You're going to arrest me if I come anywhere near your station." I was actually apologizing to her for not letting myself be wrongfully arrested.

"No, I won't arrest you. To be quite honest I need your help. I admit that at first I thought you were the killer. Hoped you were the killer."

"Very professional."

"But now I'm fairly sure you're just as much a victim as me. But not in the way you think. And I need your help to find out exactly why."

"Sorry, don't believe you."

"OK. All right. But tell me one thing – did your friend Louie, actually say, explicitly, who did this to him?"

"Yes."

"He actually said it?"

"Yes." Well, as good as.

"In that case, I'm sure he was either lying or wrong. But I do know it wasn't you, and it wasn't any kind of religious fanatic."

"How can you say that?"

"Listen, Mr Bridges. I need you to help me find out what's really going on."

Weird – I could almost feel sincerity in there somewhere, but this had to be a police trick. There was a silence on the line, then an uncharacteristic, almost embarrassed, Armlock voice.

"Will you please come in and talk to me? I promise you won't be arrested."

"No."

"I can send you a written promise if you want."

"No."

"Right, then there's only one way to convince you. I suggest you have a word with Junior Minister Greensands. She's covering something up. Apparently she was the one who called off my investigation. There can only be one reason why she's been keeping you in the dark about Beano, and that's –"

I switched off the phone. I'm not that thick. The Inspector and her confusion tactics. Leading me on, playing for time till she could get a fix on my call and send one of her cars screaming round the corner at me.

There was one more call I had to make before going to fetch Claudine. I used my old work phone for this one.

"Hello."

"Granola, it's me –"

"You've reached Granola's voicemail, please leave a message after the tone."

"Shit." I waited for what seemed like several hours for the beep to end. "Listen. Louie's dead. Killed at his house. I've got to get away till Monday. Please get out of the flat. Go to your Mum's or something. Armlock's refusing to protect us. Just grab some knickers and go. Sorry if I'm screwing things up. And for missing lunch, of course."

I felt I really ought to add something like "darling" or "I love you", but it would have felt hypocritical. I never say "darling" or "I love you" these days. So in the end, after a little sigh, I added, "I love you, darling" and pulled the battery out of the phone.

****

Dear Member,
Worried about prescription budgets? Feeling pressure to prescribe only generic drugs?
Nostrum has the answer.
Cut your costs at a stroke with our new range of own-brand generic drugs.
Details here: NostrumGenerics

****

28 Air Freshener

I dumped my car – too conspicuous –, hired a bland but ballsy businessman's saloon, and parked it a couple of hundred yards away from the studio where Claudine was filming. I walked as calmly as I could down the street. No one looked at me twice. They were all concentrating on their own struggle with the chilled drizzle that was sweeping down from the North Pole.

"Bernie." Mike wasn't pleased to see me. I wasn't pleased to see him, either. Or to have to look at him, anyway. I swear he was wearing the same check shirt he'd had on five days before. The collar looked crusted with grease. Carbuncles were probably flowering in its shadow.

Claudine was sitting against a white backdrop under a blaze of lights. She was holding different expressions for three or four seconds each. Scorn was not among them. The white coat and thick framed specs looked good on her. She didn't notice my entrance. She was frowning thoughtfully at the lens, as if musing on some tricky clause in the Hippocratic oath.

"Got much left to do, Mike?" I asked.

"No, she's a real pro," he said. Pro, I could have told him, has more than one meaning.

"I'm going to have to borrow her for a while, I'm afraid. Can you finish up in ten minutes?"

"No way!" Mike was even more pissed off now, but then who wouldn't want to spend the rest of their Saturday staring at Claudine?

"What have you got so far?"

"She's done most of your key phrases and emotions. Now we're doing some nodding, thinking, taking notes, a variety of smiles. Des wants real footage for the close-ups."

I looked across at Claudine, who was smiling with varying degrees of intensity at the camera. What was it they said about Marilyn Monroe? The camera was in love with her. With Claudine, it seemed to be the opposite. Her smile was saying that this was the most handsome, witty and intelligent camera she'd ever met. All lies, of course. She was just using it.

"Sorry, Bernie, am I boring you?"

Mike had carried on talking.

"No, no, just quietly impressed, Mike." The uppity bastard. "It's OK. I'm sure you've got plenty. Just give it all to Des, we're going to lipsynch her, anyway."

He shook his unsexy head. "I can't believe you'd take risks with the biggest contract the company's ever had."

"Biggest yet, Mike, biggest yet." He was getting far too cocky. I wondered what he'd think when he found out, probably in just a few minutes' time, that I'd been chatting with him after leaving Louie dead on his settee. He'd assume I was a psycho. Might just make him a bit more respectful.

Claudine took off her white coat and glasses and came over.

"So we go to the Marina now?" she asked.

"Yeah."

"OK, I go home to change."

"Home?" I said. "No." Now that I'd switched cars, I wanted to get out of town as soon as vehicularly possible.

"You want me to go to the Marina like this?" She was in a simple white t-shirt and dark-blue jogging pants.

"You look great." It was true. In fact, no one would care if she turned up in a nylon overall, curlers and holed support stockings. They'd assume it was all by Jean-Paul Gaultier.

"Don't be stupid," she said. She picked up a priceless-looking overcoat and flounced out, giving me the opportunity, so rare outside of American sitcoms, of doing a "women? huh!" shrug to Mike as I exited. It felt good.

Half an hour later, sitting in the car outside her building, I wasn't so sure that changing was a great idea. Where was bloody Claudine? No time for a tenth coat of lipstick. Two old women were eyeing me up from their front steps. I should have waited out of sight.

Claudine came out at last, and the ladies stopped yakking for a moment to gaze at her. She was in violet jacket and steering-wheel cover, with black gloves and stockings and a black woven shawl thing around her neck. At first glance she looked sensibly dressed for cold weather, but as she moved I saw that the tops of her breasts were naked to the air. She looked hell of a lot better in these clothes than she had while I'd been humping her the previous night.

She got in, slipping her long legs carefully under the dashboard.

"You ave a meeting with a Minister and you ave no cravat?" There was a moment's doubt in her eyes. True, I wasn't looking my best.

"I'm going to buy a new shirt and tie on the way. You can help me choose," I improvised. "You look fantastic, though. They'll make you Minister of Love." OK, corny as hell, but I guessed that foreigners can't judge corn so finely. I bubbled on optimistically as if there were no hitches between us and the meeting. How the hell was I going to spring the unpleasant truth on her so that she wouldn't immediately demand to be taken home? She was very likely to be displeased about the fact that we were to spend the rest of the weekend together. She was bound to be travelling spareless. What girl willingly stays overnight anywhere without a spare pair of knickers?

My bigger fear, though, was that she might think of me as some sort of jinx when she learned about Louie's terminal drink problem. Beautiful girls have an uncanny sense of whose elbow not to be seen on.

For the moment I found a sunny radio station, smiled companionably, and drove. The car filled with something warm and Latin. The rain had eased and the sky was getting brighter, sending the houses ahead into dramatic silhouette.

Despite all her protestations, I reckoned Armlock might make one final attempt to stop me leaving town – at the main motorway intersection, maybe. I approached it slowly, looking for parked cars or flashing lights. Nothing. I accelerated away into open country, and instantly got an eyeball shock. Frost! The vegetation was glinting faintly in the low-slung sun. The air must be bitter out here, away from the street lights and the heated houses.

The road embankments were crisp with frosted ferns, brittle leaves and sugar-coated plastic bags and bottles. The traffic was light and smooth-flowing. When we emerged into flatter country, the heathland suddenly flashed at us, its dull beiges, greens and purples prickled with melting ice. The sun was dragging itself higher but keeping its distance. It felt like dawn but so much had already happened.

It was time to fake a phone call.

I held my battery-less work mobile to my right ear (as far as possible from Claudine) and said simply,

"The Marina?" I waited a few seconds then spoke again. "Good morning, this is Mr Bridges from Coma speaking, I'm calling to confirm my arrival to see Ms Greensands in approximately half an hour. That's right, myself and the actress who will be our online doctor. Pardon? Yes, OK, I'll hold ... Hello. What? My God. No, surely not. My God. No, we heard nothing before setting off. What do the police say? ... I see. Yes, right, well I'll do that. Please call me if you get more information. Thank you. Goodbye."

I put the phone back in my pocket. I breathed deeply, shook my head in incomprehension, and appeared to forget Claudine's presence. I said a couple more my Gods. When I turned to her, her white face was intent, her big eyes unblinking with concern. She believed something pretty bad was up. I looked back to the road.

"I don't believe it," I groaned. "Louie has just been found murdered." It sounded hell of a coincidence, me picking her up as the body was being found. But so what, I was desperate.

She said something expletive in French with lots of spitting and a fair dose of "merde" in it.

"They know whazz done it?" she asked.

"They're pretty sure it was the people who mounted that moral crusade against us. The godsquad."

"The religious?"

"Yes, apparently Ms Greensands is worried for my safety." I enjoyed saying that. "She's gone into town to supervise the police enquiry. Her assistant says we mustn't try to head for the Marina yet. It might be dangerous."

"But it will be the safest place!"

"Dangerous for both of us," I added.

"No one wants to kill me."

"Are you sure?"

"I am not morally dangerous. I am only beautiful." She had a point.

"But the godsquad might want to kill you *because* you're beautiful."

"No."

"No one's made threatening phone calls to you?"

"No. When can we go?"

"To the Marina? Not till they tell us it's safe. Later on today probably, they're going to call back. Till then we'll find a place to hide. I know somewhere."

"Can't we go back to town?"

"No, Ms Greensands expressly forbade it."

"She what?"

"She said we mustn't go back."

"We must stay hiding all day?"

"I have to protect both of us."

Claudine sighed and looked across at me as if it was all my fault. Which I suppose it was.

Wildwoods, a ten thousand square metre wild-west racoon-hunter's cabin in the middle of an English field, yielded a nice varied trolleyful – some warm clothes for myself, a tasteful tie and, of course, some lady's knickers – three miniscule thongs in black, white and cream. Plus a full spectrum of condoms (the penis-only variety).

Unrealistic, I know, but as Baden-Powell no doubt used to tell his scouts, "always have a packet on you".

Claudine didn't know how generous I was being with my purchases. She had opted to stay in the car to make some calls. For the last few miles to my hiding place, she sat mute in her own thoughts, looking inscrutably across at me every now and then.

I tuned in to the local radio news to see if Louie's death would be reported. Little danger of Claudine understanding – the news is far too brief and rapid-fire. There was a piece about some cocker spaniels, fed on Laddie real steak chunks, who'd saved their owner from a fire that had destroyed a row of five houses and killed seven people. A Laddie dog is a friend for life, the reporter concluded. There was a murder in a street not guarded by the Watch. May the Watch watch over you. Nothing about Louie yet. Pritchett's mob obviously forgot to get corporate sponsorship for their killing spree.

We branched off at the next motorway exit. It almost felt like coming home.

"Ya see the Jews, them that were the religious people of the day, they said unto the Lowered, they said wah. Wah! Wah should we follow thou? What you gone give us? N He says to them, you must payer respects to me. You must *payer* respects. Plant the seed an you will receive tinfold a what you give now."

"Why don't you call your Madame Greensands? Maybe it is time," Claudine moaned from the armchair. Her first words for over an hour.

"She said she'd call me as soon as she had any news, remember?"

"No." She returned to her sulking.

"The Lowered has made this promise – give unto me now and you will profit tinfold. Git ta that phone! Don't let the devil stop ya! Away Satan, away! I will not let you stop my people trustin in the Lowered! You kent stop them! Git ta that phone an plant the seed! You got ta payer respects to Jee-suss!"

This was GTV, of course. First time I'd given it a decent watch. Pretty clever viewing it was too, massaging away at all those fears and fragilities. Maybe Coma should do the same, I thought. Get some doctors on TV, haranguing Joe Public to pledge money, blood, organs.

It wasn't too late. I could phone in to GTV and say I'd been touched by the Lowered and wanted to beg forgiveness for my sins against dear brother Pritchett. I'd ask to speak to someone in power and they could have my tearful confession on the air in two minutes flat. My career would be reborn. I was honestly tempted.

"When will you phone her, then?"

"She'll phone *me*."

"When?"

"I don't *know*."

Our time in the love-nest wasn't going well. Claudine had seemed pleased enough with the village and the Extra Arms when we arrived, and mildly impressed with the delighted welcome I'd received. I'd exchanged a few words with the staring locals and promised the ogling landlord copious servings of tourist cash in the very near future. Claudine followed me passively enough up to the double room, perhaps under the impression that it was just a resting-place for the afternoon. But she wasn't at all pleased with the knickers, or their implication, and when she saw my rainbow of rubbers, she threw a major fit. She'd done all that already, she said. She ranted at me in French for a while and then went all huffy and silent.

"Please call her now, I am very impatient." Her tone was almost conciliatory.

"Oh God, all right."

In fact it was a good idea. Armlock's spiel about pumping Angela Greensands for information on the killings was getting to me. For once, the Inspector had sounded – how shall I put it? – *honest*. I got up off the bed.

"Where you going?"

"To the car."

"Why? You ave your phone."

"I prefer to go and ring from a different place. Harder to trace. I'll be back in half an hour."

I threw her the remote control. She grunted and changed channel. I drove a few miles across country and parked up in a lay-by under dripping pines. There were no other cars about. I switched my phone on and called Angela Greensands. I got through.

"No, I have no more information than what the police have just told me," she said. "But I do know that you are no longer a suspect in either of the enquiries."

"So I'm officially innocent?" I asked.

"Oh, yes."

"Excellent, thank you. And have the police made any arrests? You know, amongst the fundamentalist groups?"

"No."

"But –"

"No arrests have been made."

"Right. OK. Inspector Armlock mentioned you called off the investigation about Beano. Why exactly did you – ?"

"I have no idea why she would think that. I don't give orders to the police. I can only assure you that your movements are free. Where are you staying?"

"With friends." Why did I lie?

"OK."

"So I can carry on preparing for Monday with an easy mind."

"Yes, see you on Monday. Thank you for calling."

"Sorry to have disturbed you again."

"Don't mention it. Goodbye."

"Goodbye."

For the first time I didn't believe her. Someone in her position would have been told about those tests. She wasn't being straight with me. Shit.

"Claudine – it's me. I'm on my way back to the hotel."

"Bridges? Exploiter of women, mocker of God."

"Pritchett? I know it's you. The cops are after you."

"You will die."

"Phil? Is that you? Stop fucking about. Give Claudine her phone back. How did you find us? Did she call you?"

"You will die."

The voice – the same badly disguised one that had threatened me before – rang off and I was back at the inn in two minutes flat, kitted out in my anti-mugger ninja gear, creeping along the first-floor landing, then listening at the door. Nothing except the TV babbling softly. If Pigshit was in there, I'd stuff a stun grenade in his mouth. If it was Phil, I'd give him a dose of paralysis gas, just to wipe the smile off his face. And if Claudine was lying in bed re-enacting her death scene in the first "See Models Die" movie, I had decided to piss my pants and go comatose.

I burst in the room, giving a quick shot of gas behind the door. There was no one skulking there. Claudine was lying on the bed laughing manically. No, it wasn't that sort of gas. She looked me up and down, from my masked head, past my tensed nozzle-finger, to my bent, ready-to-spring legs, and carried on gurgling with mirth.

"Where is he?" I muffled, too on edge to react to her mockery or the fact that she was alone and alive.

"Who?"

"Whoever answered the phone."

"Pardon? Come here, and take off your mask – I cannot hear." She was still laughing gently, her shawl had uncovered large areas of her chest, her skirt had ridden even higher up her legs. I put the spray on the bed, pulled my mask down, and then lay on the floor while she took the car key and some money from my pocket.

"You know funny thing? Really, I know that shares are not chairs." She stood over me and smiled.

She let this information sink in. Not that it sank very far into my paralysed brain. Her finger was still on the button of the paralysis spray she'd used on me. *My* spray, for God's sake.

"I have about fifteen per cent share in your company now," she said. Her smile was almost maternal. "Some of the shares that you sold. And Beano gave me some shares to fuck him. Louie suggested it. He was very intelligent man, Louie. Phil, he is good businessman, too. He told me how much you will pay to fuck me. He was right! You give *anything* for a fuck!" She grimaced. "It was quite unpleasant."

Having got this petty insult off her ample chest, she walked towards the door, giving me a fleeting but unconsoling look up her skirt. Her parting shot at me was a taunting, throaty, deep-voiced "Brrridges, exploiter. You will die."

"Way," I managed to say. She frowned, apparently perturbed by the fact that my tongue was not as paralysed as the rest of me. "Way jessa mini."

She walked back towards me.

"Phone messes ..."

"Messes?" She frowned again, bemused but dangerous, like the velociraptors in *Jurassic Park* as their victims beg pointlessly for mercy.

"Messes. 'Bridge, ex-ploy a women, you die' ..."

"Ah, *message*." She nodded.

"Why leave messes? You wi GTV?"

It was plausible. What about Joan of Arc? A sexy French girl with a divine mission to kill Englishmen.

Claudine laughed. "No, I am with nobody. It is just me and my body, working together."

"You kill Louie?"

At this, she shook her head and did a really French thing, puffing sharply as if to blow a fly off her croissant. It was pure scorn. For me, my question, for Louie? Who knew.

She gave another long squirt of gas into the room as if it was air freshener, and left me to it. I watched the droplets floating down towards me, into my open mouth.

Good thing about that gas, it's humane stuff. You don't think, shit I can't move a single muscle, I might suffocate, or my heart might conk out, or I might never regain the use of my limbs. You don't ask yourself, when's she coming back to crack my gullet, or has she already done it? Or is this death? First the loss of feeling and movement, then the freedom from worry, and finally (when?) nothingness. You don't think any of that.

You're not mad at yourself for failing to cotton on to the fact that she was the killer all along. It was so obvious! Killing Beano, the first one of us to fuck her, by making him spit black gunk like she had done in the supposedly degrading film. He'd tried to phone and warn me, poor lad. And maybe it wasn't "god" Louie was trying to say – it was "Claudine".

But why would she kill Louie if he was helping her get rich? To cover her tracks? That seemed ungrateful to say the least.

And that "Bridges exploiter" voice on the phone. She *could* do an English accent when she wanted. Maybe she wasn't even French.

But you're blissfully indifferent to such complications when you've been gassed. You're in an observer mode. You see and hear things happening, but your lethargic brain demands no action on them. It even provides a little entertainment. I watched a short film, of my mind's invention, that in happier times might have made a decent thirty-second ad for some health drink. It was all about truth versus appearances.

A Mediterranean lakeside in an evening storm. Lightning was flashing, rain was slashing down from black clouds. A handsome, bearded man in a kaftan climbed out of a small boat and waded ashore, then turned round to see his companions still cowering in the bilges.

"Come on, get out," he said.

"We can't, we'd drown!" the terrified companions whimpered.

"Look, the water's only an inch deep," the first man insisted, but the others wouldn't budge. "It's only an inch deep, I tell you," he said, wading back towards them.

But they only screamed, “he’s walking on water!” and refused to budge.

“Look!” He jumped up and down in the water, he knelt down and picked up handfuls of sand, he did a cartwheel and four or five press-ups, but the other men simply stared in awe from their rain-swamped boat.

“Well, you can bloody well stay there then. I’m going for a carrot juice,” the first man said and splashed off towards the distant lights.

I followed him.

****

j
reckon b killed beano and louie?
m

m
dunno. but if he comes round my place i'm not letting him in.
j

****

29 MORE LIGHT!

I was being carried towards, or maybe behind, a source of white light, and in the rushing blackness around me there were flashes of all colours rising and swooping in no apparent order or pattern. I closed my eyes but I could still see the lights fizzing on my retina. When I opened them again, I was speeding towards more colours and more whiteness but it wasn't fast enough.

"Go faster," I said.

"If I go any faster I'll hit a fucking tree."

I'd phoned Armlock as soon as my mouth and legs had started to work again. The Inspector was not pleased to hear from me. She cut all my paralysed ramblings short by reminding me that the case had been officially closed from up top, as I "knew only too well", and that because I'd refused to help her, she personally never wanted to see me again except as a victim in some fatal road accident. When I tried to mention that I now believed it was Claudine and not the godsquad who was going to kill us all, she told me to piss off and hung up.

I left messages for Des, Phil and Granola about the model murderess. And I got through to Mona, who sounded scared. As if Claudine was standing over her with fingers flexing, ready to paralyse then smother her, or fill her up with Cognac, or whatever method she was going to use next.

"It's OK, Mona, we know it's Claudine, the Inspector is on her way to your place right now," I lied to scare off her listening attacker. "And I'm coming over straight away, OK?" She didn't answer.

Back at the village pub, I'd had no time to explain things to the locals or the landlord, neither my curious entrance just previously (when I'd sprinted through the bar with my mask and spray and combat nerves), nor my delirious stumble-headedness as I fell back downstairs an hour or so later. I didn't even attempt to tell them why I looked half-dead, even though they all stared at me as if I was in danger of exploding. I simply settled the bill and offered to pay the cook a lot of money to drive me to Mona's place. The cook was tall and strong with leather jeans and a fast, ugly car.

We were still out on the motorway. It was dark. I was groggy.

"What are all those lights?" I asked him.

"Bonfire night, a course. Fireworks."

"Oh yes."

Here and there on the satellite estates, bonfires were blazing. People stood in silhouetted waves around them, moving back and forward with the gusts of sparks.

"Break the speed limit now, please," I told him. "If you get a ticket, I'll repay it, double."

We didn't talk much after that. I saw him looking over at me, as if he was trying to relate my twitching half-paralysis to my money, my hurry and the gorgeous woman who'd dumped me in his pub. He was going to tell his mates all about this one.

Meanwhile I was concentrating on getting my thinking muscles back into shape. I couldn't figure out why Claudine had gassed me and run. Surely the logical thing would have been to hang on in there with me until she was out at the Marina and winning herself new, more influential, fans. Her buggering off like that didn't make sense. Nor did her failure to kill me. Wasn't I worth killing?

I told the cook to come inside Mona's house with me. A witness at last, and a pair of fists. He wasn't keen.

"Listen, we said fifty to town, OK? Nothing about going into a house. Your house is it?" My insistence was making him nervous.

"Come in with me or you won't get a penny. Now." It does not do to let the Watch see two men sitting in a strange car, especially not a car with a three-metre aerial, wide chrome wheels, flames painted along the doors and "My Other Vehicle's A Mig Fighter Bomber – I Only Use This For Ground-to-Air Attacks" announced in three-inch letters across the bonnet. The Watch enjoy denting that sort of car, and the people in it.

"Ooze in there anyway?"

"Just a woman. Or two." Put like that, I suppose it sounded fun.

"Tenner extra," he said. As if to tell me there was no time to argue, a firework came screaming out of a nearby back garden and exploded deafeningly just overhead. This first detonation gave rise to two new blobs of light, one blue, one red. The two then unleashed howling jets of green tracer at each other before the red one disintegrated in a ball of white smoke and the blue one whistled its victory. The cook cheered.

"Eat-seeking," he explained. "Brilliant."

Amazingly, my key to Mona's place still worked. It was touching somehow that she hadn't changed the locks in all this time. I left the door open in case we needed to beat a rapid retreat.

There was light inside the house, and music from upstairs. At least it wasn't the silence I'd found chez Beano and Louie.

"Let's look around downstairs," I said loudly, but began to sneak up the stairs, even remembering which creaking steps to avoid.

My Native-American hunting technique was proved wanting, though, when a buffalo came pounding up behind me. The cook. If there had been any decibel-seeking fireworks about, he would have been zapped through the roof by every rocket from here to London.

Outside there were more firework flashes and a faint whooshing explosion.

At the top of the stairs I stopped to listen for creakings or door-handle turnings or the micro-fart of Claudine giving the paralyser spray a test squirt. Nothing except faint music from the bedroom and the bomp-BOMP-bomp of the cook's last steps. He was now looking intrigued. Maybe he hoped we were going to storm in on some orgy scene. I went towards the music.

Taking in a deep breath and listening to my heart doing one final paradiddle, I jumped into the centre of the bedroom.

The first things I saw were Mona's terrified eyes. The room smelt alcoholic, just as Louie's place had done. Beside the bed on the bare polished floorboards was a dead whisky bottle.

A dark duvet was pulled up under her chin. She was breathing like an empty Fairy Liquid bottle. But she *was* breathing, and alone. I leapt at her and started giving her the kiss of life. For her, I was willing to make an exception.

"Fucking hell," the cook said behind me. "You're paying me just to watch this?"

There were footsteps down in the hall, but to my surprise they started coming up instead of running away. Claudine was coming back for the kill. I took a breather from blowing air into Mona and whispered to the cook,

"If a beautiful woman comes through that door, thump her."

"You what?" He looked confused to say the least.

"Punch her back down the stairs. Police!" I shouted at the phone. "Emergency!"

The cook looked around for some way out. Poor guy, I had no time to explain everything.

"No, stay there and flatten her," I ordered. "Ten quid a punch, twenty if you break her nose."

The cook whimpered. The steps were slow but getting louder and heavier.

Mona managed to whisper a couple of words as I held her head between my hands.

"Ker ..."

"It's OK, Mona, I understand. Claudine. Yes, we know. We'll get her, don't worry."

I was just congratulating myself on the success of my mouth-to-mouth when an armed, uniformed officer slammed the cook face-first against the bedroom wall. A policewoman leapt in, legs bent, and pointed a pistol at my face. My hands lost no time in flapping towards the ceiling. My sphincter felt dangerously loose.

"Don't shoot, we've saved her!" I pleaded.

There were a few seconds of silence, apart from everyone's hyper-tense breathing, as the new arrivals tried to work out what was happening.

"Hello. Police emergency," the phone announced. "Your call is in a queue. It will be answered in ... TEN ... minutes. Please hold, your call is very important to us."

"I was just calling you lot," I said, nodding down towards the phone. "And we've got to get an ambulance for Mona here. She's alive!" I must have looked genuinely pleased, because the policewoman pointing her pistol at me seemed to relax a little. I kept my hands high and motionless as her eyes flicked down towards Mona, who was groaning softly.

"We saw the blazing car outside," the policewoman replied, "and the front door was open."

"Blazing?" The cook struggled to get free but his arm was twisted further up his back, his cheek pressed harder against the wallpaper. It was true, that last firework had seemed to glow with particular intensity. "That's my bloody car!" the cook moaned. He risked his bones to turn and tell me I'd "fucking pay for it".

"He's brain-damaged," the cook told the man breaking his elbow. He meant me. "He said he'd give me fifty quid to punch whoever came through the door." I'd only offered twenty, but I didn't correct him. I was more interested in the pistol and the finger controlling it, which now seemed to tense again for some reason.

"You – what's your name?" she asked me. I told her.

"Bridges?" she repeated. I nodded helpfully. She spoke to her lapel. "Seven-seven-oh here at the site of a burning car in Kitchener Road. Request immediate aid and one ambulance. Have apprehended two intruders. You know, Pete," she was speaking to her mate now, "I reckon they were all wrong. I reckon this Bridges is the murderer after all."

"No!"

"Yeah, he was trying to suffocate her, I saw him," the cook chipped in.

Betrayed, exhausted, demoralized by all these unfounded accusations, my poor little sphincter finally gave out.

****

Dear Member,

How often do you regret taking your phone to the marina, golf course or a dinner party? And why is it that so many of your patients pick mealtimes to call you?

It's ironic: we're told we've never lived longer or been so healthy, but somehow your patients haven't got the message.

This is mainly because certain parts of the human body age less gracefully than others. The bladder, prostate, vital organs, brain and major joints are all potential sources of pain or embarrassment to older members of your patient base. And they'll bring their cares to you, no matter the time of day or night.

That's why we at Nostrum have created a one-stop body shop for the over-70s. Send them to us for a once-a-year once-over and we provide a fully guaranteed 12-month breakdown prognosis. Life expectancy, organ-failure predictions, and all vaccination and prescription needs for the year ahead.

As you go for that 20-foot putt, you want your mind to be free.

Nostrum/PeopleMaintenance

****

30 The Bogie Men

I guess I'll get used to the high-wire fences, the reinforced glass and the thick-bellied guards. But the wind was one thing I hadn't bargained for. It was whipping between the anonymous white buildings, it was loaded with leaves, sand and the occasional gust-riding gull.

"You'll have to leave your non-essential things here," the clerk told me through thick glass after I'd passed the first X-ray frisk.

"And wear this at all times," someone else said, clipping a bar-coded photo-badge on my collar.

I was led further in. Security doors opened and shut, guards in Perspex cubicles nodded at the hygiene-masked attendants accompanying me, corridors and staircases curved off left and right, but we kept straight on, going deeper in. I never had to wait an instant for automatic doors to open. Hands were at my elbow to ease me onwards if I faltered to look out a window. The corridors were all undistractingly white.

Prison.

Of course not.

It'll take more than a pistol in the face to put Bernie Bridges off his aim. This is the Marina, this is Monday morning. I no longer need to freak out about who's been killing whom. I'm officially safe.

How did I do it? Easy. I have innocence and high-up protection on my side.

First, though, I'd had a spot of luck – the cop with the gun aimed at my skull discovered some human genes in her distant ancestry. She let me shower in Mona's bathroom and I was clean and fresh in a pair of Phil's discarded coffee-planter's trousers by the time two paramedics arrived to start filling Mona with oxygen, and discussing whether to pump her stomach in case of poison. I wasn't sorry to obey their request to leave them to it.

Outside, the Inspector was sitting in her car, apparently oblivious to the blazing hulk just across the road, which was whooshing and hissing as its metal, plastic and oil continued to convert themselves into stinking smoke. When I went over, she ignored me too.

She turned on her rooftop megaphone and bawled at the little gaggle of curious neighbours admiring the cook's street barbecue.

"Piss off home the lot of you!" They didn't move. "As for you ..." She looked at me through her car door window, which was open an inch or so. "If I'm ever allowed ..." She took a couple of breaths, closed her eyes and groaned, "just fuck off and stop wasting my time. Go and see your girlfriend Angela Greensands. Give her a big slobbery kiss from me."

But I didn't fuck off. I had things to say, quite apart from the need to deny any romantic link between myself and a certain politician. I tried to suggest that the Inspector should look for Claudine's fingerprints on Mona's whisky bottle, but my voice wasn't getting through. Now she was on the phone. She pushed a button, and her window rose to shut me out completely.

I tinkered with the idea of smashing the window, grabbing her head and spelling out my evidence with sign language up her nose, but decided against it. Seeing that Inspector Armlock really wasn't going to arrest me, that she didn't even want to talk to me, had dampened my truth fervour. Claudine would be on her way across the Channel by now and I'd done enough chasing after her.

"I demand you drive me home," I told her. "Your lot arrested me, I'm your responsibility."

She took a moment's break from her phone and mouthed, "Bugger off." Which she then did, leaving me alone with an infuriated cook whining sentimentally about the vehicle he'd rebuilt from a single spark plug, a life's work going up in smoke.

"Go and talk to them about it," I suggested. Everyone, including the Inspector, had been aware of the Watch's Land Rover parked up at the corner, its searchlights turned on this centre of activity, its occupants looking very proud of themselves.

The cook ranted on, though, and looked about to declare Blitzkrieg on my face, which was already getting pasty after all the worry of the last 24 hours. This yokel could destroy my whole career with one swing of his soup-ladle fists, I knew. A black eye would be proof that I was mixing with too many lowlifes to enter the higher echelons of the business and political world. In such cases pride is dispensable, a nuisance even, and I began to turn on the sympathy and the apology, which eventually had the desired relaxing effect on the cook's hand muscles. I gave him all my cash and told him to call me as soon as he'd got a price worked out for the car, including compensation for his distress, then left him Louie's phone number.

The Marina is set around a wide amphitheatre, maybe quarter of a mile across and five storeys high, opening on to at least ten concrete jetties. Out by the choppy sea, parties of busy people had their heads down in the wind and were striding between bobbing hydrofoils. I wondered whether next time I wouldn't arrive that way, direct from the pier, five minutes by hydrofoil instead of thirty minutes and two road-blocks by car.

My masked escorts guided me around a long curve of corridor that seemed to lead eventually to the sea. I could smell salt in the air. Strange that one of the most vital strategic buildings in the country wasn't even draught-proof.

We arrived at a major security check – a metal-detector door and a couple of guards, just like at the airport. The guards and their equipment wore very prominent company logos – Firewall Security. Beyond the metal detector, a receptionist was waiting behind yet another sealed window.

"Mr. Bridges? Ah yes, the last representative of Coma," she said. Her jacket revealed that she too was Firewall property.

"You make me sound like a blue whale." I didn't think all and sundry were supposed to know about the sudden vacancies at the company.

"Pardon?"

"The last."

"Oh, yes, no." She blushed and smiled for a moment before getting a grip on her face muscles for the sake of the security cameras. "I meant the last to arrive."

That was definitely wrong, I thought. Des was at home by his computer, and the others were dead, half-dead, or not invited.

There was another strange thing with Des. We worked most of Sunday together from our respective homes, perfecting our plans for the Ministry men. Nothing untoward there – Des was his precise self throughout our rehearsals. He talked me out of dumping Claudine as the model for our lady doctor. It was too late to change, he said, especially after I'd agreed to pay her a small fortune for her services. He was right, and anyway, at least in digital form she's easy to manipulate.

I asked him about Claudine owning some of our shares. He assured me he didn't know anything about that. Which had to be wrong. Des knows *everything*.

I hadn't sleep too well Sunday night, either. Especially not alone. Granola had gone to stay at her folks' place, so I was *really* sleeping alone. I turned the alarms up to eardrum-fracture strength and waited for Claudine to burst into my bedroom. Not as sexy as it sounds.

A brain can only take so much input. Like some comedian said, you shouldn't try to learn too much, because one day your brain will absorb a pointless new fact and shove something essential out. You'll know the capital of Lithuania, but you'll have forgotten how to walk.

That was me, failing to work things out in bed last night.

And that was me now, as I tried to stroll nonchalantly along the Marina corridors. There was too much in my head. Something was bound to give way, and I just hoped it wasn't the power of speech, or my memory of important people's names, or the control of my already weakened bodily functions.

I was shown into a blastingly air-conditioned room and asked to wait. At least here the draught was controlled, and warmer. It wasn't the direct sea breeze. I sat facing a large screen-cum-wall-cum-window, beyond which there were a couple of rows of cinema seats.

There were three computer screens on my side of the window. Everything on one of them would be blown up and projected on to the audience's side of the window. Another screen was already hooked up with Des. I typed him a message (he doesn't like using face-to-face messaging, for obvious reasons).

"Des, Bernie here. You ready?"

"Ready," was the almost instant answer.

"Know who else from Coma is out here at The Marina?" I asked him.

"No, who?"

"That's what I just said."

Des typed nothing in reply.

My audience came in, Angela Greensands leading. Not on my side of the glass, though, the other side. Fifteen or so well-groomed, well-fed men and women were facing me through the glass, smiling pleasantly. We were introduced via intercom. John Sway was there, Gimble was there, together with faces from the Ministry's website and names I'd read on some of the confidential blurb I'd received – all of them Ministry of Development officials or Nostrum people, including a couple of Americans and bilingual-sounding Continentals. No sign of my supposed Coma colleagues. Perhaps it had been a mistake.

Angela G excused herself for the impersonality of the arrangements, explaining that the kind of presentation I'd planned, especially one so quickly prepared, had outstripped the Marina's capacity for the moment. Despite myself, I felt a flush of pleasure at the compliment I only half believed. I realized I only half believed everything she said now.

I smiled at her apology.

"Then I hope this meeting will have contributed something to your *ministry's development*." My little courtly pun went down well, they chortled and nodded approvingly. They saw none of my worries, just the clever bastard they'd been brought to observe.

I stepped up, they sat down. I warned them not to expect too much, as this was only a prototype (even though I hoped they'd be orgasming about its brilliance by the end of the presentation) and began to outline the scheme as I saw it. I stressed that all the details were flexible and could be changed at the touch of a screen.

With this, I touched a screen and the Coma logo was projected across our dividing window. The lights dimmed. While they were getting their eyes used to this, I pulled up an icon labelled "Online Doctors", and opened it, reassured that Des was following every touch of my fingertip from his clifftop den.

I started with an outline of the basic two-tier structure of the service: a general health-awareness zone, and, couched within that, the areas where we would promote the seven-day cure. I spieled for a few minutes about using the public's fears and fragilities to persuade them of the need for the treatment, and then cut short the spooky stuff by introducing my provisional name for the project: The Big Sleep.

"This title is understandable by the majority of people, whether they associate it with the classic film or not."

My voice was sounding good and clear, my memory was perfectly tuned.

"And this, Ladies and Gentlemen, is where the fun begins."

As if to prove me wrong, into my little projection room slinked, or slunk, or slank, Phil and Rita.

Doing my best to ignore them for the moment, I introduced the first segment, and made a famous footballer's face fill the big screen. His computer-animated nose began to twitch and pucker, ready to sneeze or not to sneeze, and my audience breathed with him. This gave me about half a minute to go and squeeze Phil's hand, hug Rita, and whisper,

"I wasn't expecting you."

"Moral fuckin support, mate," Phil whispered back, looking chuffed with himself. Rita's smile was strained.

"Any more news of Mona?" I asked. Rita looked away.

"Don't worry, Bernie, s'all under control." Phil delivered this with an infuriating wise-boy wink, as if he'd just managed to get us all admitted into some very exclusive nightclub. As if Louie, Mona and the events of the weekend were nothing to him. It was flippancy beyond even my scope.

"But what the fuck are you doing here?" was what I wanted to ask. Instead I chose, "Angela invite you along?"

"Yeah. Wanted us to share your big moment."

Bathe in it, more like. Usurp it. That was the whole point about my big moment. It wasn't supposed to be shared by anyone, except maybe Des. I managed to swallow my irritation before the footballer's face exploded in a colourful, slow-mo, splattering sneeze.

"We'll also have ads in the street and in cinemas, with coloured sneeze pellets that will actually be squirted at the public. Biodegradable, naturally." There was appreciative chuckling from the gallery, a loud guffaw from Phil. "To vary things a little, and encourage frequent clicks, we can update the online sneeze sequences. For example ..."

I pulled up Humphrey Bogart's face, and there he was with Bacall, nose to nose from *The Big Sleep*, just about to kiss. After a phrase or two of Bogie's incomprehensible but passionate mumbling, Bacall sneezed a faceful of yuk at him from point-blank range. His computer-manipulated head turned to the audience and gave a look of distinctly un-Bogartesque revulsion. This was the worst thing he'd ever come across, we sensed, worse than a trainload of gay Nazis. No one shoots bogies at Bogie. He sent Bacall away with a seven-day cure pack that had miraculously appeared in his hands. Then, after the obvious cliché caption "seven days later", they came together amidst soaring violins for the consummate sneezeless kiss, under the final title, of course – "you have been watching Bogart and Bacall in *The Big Sleep*." There was actual applause from the other side of the screen.

"There will of course be other couples," I said, and the screen was suddenly full of icons. I love icons. What's the opposite of an iconoclast? An iconophile? An icono-licker? I gave them some classics – DiCaprio and Winslet from *Titanic* (she was admiring the portrait he'd drawn, but then erased it with a spray of mucus), Hagrid literally burying Harry Potter in goo, an English Prince sneezing all over his Princess's wedding veil, all of them brought to life by Des's Druffman magic. Each time the sneeze and the expression of disgust were differently timed and differently pitched. What with the false alarms, you never knew who was going to explode and where the gunk was going to land. Even without the mics, I'd have heard the laughs.

"We don't yet have the rights to those sequences, but any combination is possible. Here are some which definitely *won't* be used." I showed them a few of the risqué satirical couplings Des and I had put together.

Highly unlikely political and sexual embraces (carefully selected to offend no one present) got them clapping and cheering at every new shot.

I was king out there. I was moving billions of pounds-worth of minds around at my whim, I was making myself indispensable and Phil redundant. Perfect, that was the only word for it.

Then something dreadful happened. Something calamitous. No, two things. But they happened so quickly, they seemed to be one and the same event. Some people probably thought it was deliberate.

"And now," I announced, "I'd like to introduce you to the real face of our health project. Our first female online doctor. I think you'll agree she's perfect."

I tapped, more aggressively than was necessary, on Claudine's face and she came up on screen, in a full head-and-shoulders shot, sexy but serious in her white coat, strict pulled-back hairdo and heavy-rimmed specs.

There was a murmur of appreciation from the other side of the glass, which turned into a collective sigh of pleasure as the real thing, the non-digital version of Claudine, appeared in the room beside Phil.

I almost choked with the shock of it, and coughed to clear my throat so that I could call for a guard to arrest her. I shouldn't have done. There was a noise. Two noises.

"Gurk. Flatsh." With a full half-second separating the two.

They could describe a hundred things.

An ostrich laying an egg on someone's head.

A shark spitting out a Kardashian family member's implants, then the rest of him or her.

A small meteorite landing in yogurt.

Well, it was something of all of those.

31 JELLY WOBBLE

I'd been sniffing slightly for a couple of days, but no one, least of all me, had noticed. Everyone sniffs – there's the air conditioning, there's the occasional drugs, the strange smells detected in the street, and the constant worry that your deodorant isn't giving you all-day freshness. Anyway, when I tried to speak, the words got stuck in my throat, I coughed once, briefly, and produced the above.

Gurk for the twitching of tonsils, flatsh for the impact of the asparagus-grey jelly-wobble in the middle of the big window-cum-screen. Right, as fate would have it (you bastard, fate), in Claudine's digital mouth. If it had hit the floor or a wall no one would have seen. I could have wiped it up later. But I was up there in a face-to-face battle with my future, and I coughed gunk in its gob.

At first everyone in over the screening-room was preoccupied with Doctor Claudine's beauty, but when this thing began sliding down the screen, there was an unrestrained general cry of "yerk". They turned to see me red-faced, staring at my creation.

"I think we'll take a break," Angela Greensands said, and the seats began to empty. "Mr Bridges, thank you for your excellent work. Mr Harrap can continue the presentation in a few minutes." I couldn't answer, I was still clearing my throat. "Don't worry, ladies and gentlemen," she announced to her guests, "each room has entirely independent air-conditioning." Then they were gone.

When I could speak again, I asked Phil, who had put on a mask and given one to Rita and Claudine, and as an afterthought to me, what the hell the bitch Claudine was doing here. She was looking so beautiful that it felt almost indecent to be rude to her, but I managed.

"Claudine's on the board. She owns as much of the fuckin company as you do, Bernie. More," Phil said, admiration sparkling in his eyes.

"She tried to kill me," I said. "And Mona. She killed Lou –"

"Don't talk shit, Bernie. She didn't kill no one. Don't chew get it?"

"No I don't. Who *did* kill Bernie and Louie, then? And what about the phone calls?"

"I don't know oo fuckin killed oo. But Claudine was just takin the piss outer you with them calls."

"Taking the piss?"

Claudine's self-satisfied look confirmed it.

"And you were in on the big joke with her?" I accused Phil.

"Just fuck off ome, Bernie," he said, almost kindly. "You done great work settin up the job. I'll take it from ear."

I asked him how he thought he was going to carry on my presentation.

"Now then, what's left?" he said. "There's the patient interface wiv the doctor. The site map to show um that every click leads to a prescription. Then there's your very clever – well done, Bernie boy – suggestion to buy script time in the soaps. A few major characters'll get a cold an take the cure, right? I mean, if I fuck up, Des'll send me the cues."

I listened dumbly to my ideas coming out of someone else's mouth.

"How do you know all that?"

Phil smirked through his mask.

"Don't worry, Bernie, I'll keep um all amused, or Rita can. She'll grab their attention, right Reet?" He reached across to pinch Rita's ribs. She'd been silent since they arrived.

"Rita, how could you do this to Mona?" I asked. Phil's eyes grinned at me and her alternately. She said nothing.

"Mona and me weren't fuckin *married*, Bernie," Phil answered. "It wasn't till deaf us do part like it is with you and Granola."

"But you dumped her in the middle of the night."

"Yeah, bad timin. But it was gnu appen sometime. She was gettin right up my arse. Aven't you eard her whingin on about gettin Coma *back to basics*, and *not compromisin*, and bein wary of –" his voice dropped to a whisper – "you know, all this genetically-modified arsewipe bollocks." He shook his head. "On and on and on and on. Mona's a lot like your Granola, you know. She's got that moralizin streak. You sure know ow to fuckin pick um, Bernie."

"Like you'd never talked to Mona before you screwed her?"

"Just go ome, Bernie." He was almost pleading. "I got a presentation to give."

"You virus." I could almost hear my project crunching to pieces under his feet. I was swaying. "You stuck-up rich-kid germ with your Mockney fucking Cockney accent, you're just one of the old boys, aren't you? You put in a few phone calls to your school chums and get an invite to my fucking party. No respect for real achievers like me, the people with the ideas. I didn't think it still existed. Even today we can still get trodden on by the old privileged class. I thought you'd all in-bred yourselves to death."

"What are you talking about?" This was Rita. She'd been fooled by his act too, remember.

"Didn't you twig him?" I asked her. "Didn't you see through that ridiculous fake accent?"

"There's nothing fake about Phil," she said, and looked as if she was already regretting it.

"Bernie, you're an ill man. Go *ome*." Phil was getting seriously impatient to take centre-stage.

"Is he the one who turned you against me, Rita? What's he been saying about me?"

"No, Bernie." Rita looked genuinely sad. "You did that yourself. You never even tried to get Beano's stuff kept on line. You just caved in to protect yourself." This was Rita's longest speech to me for a week, and she'd got it all wrong.

"That's not fair, Rita, you know very well that Louie decided to delete all our stuff."

"You didn't even go to the meeting where it was decided. Phil was the only one who voted against."

OK, so she had a point.

"And where does shagging him fit in to this great loyalty-to-Beano scenario?" I demanded. "I mean, I've heard of being on the rebound, but you bounced faster than a kangaroo with a basketball up its arse."

"You mate are fuckin *out*." Phil's fist was bunched at me. His eyes wanted the fist to connect with my face. He'd let the anger rise at last, but he still held on to his accent somehow. His vowel-coaches were geniuses.

"He's only shagging you because Claudine wouldn't let him!" I shouted at Rita.

Up to this point, Claudine had simply been observing with her usual ironic detachment. Now, though, she grabbed my arm with surprising strength and thrust me through the doorway into the corridor.

A masked attendant was waiting to whisk me away.

For some reason, I didn't resist. I was exhausted, spent. Maybe it was the shock. That no one seemed interested in arresting Claudine. That Phil had stolen my work, my credit, my art for fuck's sake. It's just not just. And what was so gruesome about a spot of tracheal gunk? I could have wiped it off and carried on my presentation. But now Phil would be the one to get his hand shaken at the end of it all. Or maybe not – maybe they wouldn't let him on the other side of the glass, either, just in case. Maybe all Angela Greensands wanted from me – from us, I mean – was the product, the job, the ideas.

****

****

32 Wheeze

"No thank you, I don't want to take it," I told the doctor, a tall, clean man with a grey suit, white shirt, very white latex hands and a thick surgeon's mask. He had been waiting outside my apartment when I arrived home.

Now I was sitting on my sofa and he was standing by the open window wasting all my heating money. He'd already taken my temperature and stuck one of those lolly sticks down my throat.

"But it's for your own good," he said. "You'll wake up in a week free of any effects. No headache, no blocked-up nose."

"I don't have a headache or a blocked-up nose. Listen." I sniffed for him – my tubes sounded digital-clear.

"But I think you will have very soon. Maybe today."

"OK, I'll take aspirin and vitamin C. That's what you doctors always prescribe for colds."

"Not this time. Take my advice, have the treatment. You'll avoid all the discomfort." He could never have been in advertising. His voice didn't have that combination of homeliness and force necessary for ridding the mind of all doubt. Or maybe it was just the muffling effect of his mask that was reducing his powers of persuasion.

"I can't go to sleep for a week," I told him. "I have work to do, people to contact. Sorry." I tried to make my decision sound final.

"But you were going to promote the treatment, weren't you?" he asked me.

"Yes." I could see him coming a mile off.

"Well surely that means you would be willing to use it?"

I laughed.

"Listen, our company represents quite a few gynecologists, but I wasn't thinking of sprouting ovaries." He gave a polite smile. He was on very flimsy territory and he knew it. Aren't doctors the social group who take the least medication? "Look," I summarized, "it's simple. I can't spare the time to take this stuff, I feel fine, and I don't *have* to take it, do I? No one can force me, can they?"

I wondered if he knew of the campaign to make it law. Probably, seeing as the Marina had sent him, though you can bet he wouldn't take the stuff himself. People in the right places would be exempt, as they are to most other minor laws. Another good reason to get up to the top of the tree.

"No one can force you, it's true," he said, "but I would advise you strongly to take the treatment. You and your wife."

"She's been away since Saturday."

"Well when she comes back home, she should definitely take the treatment too."

"What's in it, anyway?" I asked.

"You don't know?"

"No," I assured him innocently.

"Hmm. Well, there's pollen extract to soothe sore throats, and –"

"Come on doc, you're not selling cough pastilles. What's the active stuff? The knock-out drug, the vaccine?"

He took a white cardboard case out of his bag. First time I'd seen the kit in the flesh. It was a lot smaller than I'd imagined. Square, about big enough to contain a double hamburger.

"That's it?" I asked. "Looks kind of cold and clinical."

"Yes," he said. "The kiddies' version has cartoon characters on it."

"Cute."

It opened up in the same way as a pizza box. Inside was what looked like a silicon breast implant and a sheaf of smaller packs. He pulled out a thin user's manual.

"The drug names won't mean much to you. They're just brands," he said.

"Try me."

"OK. Well, this pouch" – he held up the clear liquid for me to admire – "is a drip containing an anaesthetic called Nostrocaine, similar to that used in operations, Nostrodetoxine to slow down kidney functions, plus nutrients and fluid to stop you dehydrating. This pill is Nostrostop, a constipatory drug to prevent you from messing yourself during the treatment. Those patches contain microchips programmed to release constant doses of Nostrophenyltoloxamine and Nostropropanolamine to combat nose and throat infections. The capsule there is a large dose of an antibiotic called Nostramoxicilline to treat any bronchitis ..."

"What if I haven't got bronchitis? Why give me a massive dose of antibiotics?"

"True, some people do argue that the indiscriminate use of antibiotics could present problems in the future, but –"

"And the vaccine?"

"Ah yes." He held up a large, pink, sexy-looking patch. "Even if you don't use the rest of the pack, we encourage you to take this. It's going to be distributed on its own, too. The patches are really easy to use."

"OK but what is it?"

He looked disappointed that his sales patter hadn't got me clamping the patch to my heart already.

"It's a compound called Nostradamicine-plus, against the strains of influenza and the cold viruses that are expected to cause epidemics this year. It'll be updated every year."

"Genetically re-modified, you mean?"

"Pardon?"

"It's a genetically-modified vaccine, isn't it?" I wished Granola could see me now. She'd forgive me everything.

"I don't think you can genetically modify a vaccine."

"Well, thanks for your advice, doctor, but I'm not going to take any medicine prescribed to me by someone who knows less about it than I do myself." I stood up and walked towards my open window. A breath of fresh air is all very nice, but less so when you're paying to re-heat the stuff. "Excuse me, it's very cold in here."

He moved away from the window and picked up his bag. He gestured towards the seven-day kit. "I'll leave this here in case you change your mind." I shook my head. "Even so, I'm afraid I must ask you at least to stay at home until your cold has run its course."

"Sorry, I can't. I have people to see."

"I must insist," the doctor said, smiling pleasantly. "I have the authority to do so."

"Rubbish!"

He showed me. A Department of Health order, with his name on it, giving him the right to imprison me at home for seven days.

"What is this? Bloody dictatorship?" He looked unswayed by my fluster, so I tried a new tack. "Can't you make an exception? Please?" A spot of outright begging sometimes works, especially the old "I'll-lose-me-job-guv" line. But it didn't move this guy.

"You won't be the only person out of the office. One of your colleagues has accepted the complete treatment."

"Who? Phil Harrap?" It was worth hoping.

"No, er, Miss Moore, Kitchener Road."

"Mona? She's not ill. She was –"

"She'd been in contact with the virus," he interrupted, cool as anything.

"Wasn't her day, was it? Just as she's coming round after an attempt on her life, a team of mad medics knocks her out again because she snuffles. Taking professionalism a bit far, isn't it?" We were face-to-face now, and he clearly didn't like me breathing on him, even if he did have a mask. He grabbed his confinement order and made to leave.

"Are you sure you got Mona's permission? You didn't just pump it straight in her without asking?" The doctor backed off, making me think maybe I was right. "Well I hope you've got her signature somewhere, otherwise as soon as she wakes up she's going to sue you rigid, OK?"

He made for the door. I marched a yard or two behind him. I was determined to slam him goodbye.

"By the way," he turned as he crossed the hall, "I was warned that this problem might arise, so I've asked for backup to make sure you don't leave the building. All right? Call me if you change your mind about the treatment."

My answer was a shuddering door.

First thing to do was get out, of course. To prepare myself for freedom, I swallowed some vitamins and an aspirin or two, washed down with a gargle of lemon vodka.

"Sorry, Sir, no can do." This was a masked Firewall security guy stopping me climbing out the hall window into the back garden five minutes later. I was sitting there with one leg outside, the rest of me still indoors.

"Come on, I just want to nip down to the supermarket for a few cans. I'll bring you back something if you want. What do you fancy? A bottle of whisky to keep you warm?"

"Use a delivery service."

The bastard. His black-gloved hand tapped on my knee as if to tell it to get back inside.

"How much are they paying you to hang around out here in the cold?" I asked.

"You offering to pay my salary for life?" He laughed and tapped on my knee again.

I wandered back upstairs. My apartment windows all face the front. My neighbours opposite weren't in, so I couldn't ask to let a couple of knotted sheets out their back window. I even phoned the Watch and told them the security guy was an imposter and ought to be neutralized, but they didn't believe me.

What's more, they ratted on me, and the security guy came up for a whinge through my door, and then stayed sitting on my landing.

I cracked open a can of beer and had an idea.

I phoned for a kissogram lobster – a great sales gimmick invented by a local Chinese restaurant. At first the security guy wouldn't let the lobster in to lay out the meal, but I promised him I'd keep my mask on and refuse the kiss, and he relented. This time he accepted the bribe.

"Hey lobster," he said when I walked out of the flat in the borrowed costume, "you were female and six inches shorter when you went in."

I was stuck. Paralysed again.

Brain burnout. Frontal lobe exhaustion. But after a couple more cans of beer, I began to feel calmer. Cosy, even. I thought about Granola.

"Hey Granola. How are you? You look fine."

"You're at home, aren't you?"

"Yes, the Marina meeting didn't go quite as planned."

"Why not?"

"Come home, I'll tell you all about it."

"Not yet."

"I've given up the Nostrum job."

"I'm glad to hear it. Even if it is too late."

"Who gives a wobbly."

"A what? Are you feeling OK, Bernie? You look a bit ... funny."

"Knackered, a bit tipsy, too. I'm just going to have a quick lie-down, then I'll sort out all that crap Louie was going on about."

"What's that?"

"Oh, some bullshit about my shares. He was just trying to provoke me."

"Your shares. Yes, I need to talk to you about them."

"Yeah?"

"Yes. I'm really sorry, Bernie, but I have no option. I can't let you go ahead with the vaccine prescriptions. I'm going to pull the plug."

"Plug? What plug?"

"I'm going to blow the whistle on the whole vaccine scam. I don't think they'll trace the leak back to you."

"Plugs, whistles, leaks? Are you turning into a plumber? God I miss you Granola, why don't you come home?"

"I can't. Listen to me, Bernie. You've got to sell all your shares now. Before the buyout."

"Why?"

"I just told you. I'm going to blow the whistle on Louie and Greensands and Nostrum and the lot of them. I mean, I'm all for bending the rules in a good cause, but insider dealing in aid of an illegal cartel to market a GM vaccine is going a little too far."

"You what?" I was hearing the words but not the meaning. Was this what she had meant before, about us speaking but not talking?

"You've got to sell your shares, Bernie. As soon as I put the word out, they're going to sink like a stone."

"I sold half already."

"What? When?"

"Few days ago. Louie made me do it."

She laughed for some reason.

"So that was the director's sale that pushed the price down for them? Those bastards. Well, sell the rest now."

"I can't."

"Why not?"

"Because you were right, Granola, I wouldn't know how to go about it." It felt good to confess. I know it's hip to be hip to trading and investments and stuff, but I haven't got a fucking clue.

"I'll do it for you."

"It's not insider dealing, though?"

"No, it's revenge."

"Thanks, Granola. You're a real ingenu. I love you. Come home, please, things'll be different now, I promise." I meant it, too, I was feeling all snug and homely.

"You know I can't. Apart from anything else, some doctor just called me and told me to stay away."

"He what? The shithead! How did he find you? He's got it all wrong anyway, I'm fine."

"Do you honestly want me to come and risk catching something?"

"I'm fine I tell you. Look!" I opened wide and bent nearer the phone. She got a close-up of my perfect pink tonsils.

"Bernie!" She laughed. First time I'd made her laugh cheerfully for a long time and it was unintentional. I was feeling a bit dizzy, empty-headed, childish. I wanted her to come back and snuggle up to me. I wanted to eat cakes and biscuits, jelly, custard, cuddly things.

"Come home, Granola!"

"I *can't*. You know as well as anyone that this new cold strain is dangerous."

"Cold? Rubbish! Just do what I do. Booze and aspirins. Works a treat. Come home."

"No, sorry, Bernie. There are cough syrups and nasal sprays in the bathroom cabinet. Use them. You'll be OK as long as you don't touch their damn treatment."

"If you really loved me, you'd come home and look after me." I wasn't half-pleased as I sometimes am when we row. Our rows have given me many a chance to storm out and go boozing with Beano, then come home for a reconciliation with her well-shaped body. I was hurt, like a kid. I almost felt like banging my fists on the table, or sobbing. Why? That's not like me at all.

"Look after yourself, Bernie."

"Wait. I shouldn't have said that. Sorry. But you will come home in a week, won't you?"

"If you want me to, yes. Give me a call."

"Great."

I rolled myself in a blanket and felt sleepily glad that things were turning out so well after all.

****

Hi Bernie
Just looking at this invoice from Stanlee Printing for some t-shirts.
Got a couple of questions.
The company? Can't find it listed anywhere. And what unit cost does it represent?
Doesn't tally with quotes you apparently gave to Louie and Ms Greensands.
Get in touch so we can clear payment.
Michelle,
Understone Accounting

Exclusive Coma Member Announcement
Coming soon, Coma's universal online diagnosis service, in partnership with Nostrum and the Department of Health.
Doctors, this is not designed as competition for your own services.
It's simply aimed at keeping the snufflers out of your surgery.
You'll be receiving full details by e-mail within 24 hours.
Preview here.
This means, by the way, that there's never been a better time to buy Coma or Nostrum shares.
Buy here before the news goes public.

****

33 Coma Code

Now I was the one turning into a plumber. I dreamt of tubes and pipes, all being sluiced out by miraculously cool, sparkling spring water. I saw a microscopic SPS (Special Plumbing Services) unit, armed with laser-guided water-cannons, burrowing in to unblock the hundreds of clogged U-bends in my sinuses. A similar team was abseiling down into my larynx to give it a honey massage. It was a sweet dream.

I woke up wet with sweat, I don't know when. I rolled out of my blanket, showered, guzzled syrups and pills (from my bathroom, not the seven-day kit), sniffed vapours and flopped back on the sofa in a clean blanket. The TV was showing an instant-millionaire lottery, then suddenly an interactive teach-yourself-driving game, and then a nude gardening programme (ouch those roses). Whether I snoozed in between or just leaned on the remote control I don't know. My nose was flowing freely. It was clear at first, and very fluid, then thicker and yellower. I lay there immobile till daylight disappeared. I didn't feel hungry.

It sounds bad, but I've known worse. The Marina people over-reacted. So I'd caught a cold. So what?

That's what makes me all the madder at Claudine. She screwed me just a few days ago. She spent ages in my car and in a hotel room with me. How come she didn't catch it? She must be immune. A drug company will probably buy her to start a new disease-free species. I'll post a warning on the web. She's not really immune, I'll tell everyone, she's pasteurized. And poisonous with it.

I'm coughing up plenty of stuff, a red-grey colour, the grimy colour of, say, a squirrel's innards squashed on the tarmac. The cough is tearing my throat to shreds, but at this rate I'll soon have cleared my tubes completely.

I drank a bottle of some sweet, germ-killing cocktail, and slept again. It was night. Then day. It was hard to tell the difference because the lights were on and I couldn't always be bothered to turn and look out the window.

There was another phone message.

"You fucker. I don't care how many fuckin cops you've got guarding you. You're gonna pay for my fucking car or get your fucking face kicked in. You've got till next Saturday to pay up then you're gonna fuckin get it."

The chef, of course. He'd found me. Trouble was, I didn't know or care when Saturday was. Tough.

Time went out of joint. Day and night passed some more, but not always alternately, and what surprised me was that I couldn't even be bothered to ring Granola, Des or anyone. I was completely introspective during my expectorations.

I found myself answering a phone call. A polite one this time.

"Mr Bridges?" A female voice. "DC Martin here. Police. About your stolen watch. I just called to let you know it's been found. Someone took it into a repair shop because it'd stopped ... Mr Bridges? You there?"

I was silently rocking on my sofa. So I wasn't the only wind-up virgin in town.

"Sorry," she went on, "didn't realize I'd got through to voicemail. Anyway, get in touch any time today, Thursday. Er, in case you need to know the time, it's 10.45."

Another cop who thought she had a sense of humour. It must be a virus.

Then, minutes, hours or days later, there was a knock on the door. At first I ignored it, but it wouldn't stop, so I got up and walked into the hall.

"Bog off," I snuffled.

The knocking only got more authoritative.

Against my better judgement, I opened up, and came face-to face with an expanse of metallic grey. At first I thought someone had parked a battleship outside the door, then I noticed that the grey surface had buttons, and, hovering above them, a head.

"Yes?" I inquired helpfully.

In reply, a hand pushed me softly back indoors.

The battleship manoeuvred to starboard and there was Angela Greensands. The big guy was one of her heavies. I now recognized his suit and its underarm bulge.

I stepped forward to say hello and was held firmly in place.

But when I sneezed, the heavy recoiled a yard or two, just as the doctor had done when I'd got too close. My movements were free again. I'd clearly found the male equivalent of telling a rapist you've got your period.

"Come in," was all I could think to say. The heavy swept past me into the living room. Once he was sure there were no terrorists, attack dogs or land mines in there, he motioned for me to follow, then Angela Greensands closed the door and brought up the rear.

"Is there a problem?" I asked her back. She was busy opening a window. Again, just as the doctor had done. Even though, as usual, she'd come protected.

There was one thing about Angela Greensands that maybe I should have mentioned earlier. The truth is that every time I met her at the office, face-to-face, she was wearing a surgeon's mask. At first I thought perhaps everyone out at The Marina wore one, as extra protection. Like the Japanese do. Politicians can't afford the slightest illness, can they, or else government stops. People like her are outside our frame of judgement, I told myself. The first time I saw her full face was on her Facebook page, and then on TV. The only time I saw it in the flesh was out at the Marina, and that was through glass.

She didn't answer my question. She just strode about the room, her mask puffing in and out with every breath. She was looking less cool than on previous occasions. Something, I suspected, was up.

She seemed to be inspecting the apartment, taking in the minutiae of my private life. She looked down at my crumpled blanket and my bottle bank of medicines. She examined my art books, tested a shelf for dust, admired my vintage, year 2000, coloured computer, and tickled its old screentop webcam under the chin (well, it does look a bit like a piglet). She peered close up at one of my dad's framed scrawls (entitled "Nameless Scrawl" as it happens), picked up Granola's antique Chinese teapot and squinted at the signature on the base. She made no comment. I sank down on the sofa and watched, wondering if she was going to steal something, smash something, or just ask for the address of my interior designer.

"I had to come and see," she finally said.

"See what?"

"You."

She walked inscrutably around for a few seconds more. I was too lethargic to wonder why a government minister had felt the need to drop in and say hi. She stopped pacing and seemed to make up her mind about something.

"What I want to know is, did you do it deliberately?" she asked.

"Do what?"

She gazed into me. Through me. I noticed that the heavy, who was also wearing a mask, was posted with his back to the living-room door, blocking my exit. I suddenly began to feel nervous, as if I might soon be needing aspirin for something more than a cold.

"You do know the government's seven-day cure project is on permanent hold?" she asked.

"On hold? No. Been ill. Out of touch." I coughed to prove my point, and to make myself look too fragile to be worth punching.

"And the whole nationwide online diagnosis project is going down the toilet." She waved an arm in a chopping motion. She was angry, something I'd never seen in her before. "There were leaks."

"Leaks?" I hoped I wasn't blushing. I seemed to remember that Granola was the last one to mention that treacherous little word.

"Yes. And it transpires that questions about the vaccine were asked from here." She pointed to my innocent floorboards. "And from inside the Coma offices. Is that a coincidence?"

The heavy seemed to flex his fingers. I put a hand up to my face in anticipation of imminent assault. Coughed again to give myself time to think what to say.

"Well, I did ask questions," I admitted. "But, I mean, I addressed them direct to Nostrum."

She closed her eyes and her mask puffed out. It was several seconds before she spoke again.

"So you," she said calmly, "one of the founders of Coma, who were in the process of selling up to Nostrum and were putting together a project for me, started asking questions on hackable devices about genetically-modified vaccines?"

"Well, yes," I confessed. It wasn't as heinous as she was making out. "I'd heard rumours about a GM vaccine, I just wanted to find out what it was. Nothing more."

"Nothing more!" She laughed. It was a humourless sound, like the grunt a taekwondo black belt gives as she kicks her opponent in the head. "Don't suppose you've heard any *rumours* about me resigning?"

"Resigning?"

I couldn't believe it. People like Angela Greensands don't lose their job. They're untouchable. Though watching her now, striding back and forward, it did look as if some part of her had snapped. Just a small part – a cluster of sweat glands on her forehead, for example, or the tendons that were making her fists bunch and unbunch. Her clothes were the same as when she'd come to the office – blue trouser suit and blinding white shirt – but there were creases where there'd been only silkiness. The aura had faded. There was something different about the bodyguard, too. Yes – the earpiece was gone. He wasn't wired up any more. The Greensands team had been disconnected from the circuits of power.

"When the shit hit the fan," she snarled at me, "the PM disclaimed all knowledge of the project and made a statement declaring that government policy could not be in any way dictated by business interests. What the hell did he think the Ministry was for? Short-sighted, cowardly bastard."

She flexed her fists as if she was about to punch my old webcam in the eye.

"Not that it matters particularly," she shrugged, her anger suddenly spent. "My resigning means there'll be no official inquiry. And Nostrum may have screwed up their brand image in the UK, but they'll be back. There are other countries. There'll be another cold epidemic next year. And it won't take long for people to realize that the vaccine is the only way of facing up to the new breed of germs. If the PM wants to take the blame for letting the cold epidemic get out of hand here, that's up to him. I'm off to the sun till the political storm blows over. Fortunately my ministerial salary wasn't my only source of income." She gave her taekwondo laugh again. "Yours, however, is totally blown."

"How do you mean?"

"Coma's down – hadn't you heard?"

"Des'll fix it."

There was a grim kind of glee in her eyes.

"No, it's dead in the water. Defunct. Coma is an ex-company."

"Can't be." The fever, which had subsided while I was concentrating on what Ms G had to say, suddenly seemed to rise and clog my head again. Granola said she was going to pull the plug on the GM vaccine, but I didn't recall her mentioning she was going to fuck up my whole company. Perhaps I'd dozed off during that bit.

Angela Greensands shook her head almost sympathetically.

"Afraid so," she said. "Unlike my impeccably preserved reputation, Coma's is shot to pieces. I'm very sorry, but it's partly my fault." She shrugged apologetically. She was getting good at this mea culpa lark. "You've been found guilty of association with Nostrum. There'll be no buyout."

"Shit." Though didn't Granola say she was going to sell my shares for me? I couldn't remember.

"Yes, it's a shame." You wouldn't have thought it from the jeering look on what I could see of her face. "Coma was good. Fun, too. I almost felt guilty."

"Guilty?"

She stopped and shot me a look that was chillingly similar to the one Claudine had given me as I was lying paralysed at her feet.

She sat down in an armchair opposite me, and spoke, and her words felt like punches from the heavy's fist. Each one hit me painfully between the eyes, right on the spot where my sinuses were doing their best to drill their way out of my skull.

"Your friend, what's his name again, the first one who died?"

"Beano."

"Right. You know how he died?"

"No. Do you?" I'd guessed the answer to that one.

"I thought it was obvious. The cold bug. The new strain. He must have been particularly susceptible. You said he drank a lot. That could have weakened his immune system. He was one of the first in the country to die."

"What about the black gunk?"

She shrugged ignorance. "Who knows what he'd been eating or drinking?"

So I was right. Probably his rum-and-black addiction.

"And the thumbprints?" I asked.

She held her arms out like a magician proving that he's not hiding any cards. Then she slowly put her hands up to her throat and mimed somebody throttling themselves.

"So they *were* self-inflicted?" I said.

"Yes. That wasn't the direct cause of death, of course. You can't strangle yourself that way, because you'd pass out and loosen your grip. It's the bug. It makes your throat swell internally and you asphyxiate. But in some cases, it seems that the pain makes you squeeze your own throat, so you've got the bruises, and it looks like a strangling. The police have only just found this out."

Despite the addled state of my brain, cogs were finally turning.

"What about Louie? And Mona ...?"

"Yes," she said. "And yourself. You all caught the same bug."

"Me? But –"

"Louie was not a fit man, either. Looked as if he'd never done an hour's exercise in his life. I'm sure we'd have saved him with the seven-day cure, if he'd only asked for it. But then that was your job, to make sure everyone asked." She gave me a look that was the opposite of a mea culpa – a youa culpa, you dickhead. "You and Mona – she's your other colleague, isn't she? – seem to be luckier. It's been a few days, you're young and reasonably fit."

"But I've only got a col –"

"Shame I can't say the same for the old guy who lived downstairs."

"Grockel?"

"There's a note pinned up in the hall. Died on Tuesday, it says. Asks if you want to send flowers."

"Poor old sod. I didn't know. But that means ..." My mental whirrings were beginning to get up speed. "Basically, what you're saying is ..."

"Yes?" She knew what I was going to say, and clearly didn't give a shit. Or rather, she was pleased I was finally going to say it, like I'd learned my lesson.

"You covered all this up."

"Oh, I wouldn't call it –"

"Yes, you covered it all up. This epidemic. Just for profit. Just so you could get your bloody cure and vaccine made compulsory and watch your shares go through the roof." I began to sweat freely at the implications of it.

"No, no, not just for profit ..." She relaxed into the chair and crossed her legs. She almost seemed to be enjoying herself. "Do you know the medical definition of an epidemic? Well, it depends on the disease, but with the flu it can mean as few as 40 new cases a day within a ten-kilometre radius. Peanuts. But what happens when someone actually pronounces the word epidemic? Total panic. A lot like the stock market, really. Ironic, that. Anyway, the speedy introduction of the seven-day cure would have earned me money – there's no shame in that – but it would also have avoided unnecessary panic. The two are not mutually exclusive."

It all sounded very plausible, but there was something wrong somewhere. What I needed was Granola. She'd have seen through this well-argued politico-babble.

"Of course there were those who argued that we should go public on the whole thing straight away," she mused, like a retired general reliving his war. "But the majority of the Nostrum board were afraid that it would provoke a knee-jerk reaction. They wanted to plan their campaign on their own terms. And I must say I was relieved. By the time your friend, er ..."

"Beano."

"Died it was much too late. If we'd gone public then, I would have been crucified for covering up the dangers for as long as I did."

"You might at least have warned the people you were working with on the project. Me, for example."

"Would it have helped?" she asked philosophically. "The most efficient thing you could have done was get the project finished fast, without worrying about GM vaccines or your dead friends. By now the seven-day cure would have been made compulsory, half the population would be snoring peacefully, and you and I would be rich. Why do you think Nostrum wanted to buy your company? Did they just like looking at a French model with her clothes off? No, you fitted their requirements. And when your late colleague Louie said he had one of the world's best software creators and two totally unethical designers on hand, it couldn't have been better. It was a shame that the more unethical of you ... er, sorry ..."

"Beano." Was she doing it deliberately, to rile me?

"Beano, yes. It was a shame that he died so quickly, but in some ways you were better working alone. You weren't unethical so much as innocent of the existence of ethics. It reminded me of that old French pop song. You've probably heard it. Dominique, nique, nique." She la-la'd the rest of the melody and chuckled to herself. "Have you heard it? It was back in the 60s. Sung by a nun. No one told her that 'nique' means 'fucks'. She was so innocent about it that all the prime-time TV shows were able to invite her on. So there she was, a nun singing about Dominique fucking and she was the only one who didn't get the joke. Hilarious. She committed suicide, you know."

Despite the heavy's mask, I could see that even he cracked a grin at this.

Call me a party-pooper, but I didn't find it quite so amusing.

"Bollocks!" I shouted, and both of them clicked out of their mirth. "From where you're standing, or sitting, over there in the cynics' corner, anyone with the minutest grain of decency in them must look like a fucking nun. Coma has its flaws, but at least we allow people to communicate without their thoughts being intercepted and manipulated by bastards like you."

Angela Greensands just laughed again.

"It's tragic, really," she chuckled. "Why do you think the time was right for my project? It's because the airheads talk direct to other airheads without any interference from anyone who's truly capable of assessing information. And yet people trust the internet more than journalists because they think they're getting it *from the source*." She did an infuriated version of the finger "quotes" thing. "But in fact they're only getting it from other airheads. Or from people who know how to influence airheads. And anyway, you are so out of date with all your guff about unhindered peer-to-peer communication. Don't you know that everything said or done on the internet has been either watched or controlled by the corporations *for years*? Face it – these days, internet users are just a load of geese being fattened for an endless corporate Christmas."

"No!" Again, I got my inflamed throat to work at something approaching full volume. "You can't tell me you've got enough people to monitor everything that happens on line. It's too huge. And anyway, the net can be a force for good. For education. Healthcare, even."

"Ah, education, education, education," she replied. "Yes, maybe you're right. After all, the internet is where criminals get educated in buying illegal guns, where terrorists learn how to make bombs and biological weapons, where paedophiles educate their little penpals." She did her smug philosopher's shrug.

Something in me snapped.

"No!" I stripped the remaining flesh from my larynx with a primal scream. "Granola was right. You're a monster. Get your fucking mask off and face up to life like the rest of us. Take it on the fucking chin for a change. Here, I'll take it off you myself."

I lunged.

She didn't budge, confident in the training of her armed protector. A fat hand appeared in front of my face and stopped me in mid-charge. The heavy didn't even need to hit me. He just pawed me aside and I sprawled across the floor.

"I'm vaccinated against all the dangerous germs," she informed me blithely. "I wear a mask to stave off minor infections. Sinusitis, laryngitis and suchlike."

She stood up. I lay there and watched her move towards the door. It was the Claudine scene all over again.

"I'm glad we had a chance to talk," she said. "I feel better knowing that the leaks were just another of your cock-ups. I didn't like the idea that I'd been outsmarted. I'll send you a postcard from my sunny tax haven. I might even lick the stamp. You can sniff it if you want to get a share of my vaccines."

My two visitors made their exit from the living room.

"I hope a stonefish stings you on the butthole," I told her. "You'll have to give your bodyguard one hell of a fucking pay rise before he sucks that poison out!"

My voice was little more than a croak. If they heard me, they didn't bother to react. Luckily.

The front door closed gently and I was alone with my new knowledge. It was not a convivial room-mate.

Knowledge. Education. People tell me I spend too much time on the net. But it's the one place I haven't been often enough these past couple of weeks. That's where I could have found out how Beano died, even in rumour form. And Louie ...

I wished my mind would slip back into its stupor. Painful realizations were popping up like cold sores.

Louie had known what was happening to him, and called me over just to try and infect me. Christ. I was right. He really hated my guts.

My gullet hurt like hell. I went to the bathroom to get some more syrup.

When I looked in the mirror I got a shock. There were twin bruises, no not bruises, they were only smudges really, on my Adam's apple. I stifled a wave of panic.

It's only an illness, I told myself. Sometimes illness has a voice that can talk you into death. It's true, ask a nurse. Sick people convince themselves to die.

But this is only a cold. The *common* cold, they call it, because it's so common. It's just a cough that's gone viral.

Now I've come over very sleepy again, but in a deep, restful way. I'm going to take a snooze.

Before sleeping, though, it would be best to re-assure Granola. She might get worried if she tries to call and I don't answer. I don't want her worrying.

I want to tell her I'm lucky. Beano didn't know what was going on. I do. It's nothing special, just a cold with a bit more flu than usual mixed in. I'm prepared. And I'm strong. Angela Greensands said so. And fortunately for me, forward-thinking Granola stocked up the flat with syrups, lozenges and aspirins. I'll be fine.

My Granola. What a woman. Angela underestimated her. It wasn't a cock-up. Cock-up, my arse. (As it were.) All that plumbing Granola was on about: the leaks, the plug-pulling. She flushed Angela Greensands out of her job.

I must call and congratulate Granola.

She doesn't answer, so I punch out her folks' landline, and get their damn voicemail. (Funny that they should all be out.) I decide to leave a message.

The yelling at Angela has played hell with my tubes, though. Everything's blocked up again. My nose, too.

"Gran-erg."

Try again. A swill of throat syrup, and for a few magical seconds my vocal equipment is all but clear. I'm going to be OK. Everything's going to be fine. I tell her so –

"I ony god a code. Jussa coma code."

It may just be a cold, but it hurts like the bloody plague. I cut off my message before I start croaking like Beano, and scare Granola. I'll call back later, when I've had a rest.

One final life-affirming thought before my siesta. Des. He'll still be up and running, even if Coma isn't.

"Hey, Des," I call out across the town, my typing so much clearer than my voice. "Check out my old webcam: it's still on line. Picture quality's pretty shit, but the footage for the last half hour or so should make fascinating viewing. Can you sharpen up the sound quality? Bet there'll be plenty of people interested in seeing the real Angela Greensands in action. She really let her mask slip this time."

When I've had my sleep, I'll take a hot shower and then get down to some cool-headed revenge.

****

PUBLIC SERVICE ANNOUNCEMENT*
Beat the Bug
Miracle cure! Totally free of charge!
Get your seven-day cold cure absolutely free, direct from the manufacturer.
No need to ask your doctor! No need for a prescription!
This miracle treatment for all forms of colds and flu has been found in tests to eliminate symptoms in 100% of cases. Yes, that's 100%.
Try it once and we guarantee you'll stay with us for life.
Miracles do happen.

* Sponsored.

****